MORGUE to Love

a Last Responders Romance

by Megan Montgomery

ADVANCING WOLF PUBLICATIONS
PULP CLASSIC

book cover by Kris Madden

pulp classic edition 2023

dedication

For the last responders, funeral professionals,
and anyone who works with the dead.
May this book bring a little light and humor to your day.

CONTENT WARNING: CONTAINS DEPICTIONS OF AUTOPSIES, EMBALMINGS, AND MORBID HUMOR. IT'S NEVER INTENDED TO BE CALLOUS OR GRATUITOUSLY GORY. THE GORE IS ALWAYS USED TO EXPLORE THE NATURE OF DEATHCARE: THE MEANING, BEAUTY, *AND* HARDSHIP OF THESE PROFESSIONS; THE STRENGTH OF THE BONDS BETWEEN DEATHCARE WORKERS, AND TO BETTER DEPICT THE CHARACTERS WHO PERFORM OR WATCH THESE PROCEDURES (I.E. IT TAKES ON A CLINICAL LENS WHEN VIEWED THROUGH SOULA'S EYES, "GROSS" FROM WAYLON'S, ETC.)

chapter one

Soula—Now

BETHANY TOSSED HER BLONDE curls behind her shoulder. The glossy ringlets caught my attention as they sprang perfectly back into place. That was my beacon. There wasn't a bar, burlesque, or honky-tonk in the whole state of Tennessee where I couldn't immediately spot my platinum-locked friend. I forgot how much I'd missed this.

I dodged tourists and cowboys (i.e., tourists and tourists dressed as cowboys), avoiding contact with the living at all costs until I sidled up next to her at the bar. My best friend had nixed her scrubs and sober black suits for her colorful, 50s-era street clothes and tonight, she looked every inch the film noir femme fatale—perhaps Technicolor would be more appropriate—as she stood with one platform espadrille crossed in front of the other, sipping her highball in her skintight, tiki-print dress.

I changed my clothing too. Jeans, t-shirt, and my favorite brown leather boots. But I didn't deserve even that much credit. If it wasn't a professional hazard to leave the office in scrubs, I probably wouldn't have bothered. I never went *all out* like Bethany, but then, I didn't have the bombshell curves or the corresponding personality that was best highlighted by throwback pin-up girl dresses and sultry glances at men across the bar. And forget about sculpting my flyaway hair into anything more than a messy bun after a quick shower, even on nights like tonight.

I hooked my boot heel on the brass rail under the bar and nudged Bethany's shoulder in lieu of a hug. I'd seen her since she got back to town, of course, but tonight, we were officially celebrating her new position at my dad's company. It had only taken me years of begging him to finally hire someone outside the family, but he and I both knew that someone could only be my grad school roommate and best friend, Bethany West. She was the best in her field.

"How was your week, Darlin'?" Bethany quirked her coral lips and her eyes twinkled at me.

"Rotten. Thank God it's almost over." I waved my hand, signaling for the bartender, and Bethany slid her glass over to sustain me in the meantime.

"Aren't they always?" She drawled.

"Not always," said a familiar and entirely too chipper voice behind me. Decca wedged in between me and Bethany and plunked a heavy elbow on my shoulder, making me choke on the cloyingly sweet cocktail. "Sometimes the bodies are fresh."

I wriggled out from under her; the bemused grin on her freckled face told me she'd intended to provoke just that reaction. We'd been friends for too long and had gone through too much education—and other things—for her to miss an opportunity to annoy me.

Tonight, Decca was dripping in layers of diaphanous black and chunky jewelry that brought to mind ancient live oaks dripping with Spanish moss. Looking at the three of us, I was sure no one here realized we were intentionally here at the Bunganut Pig together. But we didn't need to share the same style to bond. We bonded because we had one thing that separated us from the rest of society.

"Who're we waiting on?" Decca asked.

"No one. It's just us tonight." I explained, secretly pleased that my lab tech needed to take her kids to some sports lesson. Tae Kwon do, maybe? I didn't want this to become a work thing. I needed a release from the office.

"Good. I'm thirsty, and it looks like Bethany's already started. I don't know who's playing tonight, but I'll need at least a buzz if my ears have to be assaulted with an autoharp."

Bethany nudged me to look up at the tv. Her attention had been focused forward the whole time Decca and I have been here, and now I saw why. The bar was airing the early news. Male voices cheered across the bar. It was an odd way to punctuate the news story about an unidentified male found DOA in his apartment after his liquified body was dripping down his neighbor's ceiling fan. After that, someone muted the tv, and I had to rely on the terribly delayed closed captioning, trying to piece together photos of gnarled metal with the words "pile-up," "at least three deaths," and "drunk driver."

Decca picked up on the not-so-secret communiqué. "Looks like summer came early this year. I'll get the first round." She gave me an apologetic look.

"Who do we have to murder to get a drink around here?" I asked, not having seen a barkeep since I set foot in this joint. Unfortunately, I overshot the volume of my question and timed it perfectly to synchronize with one of those sudden lulls in ambient conversation. Several unfriendly heads from the troop of besuited men across the bar swiveled in my direction.

I tried to avoid glancing up, but I could feel eyes searching and finding. Boring into my cranium like the Eye of Sauron wondering what creature could commit such a social faux pas as to speak, loudly, when the musical act was about to enter from stage right—hence the lull. Bethany stepped onto the rail and leaned over the bar, signaling for another drink and stealthily squeezing her high, round cleavage even higher and rounder between her arms. She tossed a seductive smile over to the group of businessmen, but her wink was for me. It was her subtle way of signaling for the spotlight to follow her, leaving me in the cool relief of darkness, the kind of unrehearsed choreography that only the truest of friendships knew.

She caught the eye of the bartender too, who must have been purposely avoiding her in an attempt to remain *meh* in the presence of a stunningly gorgeous woman.

"Dick," Bethany said under her breath.

I waved her off. "I'm surprised. You're usually my free-drink ticket. Or at least my get-the-bartender-to-notice-me ticket. Maybe this guy likes playing hard to get."

"Not the bartender. That blue suit over there. He actually licked his lips at me. Does that even work with women?"

"Ew." Decca cringed. I hadn't noticed. I was too busy retreating into myself.

"He probably recognizes you. That's gross. No offense, Beth."

Bethany shrugged. "Ugh. It's fine. Occupational hazard. I've already forgotten about him." She sighed and shook off the bad vibes. "It's been over a year since we've done this and we're celebrating. Now, who're we going to be tonight? Hair stylists? Librarians?"

"I say we stick with nurses," Decca sighed. "It's exhausting to play a hair stylist. Men expect us to be too dramatic and performative in bed."

"I just don't feel as convincing as you two," Bethany said. "I don't know enough about medicine."

"You know how to find the major arteries and how to check for cardiac signs, right? What else is there?" I asked.

"On behalf of nurses everywhere, *'Ouch.'* I'm going to assume there's a little more to it than just knowing if a person's dead," Bethany said.

"Though that could come in handy if you ever got yourself a sugar daddy at some point," Decca added.

"I'm not putting down nurses." I shook my head. "I love nurses. I'm just saying a hookup won't be quizzing you on your nursing duties or the physiology of sexual organs."

"As long as you put his sexual organ inside you," Decca laughed.

The bartender finally showed up, glaring at us. No, not at us. At me. I rolled my eyes. Apparently, I would not win this whole *being in society* thing tonight. There was no point in trying.

"Can I just have a beer?" I glared back at him. He had nothing on me.

He looked up to Decca, who ordered her usual Manhattan.

Bethany bounced on her toes. "I see a table opening up. I'm going to snag it."

"I'll bring the drinks." I said, taking out my card to start a tab.

When the judgmental asshole returned with our alcohol, he started to say something to me, but stopped.

"I'm sorry?" I asked, really meaning, "*What the fuck did you just say to me?*"

"It's not my place, but...it doesn't seem fair to lie to men."

"What the fuck did you just say to me?" I couldn't hold it back that time. I looked around for my friends, but they'd gone. No one had heard the sheer... weirdness of his accusation.

I raised my voice from its usual whisper. Eye contact was commencing. This interaction was as serious as a myocardial infarction.

"I don't want to be rude but...." *(Yes, you do.)* "You don't want guys to lie to you about their professions, right? Maybe you should try being honest."

"Thank you for your opinion. *Honesty. Really?* I'll have to try that one." Something stopped me from gathering the drinks. Oh hell, I'd already raised my voice above its usual whisper. What was one more sentence? I was in a rare mood not to let it go tonight.

I turned back to him. "You know what? How about you spend one day elbow deep in the pneumothorax of a decomposing corpse and see how easy it is to shower the scent of *putrescine* out of your hair before you try to find a relationship? No, not even a relationship. A date. Just one single conversation with a man who doesn't bug out his eyes and run when you tell him you chop up dead bodies for a living. Then you can mansplain relationships to me."

The bartender said nothing. The whiteness of his pasty face told me honesty wasn't always the best policy.

A thing I've known for a long time.

I grabbed our glasses off the bar and caught the eye of one of the dark suits across the way. Since I was in an eye contact mood, I didn't recede immediately, but I didn't smile either. I wondered if he had heard any of my scolding. Too bad. He was handsome.

This was the problem with honesty. Too many nights with no orgasms.

chapter two

Soula—Now

DEATH RAN IN MY family.

Not as in *we died frequent and/or untimely deaths, leaving weeping, white-gowned widows or outrageous gambling debts behind.* Nor did we operate some sophisticated, underground mafia-type establishment, killing "when necessary." And alas, the Smythe family was neither cool nor aloof enough to claim any type of immortality.

Instead, Grandpa Capability Smythe bequeathed his deathly legacy (and, undoubtedly, some gambling debts as well) to his sons, John and James Smythe, in 1904. They passed down a sprawling Queen Anne Victorian mansion (with its recent addition of the coach house built behind the lily garden) to their own sons, cousins Joseph, Ralph, and Robert in 1962. Their underwhelming aptitude made the business stop short in that generation, though, because sometime in the 80s, it plummeted into the hands of my own father, Jim.

Being the only third-gen cousin who held even a vague interest in continuing the family business, he accepted, with a shrug, the entirety of a Victorian mansion in dire need of exterior painting and olive green interior carpet removal, a coach house that wasn't quite long enough to accommodate the newer cars so the manual aluminum doors rested ever so slightly on the bumpers of the longer hearses of today, and the sole proprietorship of Smythe & Sons Mortuary.

I grew up in a funeral home. Oh, but there was the adjacent graveyard as well. Not the serene, park-like resting place where families would picnic and grave markers nestled unseen in the well-tended grass, lest they remind someone of their own eventual mortality.

No. This was the gothic, Halloween-edition graveyard, complete with lichen-etched stone tombs, crumbling mausoleums, and cracked and illegible granite slabs that *sort of* marked the graves of wealthy Antebellum plantation owners. If I had to choose anywhere to get chased around by my idiot brothers, it'd be there. Really good hiding spots. But it did little for my reputation at school.

Then my father went and did something incredibly cool in retrospect—though it felt like an act of villainy my brothers and me at the time. He built a crematorium on the property. That permanently sealed the casket of my social life at Franklin High School.

Sometimes, the *family* in *family business* meant very little; a thing that would eventually be passed down until it was in your holding, like a share of Disney stock. In the Smythe family, *family* was more like *free labor*. Only, it was free labor that us kids weren't *pressed* into, as much as *guilted* into. If we just did this one quick pick-up or if we spent a weekend helping dad stock the embalming room or cleaning out the cooler, one day Mama might be able to afford real Tupperware and we wouldn't have to divvy up the leftover moussaka into eight-year-old Country Crock containers.

After participating in the family business since the gap-toothed age of eight, death had been just another part of life. My brothers, Gus and George, felt likewise. They were just as comfortable with it as me, which was a good thing considering we were the next generation in line to inherit the place.

Except, I ruined that idea and broke my mother's heart by attending medical school instead of mortuary school. And Gus broke it again when he went to Greek Orthodox seminary to atone for his Big Bad Sin.

And after Dad bought out our shares and redistributed ownership, bringing Bethany on as Funeral Director and co-owner, the shame of it was; we still had to open every margarine and ricotta cheese container in the fridge to find something to scarf down for lunch, so Mama's guilt trips had all been for naught.

But it wasn't the living among the dead that bothered me. It was *me* living among the dead that bothered *other people.* Sure, by the time I got to high school, some goth kids followed me around like I was Robert Smith, but during that time, I craved normalcy. It was hard enough explaining why I was eating pastitzio and not peanut butter and jelly for lunch and navigating the live bodies swarming the school while I constantly swam upstream, living in a mortuary—nay, not just a mortuary; a body-burning, haunted mansion mortuary next to a dilapidated graveyard? It didn't make *honesty* my ally.

THE CAROLANNES TUNED THEIR instruments while making those ubiquitous inside jokes with the crowd that all these Nashville bands did. It made me uncomfortable. Should I fake-laugh along with the audience? Let my eyes glare, unfocused, at the mandolin strapped to the woman on stage right?

Decca and Bethany easily ignored the banter between the band and their fans as they scanned the faces of the crowd for smiles in their direction. It was easy for them. *Smiles* came easily. The getting and the giving of them. Both of my best friends were stunning in their unique ways. Bethany was radiance personified with her golden halo and a heavy dash of vintage vixen. Decca was a gothic pixie with winged eyeliner and short black bangs; cute even while hiding under that stupid fucking hat she liked.

I looked... smart. I didn't enjoy getting done up and absolutely hated every moment out of leggings. My hair frizzed in the winter, when it wasn't humid enough to curl right and shrunk up to just below my shoulders in the summer. I spent so much time in the morgue no one saw it, anyway. On decomp days—like the one I had today and the one that, thanks to the news I knew I'd have again tomorrow—I autopsied bodies that, shall we say, weren't found promptly after death. The downdraft system was nearly, but not quite strong enough to keep the smell from permeating my hair down to the core. Most medical examiners were so used to the putrid bouquet of decomposition they didn't even notice the smell anymore, and I was no exception. Only after I saw children holding their noses at the supermarket, their parents whisking them off to another aisle, did I recognize that the smell making them retch as they shopped for their frozen pizzas was, in fact, me.

Now I took long showers and added disinfectant to my shampoo before I went out after work.

Tonight, I looked clean. I smelled like... not death. And I was ready to entertain my acceptance of a limited-time socio-physical arrangement. *Bring forth the men.*

And the booze, it seemed. When our server brought our drinks over, Decca insisted on a toast. "To friendships that can withstand death and dismemberment."

"To making partner and working with an all-around swell guy, Jim Smythe." Bethany raised her Mai Tai.

"To getting laid." I raised my beer and promptly took a swig, declining the clink.

"How bad was the decomp today and are we getting it?" Bethany asked by way of small talk. Smythe had a contract with the town of Franklin, so I'd be seeing Bethany at the morgue pretty regularly when she came for pickups.

"A week maybe. Not too advanced for being outside. It's not that hot yet. And I'm not sure who they called. He was likely a transient. He was found on the tracks down by the Harpeth. Lower extremities crushed. I couldn't locate next of kin to notify so I don't think you'll have to worry about presentation. Tomorrow, though..." I shuddered to imagine what the team would cart in for me.

"Ugh, remember that mass casualty simulation at FAC? We were so green. In more ways than one," Bethany said.

"That was the first time we met Bass, and he showed us the de-gloved fingerprint technique. I do that once a year, maybe." I stared at my own, fully fleshed hands and checked a text I just received from Dr. Li.

"I remember your first case, Soula. It was a decomp, too," Bethany said.

"Found in his recliner by the police after the mail carrier called it in."

"For the smell." Decca shook her head. It was a common occurrence, and for those of us who were old hat at what normal society deemed horrifying, it was no longer gruesome. Our medicolegal investigators were called out to scenes with bodies in varying degrees of decomposition a few times a year. At the morgue, it was my job to examine them to make sure the deaths resulted from natural causes—heart attack, stroke, complications from a well-documented case of diabetes that was unsurprising after reading their patient charts, etc. I'd do a tox screen if there was any vitreous fluid left in the eyeball and after x-rays and a quick external to rule on manner, I wouldn't sift through what was left unless the police truly suspected foul play. The insect and bacterial populations already rendered most of the organs useless, anyway. Tomorrow, however, was another matter. Dr. Li's text warned me that, for whatever reason, homicide would be present for the autopsy. I sighed internally. I hated when the police were present.

Decca was the academic of the cohort, as we were once aligned in varying degrees at UT's Forensic Anthropology Center, or the Body Farm, as most people know it. She moonlighted as a grief counselor and death doula when she wasn't travelling all over Tennessee performing her duty as the state Forensic Anthropologist. She shouldn't need a Ph.D. to run gigs the way she did, but in this economy, you have to pay your student loans back any way possible. At least she could feel good about the many hats she wore. She was a hearty advocate for the end-of-life plan, and absolutely hated for anyone to die alone, so she became a Grim Reaper of sorts, helping the dying cross over and their loved ones mitigate their loss.

"This is why our society needs to embrace mortality to a greater degree," said Decca.

"So that you're not a pile of sludge by the time your family starts asking about your social security check?" Bethany asked.

Decca pressed her lips together to avoid Bethany's goading. "To have a richer transition into the next phase."

"I just appreciate it when they don't die in the bath," I said.

"Ugh, skin slippage." Bethany cringed.

"The worst," agreed Decca.

Bethany played with her straw and took a dainty sip of her drink. "No." She swallowed. "The worst is when the family wants a fucking open casket after they die in the bath and we have to explain, tactfully, why we absolutely cannot grant that wish. But then there's your brother, who insists we '*absolutely can do a reconstruction.*'"

Bethany faked a dead-on impression of George's voice. It wasn't hard, since my brother was basically wooden.

"In case you ever wondered why I bucked the family tradition and moved to the morgue, George is exactly why." I shuddered. "Give me a degloved hand and maggots any day over living, breathing, *grieving* human beings. Or my brother."

I took a large swig of my beer and, in my George-induced irritation, tipped it down too fast. Foamy liquid dribbled down my chin. Signaling to the server for another round and more napkins, I caught the man in the dark suit, breaking eye contact with me. He smiled sheepishly.

It wasn't a creepy smile. It wasn't a leer. And thank God he wasn't licking his lips like his friend. It was a quiet, nice smile. With an almost imperceptible shrug. I looked away in case I read him totally wrong.

I flat-out didn't understand subtlety to the extent that I no longer tried to disguise it. I preferred to be direct and for others to state their intentions clearly until the initiation stage passed in a relationship, but I rarely got there with men.

"I think that handsome man in grey is flirting with you, Sou." Bethany nodded to the smiler.

Decca flicked her eyebrows up. "I've been watching him glance over at you. You should go talk to him."

"Ugh. I don't go talk to anyone. Anyway, I'm pretty sure he heard me yell at the bartender about why it's acceptable to lie about our occupations. He knows too much."

The folk-grass duo on stage finished their song and another round of drinks arrived. My hand was sticky from something and I rubbed my fingers against my jeans to give them something to do.

Bethany's phone buzzed, and she groaned before checking her screen.

"Hey! It's our first night out in a year. We're not on call tonight." She held up a finger for me to wait a minute while she answered the call.

That answered that.

Snippets of Bethany's quiet, one-sided conversation, the same conversation I'd heard a thousand times from Dad and George's end, cemented that assumption.

"Yes, of course I'll go." "How's the family?" "I'm on my way now." "Text me the address?" Bethany's tone of voice changed. She became respectful and subdued but not quite somber when she put on her work voice. Both of my friends had one. My work voice was my all-the-time voice. I expected that was because, as a pathologist, I communicated with families of the deceased only to extract raw data to determine cause and manner of death. Decca's work voice was the most woo-woo, since she believed she was helping usher souls into the afterlife. Bethany's was the most businesslike, since she was ultimately a saleswoman—albeit an extremely ethical one.

She hit the button to end the call. "You know your brother. He doesn't believe in *on call*. 'Bethany, as partners, we need to avail ourselves of those grieving at the expense of our own lives.'" She spat out her boss' directive verbatim.

"He just wants you to be as miserable as he is," I said. Part of me was worried George would take advantage of Bethany's newness as partner and try to work her to death while he lazed about, but then remembered George had no life outside the mortuary. He wouldn't push her to do anything he wouldn't do himself. It would be interesting to watch this dynamic play out.

"It's okay. He needs help, and I need to change first. Obviously." Decca and I shrugged. Such was the life of the cohort. Always at the beck and call of Death.

chapter three

Soula—Now

Decca left with Bethany. I suspected she felt some misplaced guilt after our conversation about bodies being left unfound for weeks and went to support the family of Bethany's body pickup.

That left me alone on our girl's night. Honestly, I was a little relieved. Today just felt off. I was a little headachy, and a lot tired after a long day. The band's instruments were too loud for the vocals, and this bar was too people-y. I fought the crowd up to the bar, squeezing into what I thought was standing room, but was really the servers' pathway to pick up drinks for their tables. When a tall woman bumped me from behind, we had a glare fight. I waited until she huffed off to slink into a new spot.

The smiling man in the dark suit was standing at the beer taps. We locked eyes, and he backed up to make space, nodding me over. I had no choice if I wanted to pay my tab and retrieve my credit card. Maybe this was my chance to ask him what made a man so goddamned happy that he smiled at strangers. But who was I kidding? I didn't talk to people.

I eased my way into the non-space next to him. "Thank you," I said rigidly. I could be polite when I had to be.

"It's busy in here tonight." He smiled.

I nodded and mentally used the Force to get a bartender's attention.

"Your friends left you." It was a statement, not a question. A very odd statement. I dropped my arm and looked my future murderer square in the eye, backing away slowly. "Bathroom."

"Oh, no. Sorry. I just noticed you before... several times." He shrugged. It *could've* been a sweet gesture. He could've also been planning how he was going to get me in the back of his van. "I don't want you to think I paid too close attention to just you. It's part of my job to be observant."

"Thanks a lot." So much for the eye contact. And the smiling. It wasn't for me, anyway. He was just doing his job, ma'am.

"No, wait. Let me rephrase. I'm sorry for thinking your friends ditched you or whatever you thought I was trying to say. I'm sorry. I have... no game. I just... I think you're very attractive and I'd love to buy you a drink if you don't have to rush out of here. There. Got it out."

I really wanted to smile, but I also had enough self-respect to try to prevent my own murder.

"I promise I'm not a serial killer. Look. I realize this might be even worse, but it's better to come right out and be honest, right?" He pulled a leather wallet out of his jacket pocket and flashed a police ID. I looked at the photo. Same face, although his smile was much freer. Almost goofy. I looked up at real-life him. He had all the authority of a Sunday school teacher.

"Detective Wells?" I'd never seen him around the morgue. The faces of most of the murder squad in the Nashville and Franklin departments were familiar to me.

"I'm new. Just made detective. You're the first person I've shown the ID to. This is the team taking me to drinks to celebrate. Or that *was* the team. They seem to have conveniently wandered off." He gestured to the suits clustered around a standing table, watching the band. I didn't recognize any of them either.

"Waylon." He offered his hand.

"Soula." I shook it appreciatively. When the bartender noticed me, then noticed the man above my shoulder. I received a reproachful glare, but he came over anyway.

"What can I get for you?" He asked insincerely.

I looked once more at Detective Wells. Waylon. He smiled again, warmly. There was something about his face, his scruffy, short, almost beard, his roughed-up hair that was probably blonde in his childhood but had now darkened into a nondescript dishwater, his irises that were just a shade lighter than my darkest blue jeans.

I was welcome with him. He looked like a cozy fireside, and I was encased in ice. I found myself wanting to stay. I wanted to be here with him, smile with him, bask in his warmth and melt away that nasty, grimy top layer of ice that spent way too long in the freezer.

"Whatever's darkest on tap," I said and smiled back.

Halfway through our beers, he still hadn't asked me what I did for a living. At that point, I didn't care if it was because he overheard me and the bartender earlier, or if his cop buddies recognized me and clued him in. I was just happy I didn't have to lie. And it was almost refreshing talking about non-work aspects of my life. Except I didn't really have any non-work aspects of my life. Unless you counted fencing club on Tuesdays and Sundays.

That left me answering his questions in the vaguest possible way, diverting them back to him as quickly as I could. It was a game of hot potato. I couldn't get caught holding the question too long, or I might get burned by the gory truth of my life.

The Carolannes finished the last song of their set, a bluegrass cover of a 90s R&B hit that was annoying as fuck. "Thank God that's over," I let slip. Waylon narrowed his eyes.

"You don't like the band?"

"Is that a sacrilege? Maybe they were a little off key or something." He took a long drink from his glass, his eyes never leaving mine. "I don't know much about music. I'm sure they were great."

"No, you should trust your ear. They weren't stellar. But everyone else seems to love them."

"Ha. That's a prerequisite for me *not* to love a thing."

"You're a contrarian. I like it." His voice was deeper when he said it. More gravel. Less *Sunday school.* He put an elbow on the bar and leaned closer to me. He didn't have to, now that the show was over, and we weren't deafened by "ironic" newgrass covers. But it gave me a chance to study his eyes in greater detail. His eyes were easy to look at. They weren't dark blue, they were regular old blue eyes, but the left one had a dark ring around his outer iris—Oh, and the right eye wasn't completely blue either. A swath of brown shot diagonally through his iris.

"Heterochromia," I accidentally said aloud, noting it in my mental file. He quirked an eyebrow.

"Most people don't notice. Or know that there's a name for two different eye colors." He studied my own eyeballs. I knew it was his way of giving me leave to keep looking. And look I did. It was always fascinating when the genome split in such a delightfully odd way, but I was more than fascinated. I was enamored. I didn't know which eye to focus on, the left with that ring of darkness punctuating the blue of the iris before that pure white sclera, or the right, with its slash of warm, whiskey brown that matched the faded freckles that dusted his nose and upper cheeks. Tiny signs of an idyllic childhood that was probably spent playing little league and fishing in the creeks. Wells struck me as the kid who'd intentionally pick the loser to be on his team in gym class. As a loser myself, I appreciated that.

His eyes searched the rest of my face, my lips parting when his gaze lingered over my mouth. He sipped his beer again. I did the same, although beer wasn't what I was thirsty for.

"Where's your favorite place to listen?"

Back to music again. Okay.

He directed his question out to the crowd, but I knew he was determined not to look too long again. At any part of me.

I did love music, and I had genuine answers. I just didn't want to provide them. There wasn't much point in dawdling when, honestly; we were really only after one thing, anyway. His friends didn't seem to miss him and he didn't pay much attention to the band when they were playing, so it was now or never.

"Do you live alone?" I ignored his question entirely.

"Uh, yeah. Except for Kudzu, my lab mix." He nodded to the bartender for another. "Can I convince you to stay for one more?" He taunted me. Or so he thought. I said nothing, happy that my beer was finally not too cold for me to drink.

"Is your bed made?" I asked. You could tell a lot about the character of a person if they made their bed. I righted my pillows and straightened my sheets and comforter but left them turned down for airflow and to prevent bacterial breeding between washes.

"Yeah, sure." His eyes looked quizzical, but he was game. "I didn't in college or anything, but now that I'm a grown-up..." He gestured to his suit with a smile you'd see in an advertisement, "I like getting into a made bed every night. Feels nicer." I agreed. And he passed the test. I didn't like going home with men and finding their rooms looking like a frat house. Or what I imagined the inside of a frat house looks like. That kind of Greek life was not for me.

"Would you like to bring me home?" I asked.

He scrunched his brows together and recoiled like a spider just crawled out of my mouth. *Well shit, I read this wrong.*

"I'm sorry if I offended you," I backtracked. "I find it easier to be honest and just flat-out ask before wasting any more of your time. I'll just... go. Thanks for the drink."

Turning away from the bar, I downed my beer and walked to the door.

After one last swig, I dropped my glass on an unoccupied table and a hand brushed my elbow. I fought the impulse to rub my skin where my shirt tickled my arm and looked back. Detective Wells. *Waylon.* I hadn't noticed his cologne when I was standing next to him at the bar, but now I was greeted with a hint of pine trees and something darker, a musk, maybe? I could never tell. It was nice. I loved cologne like I loved music. When it was *my* kind.

"Soula." He said it softly. A nice sound. Then he waited. He probably thought he offended me by turning me down, but it was cool. I didn't know how to reassure him. Maybe I offended him? The tormented look on his face made him even more handsome, but I couldn't know what he was feeling if he didn't tell me. I was about to open my mouth to excuse myself from him again, but he sighed. "Of course, I want to take you home. But I'm not in any..." He clenched his teeth together and ran his hand through his hair, disheveling it rakishly. I looked at his sandy hair and a rush of heat flared in me. He looked at my lips and lost his words for a moment. "Are you sure? You don't want to go... slower, or something?"

"No," I said, plainly. He took a deep breath and steeled himself in preparation, or thought, or whatever, but he didn't say anything. Instead, he reached his hand out to mine. I slid my fingers through his and he traced the back of my hand with his thumb before opening the door and dragging me out of the bar.

chapter four

Waylon—Now

THE FIRST THING I noticed was the way her hair seemed to float around her face like she was in zero gravity.

She was talking so animatedly to the bartender, presumably shooting down his advances, and I figured I wouldn't have a shot with her, either.

But there was something magical about the way her hair moved. I'd only seen that in my nieces' Disney Princess cartoons. And on my nieces' heads, too, for that matter, back when they were in preschool and watched Frozen like their lives depended on it. Their hair didn't know if it wanted to be curly or straight, so it sorted itself out somewhere in between, bouncing around their shoulders as they issued commands in their Anna and Elsa nightgowns. I never saw an adult with hair like a Disney Princess, though. That's exactly what I was thinking about when she caught me looking at her. Right after she caught Jake leering at her friend. Then I saw her face soften just a tiny bit when she looked dead into my eyes after her argument. That was when I noticed how pretty she was.

That was the second thing. She wasn't just pretty. She was fucking gorgeous. Like a Disney Princess.

Jesus, Waylon. Stop thinking like a four-year-old.

Naturally, I was a total cheeseball. I always wished I could be that dark, brooding guy. The type all the women went crazy over. The one who kept his cards close at all times. I blamed my expressive face. I could only act like a bad motherfucker for so long. Then my time was up. After working hours, I couldn't help but be... nice. Especially around women who look like Belle and act like Maleficent.

I guess there was a third thing too. If she shot down the bartender, she must not have been out looking to get laid. Not specifically anyway. That was definitely not on my plan for tonight, either. But she chose *me* out of nowhere.

That was why I hesitated before rushing back to her. That, and I was busy dropping some cash on the bar to cover our beers... and sucking in the drool that was surely leaking from my gaping mouth after her proposition and repeating to myself what I thought I had heard.

I've had a lot of women come on to me. But usually, those women would have been happy to take home almost anyone in a suit with a decent haircut. Soula didn't seem like she'd be the type to drop that bomb in my lap. But her honest and direct communication hinted at a confidence and made me want to plunder her depths. In more ways than one.

She tugged her hand out of my mine and walked faster, in the wrong direction.

"Soula? What's going on?" She stopped mid-step over a crack in the sidewalk and pivoted her attention back to my mouth, a place her eyes sought frequently. I wanted to press her up against the bricks and taste her Coffee Porter-soaked tongue. I put my hands in my pockets to disguise what was already happening in between them.

"Isn't your car around back?" She pointed around the building. "Are we getting an Uber?" Again, the open sincerity of her parted lips and big black eyes. Fuck. It was hard to reconcile her adorableness with her sexiness, but I was looking forward to finding a way.

"If you don't mind walking a few blocks, I live close."

"Oh. That's nice you get to drink close to home," she said, taking a cue from me and fitting her hands into the pockets of her tight jeans. She hopped closer to me.

"My party, my rules." I grinned. I hoped I could get her to open up with her words as well as her beautiful face. Suddenly, I wanted to know everything about her, but I already gathered that she didn't like outright questions. This would be a process. A slow, peeling back of layers over dinner dates, Netflix binges, and hopefully lots of chilling.

It was a warm night, typical for spring in the south. I loosened my tie as I ambled along, stealing glimpses at her and failing to wipe the stupid grin from my face. She marched ahead, annoyed, like I was intentionally slowing down her pace.

Just wait, Princess. Just wait.

When I turned left and started up the concrete path to the front porch, I heard her breath hitch.

"This is your house?"

"There a problem?" I asked.

"Did you get this place as part of a divorce settlement or something?"

"Never been married." I wasn't seeing the problem.

"It's not what I expected. It looks like a family lives here."

"I've been told it's quaint." In truth, I found the property, complete with white picket fence and lack of central air, grandma-ish, but it seemed to win points with any woman who saw it, not that there were many. I sighed. "There's a bit of a story with this house and I got it for well under market. It suits me and the dog until I can finish the reno."

I planned to do most of the work myself, but I'd been so busy at *work* work, I'd only had time to rip out the puke-orange carpeting.

"Hmm." Soula shrugged. She didn't seem amused. She barely seemed interested. Maybe this was a bad idea. Maybe she was a serial killer who plucked her victims out of bars when they tried to flirt with her. I chuckled, considering the irony of a homicide detective bringing a woman back to his place to murder him in his sleep. She stole a side-eyed glance at me.

Seriously though, maybe I'd keep my gun close to the bed.

She demurred when we reached the somewhat dilapidated porch steps and followed the pattern of my treads. Kudzu whined through the door as I found the right key and twisted it in the lock. The dog burst through the door and ran onto the porch, circling me and licking at Soula's elbows, sniffing her boots, and leaning against my legs, begging for love.

"Hey, girl," Soula said, reaching out to let Kudzu sniff her hand before rubbing her ears. She seemed genuinely happy, smiling widely. She didn't strike me as a dog person and Kudzu was a *lot* of dog.

"You miss me? Huh, Kudz?" I gave her one last pat on the side. "She'll calm down as soon as we go in. This is just what she does when I come home," I assured Soula. I don't know why I felt the need to explain dog behavior to her. Or why I was feeling nervous about the rest of the night. I was second-guessing everything.

"Do you need to walk her or something before...?" She stepped through the door and turned back to me.

"No, I already did that when I got off my shift. This is just—"

"What dogs do," she finished.

We faced each other, nodding and smiling awkwardly. I expected her to peek around, see what kind of man I was, what state I left the house in. Luckily, I just cleaned the bathroom, so there were no whiskers clogging the sink or stray hairs in the shower. Even washed the skillet from my eggs this morning. I impressed myself.

But Soula didn't look around. She just looked at me. Waiting for me to...

"What can I get you to drink?" I asked, killing time. "I'm out of beer, but I've got some local bourbon?" I stepped around the corner to the kitchen, grabbing two glasses off the bar cart along the way.

"That's fine. Ice please." I twisted the cork and the whiskey glugged out over the ice in her glass. She took it from the counter before I had the chance to hand it to her, but she didn't sip it. Instead, she brought it to her nose, inhaling the smoky aroma before lowering the glass, gazing into it as she swirled the ice.

I held out my own glass. "What should we drink to?"

She thought for a minute and leaned her hip against the formica counter as a smirk peeked out from behind her stony facade. "To finding the killers?"

Ah, I started to see the light. True crime fan. Probably listened to all the podcasts and had favorite serial killers. Sleeping with me put her that much more in touch with the hobby.

Could I be okay with that?

"To finding the killers." I clinked her glass lightly, and we drank. It wasn't the best bourbon. A little too smoky and it burned on the way down, but I liked that it was from a local distillery, and it wouldn't tempt me to drink too much. Tomorrow, I had a morning shift in the morgue that I was dreading.

Soula placed her drink on the counter and traced her fingertips along the smooth countertops until they met mine. Then, without saying a word, she stepped out of one boot, then the other, shrinking about two inches in height.

"Getting comfy?" I grinned stupidly. She smiled politely back, her eyes never leaving my mouth.

Yeah. True Crime fan or not, whatever her reasons for wanting to sleep with me, I was on board.

"May I take off your jacket?" She asked. I forgot I was still wearing it. No wonder it was so muggy in here. She reached up to my shoulders and slipped her hands down my arms until I caught it and laid it across the counter.

"I should get the window unit going, or it's never going to cool off tonight," I said, stepping around her and heading into the bedroom. I fiddled with the knobs and flicked on the switch until cool air blew in my face. Before the heat built up again between us, I needed to cool down.

I wrenched off my tie and tossed it on the dresser before unbuttoning my cuffs and rolling up the sleeves. Thinking about the rest of the night, I figured I'd open my Spotify app, let her choose the music, and chill on the couch for a while, getting to know the mysterious person I let into my home.

But I turned around and there she stood in the doorway of my bedroom, holding both our glasses and blocking me in. Or maybe waiting for an invitation to enter. I wasn't sure which. She suddenly struck me as not just aloof, but more like some kind of erotic vampire. Only one who wore jeans and a t-shirt and lived in County Music, USA.

"So..." I paused. "Do you want to talk?"

"I don't know if you noticed, but I'm not particularly great at talking." She said it to my mouth but her eyes flicked up to mine to judge my response. It occurred to me that for all her confidence at the bar, she might be just as nervous as I was. *Fuck. Why was I nervous, anyway?*

I crossed the room and retrieved my drink from her hand, brushing her fingers more than strictly necessary. Then I took her glass, wet and cold from the ice in the heat of the room. I had the urge to rub a whiskey-dripping ice cube down every inch of her body to cool her off on this humid, windless night.

"Soula, tell me what you want. Please." I didn't mean for my voice to break when I said that. Nor did I intend to beg. I couldn't seem to gather the right words with her. It was like her taciturn nature obliterated my own ability to chat the ears off a donkey.

"I want you to touch me." She whispered, as if embarrassed. My throat made an involuntary voice that was probably hideous.

"Where?"

"I really have to say it?"

I took a sip of whiskey and asked again, my voice lower now, in control. "Show me where."

"Here." She ran her palm over her throat, damp with sweat. My hand closed over hers. Instead of touching her skin, which would have resulted in the spontaneous combustion of my body, I guided her own hand across the velvet sinew of her chest, up her neck and down again, to her hip. I bent her arm behind her back, arching her closer to me. She drew in a shuddering breath. "That's good," she smiled.

"I'm kissing you now," I said, already dipping my head down and nearly brushing my lips against hers with my words.

"Yes," she responded on an inhale.

I backed away a few inches to watch her as her eyes fluttered open and closed. Her skin glowed in the last light of the sunset, and she was dewy with heat and desire.

She no longer looked tense, hesitant, or socially awkward. She was in her element. Commanding me to do her bidding by the sheer force of her honesty and desire for this.

We were in a spell, she and I. I was dead to the world and couldn't see how I'd ever come alive again. If I kissed her, I knew that would be it for me. Nothing else would be better than this.

"Soula, look at me, please."

Her eyes opened drowsily. "How about this? If I kiss you," I said, "I'm going to kiss every inch of your body. I'm going to slip my fingers between your legs and make your clit slick with my kisses. Then, after my tongue has had its fill of your taste, I'm going to fuck you however you want it. Tell me if you don't want any of that."

"Oh my God, you say things like that?" She laughed. "I didn't know anyone actually..."

My face didn't change.

"I mean, yes. That. I want all of it. Please. Place my order." She said it like lights were flashing in her rearview mirror and she was trying to sober up fast. But her mouth was hanging open and her pupils were blown. This wasn't going as smoothly as I'd hoped, but it was going.

I kissed her. Harder than I wanted to. We were both too eager. "You taste like bourbon," I said.

"You do too. I don't really like it, but I like it on you." She tugged at my upper lip and licked the tiniest corner of my mouth while a smile spread across hers. She was playful. I never would have guessed that.

She tugged on my belt loops and pulled me closer. My erection swelling almost painfully, I didn't hesitate when her hips inched forward, seeking me out. I pressed back, needing the firmness of her belly, showing her what she did to me, and easing my need.

I pulled my lips away from hers to explore other areas. Her ears were delicate and when I breathed against the spot below her earlobe, she giggled. Gripping the row of buttons against my chest, her fingers trailed slowly down the placard of my shirt until she reached the waistband of my pants. "I love this suit," she said, yanking at my belt but not even touching the buckle to give me the slightest relief.

Just when I feared she might want me to remain clothed during this transaction, she began unbuttoning my shirt, slowly, distractedly between our kisses and her reaching down to ensure the hardness inside my slacks was still there. One slow button slipped through the hole. Two. God, I couldn't take much more of that slow pace of her fingers. She teased on the third one, laughing against my kiss. I tried to help her with the fourth button but she knocked my hands away. Before the fifth, she slid her fingers inside the starched cotton, raking her fingertips against my stomach, up my chest and back down to the sixth button which she undid even slower this time, opening her eyes and daring me to speed her up.

I couldn't wait anymore. I needed this belt off. I needed her clothes off. I needed to touch her. I needed to be touched.

With a quick tug on the hem of her thin black t-shirt, she raised her arms to let me pull it over her head. Letting it drop to the hardwood floor, I took in her body anew.

The tops of her breasts spilled slightly over the cups of her bra. It was the kind that wouldn't disguise her nipples if they hardened. *Had they pushed through her thin t-shirt in the cool AC of the bar, and I hadn't noticed?*

I could see her dark nipples now, through the sheer, glossy fabric, aching to be released from their torturous enclosure. My mouth watered.

Still fully dressed in my shirt and slacks, I knelt at Soula's feet. Too impatient to remove the wire and mesh contraption, I bit at the fabric at the apex of her breasts, sucking her hardening tip into my mouth as much as it was possible, biting and rolling my tongue across the little bump. I groaned in frustration, not gaining enough purchase through the fabric, but so desperate to have my mouth on her that I wasn't thinking straight.

A laugh rumbled from somewhere deep in her chest, and the earthy sound released something primal in me. She wasted no time reaching behind her to unclasp her bra, freeing her small round breasts to be feasted on by my tongue.

Of course her breasts were perfect. She was a goddess, and I was in heaven kneeling below her, sucking on the highest peak of a small and gorgeously round breast. Our eyes met as I pulled away from one, leaving a wet sheen behind, and attaching myself to the other because I was greedy for every part of her all at once. The feel of her tits on my tongue was so fucking sexy I had to remind myself to breathe. She leaned into me, moaning, and I delighted at her sensitivity. Her fingers laced into my hair and gripped, gently tugging me back to my feet and our mouths back to home base.

She opened her jeans and shimmied the tough fabric over her hips. In the meantime, I had enough of being upright. I wanted this to last forever, but I was compelled. Drugged by her scent, I couldn't wait to taste her.

Soula was such a tiny thing I could scoop her up in my arms mid-kiss and perch her on the edge of the bed. Her knees spread wide for me, but I pushed them even wider as I nestled between them on the floor. The only thing barring me from seeing her stripped completely bare was her white cotton panties. Of course they were white. But as hot as she looked, sitting there in her innocent little boyshorts, I needed more. I needed all of her.

I lifted her ass off the bed just enough to tug the last remaining strip of fabric from her body. Already, honeyed moisture slicked her bare pussy.

I was torn. Part of me wanted to tear into her like a lion with a fresh kill. Another part wanted to ram my cock so far inside her she could taste it. A third part wanted to worship her. Just look tonight. The next night, nibble off a little more. The next, a bigger chunk. Spend the next year, the next decade just learning her, savoring her body, wringing every drop of pleasure from her neither of us would ever need another hobby.

Fuck it. She was as wet as I was hard. She leaned back on her hands and looked at me like, "What are you going to do, buddy?"

My breaths felt labored, my cheeks hot. Even so, I wanted to take my time. I wanted to just look and look again. It was all happening too quickly, almost like a dream. There might as well have been unicorns and rainbows... and a Journey song playing in the background. This floaty-haired beauty was lying open, bared to me, physically and emotionally, in glorious, throbbing radiance.

I finished unbuttoning my shirt while visually taking in all of her body. Her challenging look softened and lingered on my own body as I unbuckled my belt. My eyes slid over her inner thighs. The lights and shadows that played over her strong thighs beckoned my touch. Her knees were a little knobby and her calves were chiseled. She must be some type of athlete. My mind briefly flashed over what sports we could do together. If we ever got out of this bed, maybe she'd join the sheriff's co-ed softball league.

I let my pants fall and knelt on the bed between her thighs. I needed to feel her body against my skin, needed as much of her as possible, and all at once. I was already addicted to her. She met my mouth fiercely, needing mine as much as I did hers.

Finally, I worked kisses down her body, lingering on her belly. It was one of my favorite parts of a woman's body, the belly. Highly underrated. Soula's was beautiful. Curved to support wide hips, but with muscular dips. Finally, I moved lower, and she breathed out, lifting her hips unconsciously. She had let me look at her and feel her skin for long enough. She deserved her pleasure.

I kissed her tidy little butterfly mound before gliding her lips between my fingers and flattening my tongue against the cherry inside. I may have groaned. I couldn't be sure. God, she tasted so sweet. A cask of Tennessee whiskey, smoky, musky, and far better than the stuff I poured tonight. I'd been imagining the way she'd taste since I saw her cheeks glowing red after laying into that bartender. The reality was even better. Her pussy was glowing red for me and by the time my fingers eased into her vagina, she was already quivering from her orgasm.

Fuck, she comes fast.

I looked up, expecting to meet her eyes, but she wasn't watching me. She was silent, lying with her head flat on the comforter, gripping the cotton in her fists and inching her body away. It was so... polite, so suddenly restrained. I smiled, reassuring her, planting a firm kiss on the softness inside her knee.

But I wasn't ready for her to stop coming. Not yet, at least. Not ever, if I was being honest.

"Oh, no you don't. We're not through with you yet," I laughed, tugging her hips closer.

"You don't have to," she breathed.

Yes, I do.

I tried to communicate just how much I needed it with my adoration of her beautiful pink folds. My tongue thrust into her vagina and swept her juices up and around. She had surprised me with that bare pussy, but I loved that it hid nothing in that goddess-like V between her legs. I felt a sudden camaraderie for those Ancient Greeks who worshipped Aphrodite in their temples. She had nothing on Soula.

I lapped and sucked, my tongue claiming every fold, every angle, every texture until I knew exactly how she wanted it. When she came again, I barely heard Soula's breath catch in her throat. I hid my idiot grin between her legs as I planted kisses inside her strong thighs.

I barely noticed that I had already come on the hardwood floor, without touch or breath or even the inadvertent graze of a rogue leg, just from the sheer delight of pleasing her. Had it really been that long since I was with a woman?

When her breath returned, she sat up, looking at me like I was a stranger. I didn't know why, but it stung. Here I was getting to know her most intimate details, thinking she was feeling the same strange, almost spiritual connection I was. I never occurred to me it might be one sided. Surely something so powerful, so right, so earth shattering, should be felt around the world.

Nope. She gave me that look I got when I knocked on someone's door and flashed my badge. Curious, but warily polite.

"Are you..." Fuck, I didn't even know what to ask right then. "Are we good? Did you not like that? We can stop if you want." *Dear God, please don't say stop.*

"I'm good." She nodded. "That was... you were very focused on *me*. We can do you now." She moved awkwardly, reaching for my cock, but I'd already come, the milky pool still on the floor.

"Um, hang on." I caught her arm before she could touch any part that was still too sensitive. *Real cool, Waylon. Real cool.*

"How about we just chill for a bit?" I needed to re-assess what the fuck was happening now that my head was out of her fabulous pussy. "Come on up here." I climbed on the bed and laid against the pillows, opening my arm for her to nestle in.

She looked annoyed but stretched out, not quite next to me, on the other pillow, staring straight at the cobwebs on the cracked ceiling I hadn't gotten around to cleaning yet, let alone patching.

I rolled onto my side to see her better, ignoring her pert little tits with the perfect eraser nipples. Right now, I needed to evaluate where I had lost her. Making my cock hard again wouldn't help with that.

"You have a leak." She pointed to a coffee-colored stain in one corner of the ceiling.

I grunted in response. It was good she didn't know about the blood stain behind the headboard. The only reason I could afford a 3000 square foot house in this town.

"Used to, I guess. Hasn't leaked since I've lived here, but I also haven't gotten a contractor out since the initial inspection, so...."

"How many bedrooms?"

"Four. But there's an attic space I'm thinking of converting. I might turn one of the smaller rooms into a bigger master bath." I watched a lot of HGTV during my off hours.

"This is a good house," she said, her eyes still examining the ceiling. If she thought that, then it was doubly good she didn't know about the stain.

"Do you want me to leave?" Finally, she turned her head toward me.

"No! God, no." Terror seized me. "Do you *want* to leave?" Why was this so awkward? I wasn't *that* out of practice.

"I thought we'd keep going, but I shouldn't have assumed. If you don't want to, I—"

"No, no. I want to." Fuck. The evidence of how much I wanted to was smeared on the floor at the foot of the bed and I was still half hard. "I just thought we'd take a break. Talk a little. Get to know each other."

She frowned.

What was happening here? She seemed so into the sex, but it was almost like she shut down when I wasn't touching her. I had to experiment.

Reaching out, I traced my fingers over her knee, up her strong thigh, and across her belly that I loved. Maybe I could find a ticklish spot. Maybe she liked more of a firm touch. I didn't know nearly enough about this woman yet. Hooking my hand under her knee, I pulled her thigh across my lap. She moved easily with it, straddling me, laughing a little and coming back to life. When she lowered herself down, she was perfectly aligned. Her lips parted, wet labia kissing my cock in the most obscene way. When it surged against her, she smiled lazily. My eyes closed. She felt so good already and I wasn't even inside her.

She didn't touch me. Not with her hands. Instead, she brought them to her own nipples and pinched them as she bit hard into her lower lip.

I let out a very unsexy squeak in admiration.

"Let me help you with that." I sucked one nipple, twirling my tongue around its tip before sliding it back out and lavishing the same affection on the other. She groaned, rocking her pelvis until her clit found the underside of my cock. Then she rode it to another orgasm while I reveled in her breasts. The receptiveness of this woman was mind-blowing.

When she pulled away suddenly, I didn't realize what she was doing. My eyes fluttered open. Taking matters into her own hands, she expertly dove into my nightstand, hunting for and producing a condom.

"You want?" She asked, still pulsing her pussy against my shaft in tiny, agonizing movements.

I could only nod.

In about five seconds, she had the condom rolled on and was back, seated deeply on my cock.

The sudden pleasure of her was almost too much to handle. I gritted my teeth and breathed through my nose as I held back the impulse to move. Instead, she moved, slowly rising on her knees and back down. I gripped her hips, holding her still, feeling how deep I was inside her. Unthinking, but trying to find my horizon after the exquisite storm of her pussy.

I needed to take this slower, but she looked disappointed or worried or, shit, I couldn't tell, but I couldn't have her looking at me that way.

"Can you reach your nipple to your mouth?" I asked, my voice strained.

She blushed but nodded.

"Lick it." She cupped her breast and brought her mouth down to it, her long tongue reaching out to flick at its peak as her eyes watched me. She was unsure but willing enough. This did nothing to help me slow down.

"Close your eyes," I directed. "Does it feel good? Your tongue?"

"Yours feels better."

"Fuck." My fingers kneaded and dug into her hips. With her legs around mine, they felt swollen and plump and delicious. I moved her body back and forth, easing her clit over the base of my cock as my length filled her, trying to tease out a third (or was it fourth?) orgasm.

Then, for no reason, she stilled, looking down at me with wild eyes as she sat, pinning herself to me, daring me to please her. Please us.

"Suck your nipple, Soula. Taste how sweet you are." There was no more embarrassment as she drew her nipple fully into her mouth, her eyes drifting closed. As my thumb sought her clit, with just barely a brush, she released her breast with a pop and cried out.

"Soula," I moaned. Her pussy clamped around my cock and pulsed so violently I came with her.

Holy hell.

We hadn't even moved. We hadn't thrusted. My orgasm came when her pulsating pussy milked my cock in some rare and torturously simple form of pleasure. Even Soula made a noise that was more than a whisper that time. Her face was shocked with wildness. My head dropped onto the pillow, and she sat on my softening cock for probably too long. We stared at each other, both so stunned we couldn't even process what had just happened.

But I knew I never wanted it to end.

chapter five

Soula—Now

Detective Wells went to the bathroom, presumably, to dispose of the condom and do whatever men do after sex. *Were they supposed to pee like women?*

I heard the water running in the sink while I slipped out from the sheets and located my clothes. By the time he flicked the light off and stepped out, I had already dressed, deposited my whiskey glass in the kitchen sink, and was hunting for the Uber app on my phone.

"You're dressed?" He looked confused. I got that reaction a lot from men.

"Yeah. I prefer being clothed when the Uber shows up, you know?" I was momentarily preoccupied by my phone after the location services listed the street address of this house. There was something familiar about it. Wells was still standing in the doorway of his bedroom in his boxers. He had the body of a scholar, which I liked. Not that he was terribly out of shape or skinny as a rail. He was thin, not skinny, and had enough muscle to carry me across the room, but not too much that his biceps had to squeeze uncomfortably into his suit jacket. He looked like he might have chosen soccer if his parents made him pick a sport, but he also looked better in a suit than out of one. I happened to love men in suits, so that was okay by me. Men in suits always seemed to suggest they worked hard to please a woman, rather than thinking abs alone were all it took to bring a woman to orgasm.

It was a shame this was over. I really enjoyed his pleasing of me.

"You ordered an Uber?" he started toward me.

"Well, yeah. I mean, of course," I stuttered. I never understood it when I got this reaction from men. Wasn't I a dream date for that alone? Didn't everyone want their one-night stands out the door as soon as the afterglow dimmed?

"Well, you could stay, you know. The night. Or just for a little bit. We could hang out, watch something?" He tried to rearrange the hurt look in his eyes but it didn't really work. It just confused me. And when I was in a confusing social situation, I reverted to the way I best knew how to be: formal.

I stood up straight. "Thank you for the offer. I've got a busy day tomorrow, and I've taken up enough of your hospitality already. I can wait outside if you want."

That's what it was. Outside. The lightbulb blinked on above my head. *It was his address.*

I had a case here. My medicolegal team did the on-site work, but I did the autopsy and filed the paperwork; a woman who lived—and died—here. She was shot in the head with a .9mm in the bedroom and managed to drag herself out onto the porch before dying. The neighbors found her a few hours later when their dog came home with blood on his snout. It was probably a good thing he was a new detective and didn't know enough about the history of his property to be squeamish about sleeping in a murder bedroom. No wonder he got the house for a song.

He crossed the kitchen to get a glass of water. I backed up instinctively, though I wasn't sure why. I shouldn't feel the need to recoil from his touch at this point. Not after what we just did. Not after how naked we were together, and not just physically, either. My emotions had been stripped raw at the end.

But there was something so warm and good about him, it threw me off. I didn't know how to *be* around him. Usually, my attraction to a partner waned after the actual partnering. Then, without that rush of the initial, overwhelming attraction, I felt free. Like I no longer had to disguise my personality—or lack of it. At thirty-one, I already knew I wasn't designed for relationships. My whole life had been instilling that in me. But Waylon and I had done the partnering, and I still wanted him. Maybe even more than before, which meant it felt like a piece of me was ripping away, leaving him.

He took several long gulps of his water before speaking to his glass, as if there were answers at the bottom. "You should wait inside. It's not the best neighborhood."

Maybe he knew about his house after all.

"What type of work do you do, anyway? I think I failed to ask." His voice was clipped, almost bitter, but I shrugged it off. We had the sex, and I was getting out of his hair as fast as I could, what more could he want?

This, apparently. Small talk. Since he hadn't brought it up before the sex, I thought I was in the clear. That I wouldn't have to pull out the fake nurse narrative Bethany, Decca, and I agreed on.

"I'm a doctor," I said, surprising myself with the truth. At least, the partial truth. Wells would be used to people hiding from him and was sure to sniff out a lie.

"Neurologist? Surgeon?" He guessed. Not half bad. I was impressed he didn't guess pediatrician. I did almost go into general surgery. And neuro was a major component of my work. I certainly had the temperament for either specialty.

"Uh huh." I kept it vague.

"I get it." He smiled sadly. *Or was it bitterly?* "You don't want to tell me. I'm just a cop. I wouldn't understand, right?"

"No, that's not right. I..." I wanted to tell him. It was the first time I actually wanted to tell a man what I did. Not just what I did. *Why* I did it. I wanted to explain that by carving up corpses I was saving lives—or at least, that's how I saw it. "You're right. I'm a surgeon." I chickened out. In my defense, I didn't think it was fair to send him running to the toilet holding his guts because he'd just slept with a woman who "hacked up bodies" for a living. Even if he was a detective and dealt with death in his own career.

"M-Men don't often get it," I said. Another half-truth. I wanted to give him *something*.

"Why? Because of the schedule? The being on-call? Soula. Come on. If anyone gets it, it's me."

"I'd—" my phone buzzed in the back pocket of my jeans. *I'd love to tell you*, I was about to say. I almost got it out. But this was for the best. We could part amicably. Go our separate ways and hope our paths never crossed—as unlikely as that was, since cops frequented my morgue after any local homicide. I just had to cross my fingers no one would ever be murdered or accidentally killed in Williamson County for the length of my tenure there. *Yeah, right.*

"I'm guessing that's your ride?" He asked, stepping back to allow me to pass. He gave me such a wide berth, my chest ached with reluctance. I didn't want to part from him.

I nodded and looked up at him. "Thanks for the sex," I said pathetically. I even rolled my eyes at myself. "You're very good at it. I hope you enjoyed my part of it. Anyway—"

"See you around, Soula." He opened the front door and I stepped onto the porch. I couldn't help but inspect the wood for bloodstains, but it looked like all the marred boards had been ripped out.

I didn't say goodbye. For the first time, I didn't want to leave. Goodbye just made it harder. I opened the door to the silver Prius and when I looked back, Wells closed the front door with a half-assed wave.

chapter six

Soula—Then

I MUST HAVE BEEN twelve. Thirteen, tops. Mama sent me to hunt around in the supply closet for a particularly pale shade of Rose Plasto-tint embalming fluid. One with a larger-than-normal ratio of moisturizer to preservative.

It was a cold winter for the south. Our pipes had burst in January and the frost still didn't seem to be thawing now that it was nearly March. Ice dripped off our oak trees and we saw more transient deaths than normal. It was so frigid in our massive supply closet, the tissue-building waxes and reconstruction materials had to thaw before use. I shuddered violently against the chill of the long hallway and brick-lined room adjacent to the exterior wall that it made the preparation room feel topical in comparison.

There was mom, her thin shoulders slouching on her tall stool next to the body of an older woman as she studied the decedent's face. Mama must have been exhausted. Usually, it took more energy for her to stop talking, or stop moving, than it did to maintain her usual frenetic pace with which she steamrolled through life. Watching my mom watch this woman made me uneasy.

I handed her the bottles of arterial fluid and after an eternity (probably a second) she reached for it, her eyes never leaving the corpse. Everyone had off days. This was probably just one of Mama's. It was late and she'd prepared several bodies for viewing that day. It was a long time to spend on her feet.

"I have homework, so I'm gonna..." I gestured to the door. Legally, I was prohibited from even entering this room, even though it was located inside my house. In most states, you had to hold an embalmer's license to witness an embalming. Exceptions could be made for those considering the trade, who wanted to shadow a funeral director. And of course, there were always interns, but this room was technically off-limits for tweens. Especially those with homework still to finish.

"I think you might like this one." She said, her energy surging back to it's normal state as the liquid from the bottles chugged into the embalming machine. Vessels had been raised. The needles placed in the dead woman's blood vessels; one tube in the carotid, to pump in the preservative, one in the jugular, to get rid of the blood. Mama flicked the motor on, and the telltale hum started. I sighed, taking Mama's place on the stool.

Before my very eyes (or, like, an hour later, I couldn't really remember since I was twelve or thirteen) the old woman's form rose. The rosy glow of the Plasto-tint coursed into her arteries, through her heart, and trickled down through the smallest veins, plumping her skin full of the dew of youth and artificial life.

The corpse's sunken cheeks were filling out, her skin unfurling like a blossom for one last viewing. I looked at my mom and she appeared satisfied.

"Holy shit," I said. Mom didn't even yell at me for cursing. She just nodded. "I hoped that would do it. We're lucky she's so young. Still has all that collagen in her skin." She put her hands on her hips. Another

Act of God overseen by my mom, Ourania Panasolakis Smythe. I was too mystified by the reverse horror show to roll my eyes.

"What happened to her? How old was she?" I had all the questions.

"You know that tacky glass office building by your brother's school? She worked there. They said she was working late last Friday, catching up on filing or something. She was the last one on the floor. They think she opened a filing cabinet, turned around, maybe got sidetracked or something and swung back around in her office chair and slammed her head into the drawer that was still sticking out."

"Okay but," I said, looking back at a face that was quite pretty now that she was no longer grey and wrinkled, "that would suck, but even if she gauged her eye out on the metal corner, it wouldn't be bad enough to kill her."

"It didn't. Not exactly. She hit her head hard enough on the cabinet, hence the bruising around the temporal, but her fall to the marble floor caused the subdural hematoma. She was probably knocked unconscious, but since no one else was there, they couldn't call for help—"

"But why the desiccation? And none of the early signs of decomposition?"

"I'm getting there, Soula. Don't interrupt your mother. Anyway, three-day weekend. The cleaning crew usually comes Sunday night but came Monday night instead. Sunday would have been too late to save her, anyway. I always hated that ugly building, you remember? I knew something like this would happen there." Mama spat on the linoleum tile floor—to ward away the Devil. "Remember, Soula? I always tell you how much I hate that place whenever we pick Georgíos up from school. That place is what killed her."

She was momentarily lost in her own superstitions. I didn't dare interrupt her again. I really did have homework to finish, even if it was just a fourth and final proofread of my Midsummer Night's Dream paper.

"They turned off the heat, those sons of bitches," Mama huffed. "That's why she looked so bad. It was so cold in there, it shrunk her skin down to her bones. Poor girl," she said to the corpse. "We wouldn't let your family see you like that. *Eìonía í mními.*" Mama did her cross and said the traditional Greek blessing for the dead, staring daggers at me. I repeated the condolence.

May her memory be eternal, indeed.

"Go, go, Soula. Do your homework." She shooed me away as she gathered her cosmetic supplies. I tore my eyes away from the young female on the table and hopped off the stool. Just as I was about to leave, Mama shouted, "Thanasoula?"

I turned back, noting the use of her most precious nickname for me.

"Whatever you do, never work in that ugly glass building. I mean it."

"Well, Mama. I'll probably work here, so you don't have to worry."

"That's my good girl."

She needn't have worried. Death by filing cabinet scared me away from ever entertaining a career in the corporate sector.

Waylon—Now

"DAMN, WELLS. I DON'T think I've seen you so quiet. Or crank out so many chin-ups. Maybe this should be your cue to ease up on the conversation in the gym," Reyes hoisted his gym bag over his shoulder as we left the locker room.

"I know I should give it back to you, but this time you're right. That is my problem. I give it all away. Right at the start. I have no boundaries."

"You have boundaries, man. You're just honest. And you expect the same level of honesty back. But she didn't lie to you. Not really. You were just acting under false assumptions. You banged a real hot girl, and she didn't want any strings. What I don't get is why you're being such a sweet angel baby about it." Reyes emptied the rest of his water bottle into the shaker container and glugged down his protein shake before opening the door. I followed him out onto the cracked asphalt. It was hot today. And bright. The parking lot reeked of tar, and last night I drank way too much of that shitty bourbon after Soula left. I was surprised I could even finish my work out without puking.

"Since when is honesty a problem? Don't you get sick of the lies people feed you? About the dumbest shit, too. I get it so much at work, I need a break in my personal life."

"No, see, that's what you don't want. Honesty on a first date. First dates are supposed to be mysterious. It's not lying. It's putting up a fucking wall, so you don't get hurt."

"This from the married guy with five kids?"

His shoulders shook. He didn't smile. Or laugh. The shoulders were my only indication he was amused. "I am the wall. I don't need anything built around me. And Tiff carries a sledgehammer." Reyes was right. The word *formidable* came to mind looking at him. He wasn't any bigger than me, but his perpetually grim face and shrewd eyes made me look even more like the *good cop*.

"Maybe." I leaned against the SUV with my gym bag still over my shoulder. "And I'm not a sweet angel baby. I'm just getting old. One-night stands are for college. I want a family one day, too."

"Not with a one-night stand, you don't. I knew I should've gone with you last night. You need me to keep you out of trouble. What else have we got today?" Reyes asked. "Rescuing orphaned kittens?"

"I don't want to think beyond the extra-large coffee that's next on the agenda."

We'd completed our workouts, showered, and changed. The morgue didn't open until 9, so we had time. I looked at my phone. "After the ME's office, it's back to the shop to stare at footage for hours for a bullshit case." I could only hope some baby animal walked across my path today. It was looking pretty bleak.

"Just a heads up, the ME's not one for leaking early leads, and *I* have an *in*, but maybe you'll have better luck with her. Since you're such a sweet angel baby and all," Reyes grinned before throwing his bag in the back.

chapter seven

Waylon—Now

REYES SLAMMED THE EXPLORER in park and gave me a look out of the corner of his eye.

"You sure about this? This case is...." He shook his head. "Dr. Smythe really isn't going to release any information until she's done."

"Yeah, you said that—"

"Like, *done* done—knows manner, cause, tox, every fucking detail. And she's no people person. Hates an audience unless it's pretty obvious it's a homicide and this..." he shook his head. "I know it's your first suspicious but come on, man. There really ain't nothing suspicious about it. You sure you want to see that shit again? You looked a little green yesterday."

"That was at the scene. This'll be different. The stainless steel. The antiseptic. Probably won't even smell. I just need to see it through."

Reyes nodded. "Alright. Cause I told her this was timely."

"She believed you? The vic wasn't found for three weeks and you're putting a hustle on her?"

"No fucking way. But she agreed to initiate you anyway." My partner laughed, his teeth glowing against his tan skin. So much for not showing his emotions. I led the way up the concrete stairs with the rusted-through handrail. The stairs into the morgue looked like a death trap itself.

I had never visited the Medical Examiner's office during my very brief time as a beat cop. In my previous career, I'd gone in once. Ran in the front door, grabbed a stack of manila envelopes from the receptionist, and hightailed it out of there before jogging back across the street to the courthouse to assist the old DA.

This was different.

It's not like I hadn't seen dead bodies before. I was called to a DOA several times a month. I'd seen *this* dead body. But that didn't make me like them any better.

"Got your smelling salts, Wells?"

I was hesitating too long. Nevertheless, I did have an ampoule of ammonia in my pocket. Not that I'd need it. "I'll be okay." I took a deep breath of fresh air—my last for the foreseeable future—and rang the buzzer.

A young woman with green and black hair, multiple facial piercings, and colorful neck tattoos opened the door almost immediately, leaning out to beckon us inside.

"Gentlemen," she greeted us.

"Hey, baby. What's up?" Reyes stepped in first, kissing the woman chastely on the lips.

"Same old, same old. People need dissecting. Hey, new guy." She nodded at me.

"Tiff, this is Wells. Wells, my wife, Tiffany Reyes," Reyes introduced us. Tiff held out her hand and shot a nasty look at the man standing next to me.

"I didn't realize he was married to the morgue," I said, shaking her hand. "Great to meet you, Tiffany."

"Tiffany's like, super Valley Girl. Everyone calls me Tiff. I'm the autopsy tech. Dr. Smythe's filthy, right-hand woman." She smiled, and I glimpsed a flash of silver embedded somewhere in her gums. I liked her immediately.

"Come on back and let your noses become intimately acquainted with the county morgue." Tiff guided us through the bowels of the building like it was the most gruesome walking tour in history. "I'm warning you now, we're in the decomp room but the down draft vent is old as fuck and can only handle so much stench."

Tiff called to attention the fact that the smell of death hadn't yet accosted my nose. Merely strong cleaning fluids and the general mustiness of a midcentury building. In that respect, it wasn't much different from a hospital or Kudzu's vet clinic. I sighed in relief. I had stupidly built up the disgust factor. Reyes only made it worse.

This probably wouldn't be so bad after all.

"Has she already started?" Reyes asked. I hadn't met the Medical Examiner assigned to this case. All I knew was that her name was Dr. Smythe, and she was very thorough. And a stickler for rules. That suited me just fine, since that was also my M.O.

"Doc's finishing up a call. Then she'll be in to open the chest. I've already completed the external exam, so if you want to join me now, feel free. Masks are over there, but I'm warning you now, it won't help." She elbowed to the counter where the PPE was housed. Reyes and I both swiped a set of surgical gloves. "Oh, no. You'll need a gown, too. You'll never be able to dry-clean the smell out of that pretty suit otherwise." After we were gowned and bonneted, Reyes looked at me with raised eyebrows and glanced to the ammonia packet taped to one of the cabinet doors. I patted my jacket pocket, and he nodded.

"Through here," Tiff backed into the decomp room—literally, the room specially designed to autopsy severely decomposed bodies—as she jerked the thick plastic shield over her surgical face mask.

As soon as the door opened a crack, I imagined a green wisp of putrid smoke wafting toward us. Shit. This was worse than I remembered when I'd processed the call. And that was when I was in the house *after* the body had been removed.

Body removed. Not the smell.

Reyes coughed. "You sure about this? My eyes are tearing up." He didn't like it any more than me, but this was my first assignment. I needed to make a good impression with the captain, who thought I was some kind of boy scout. I wanted to solve this quickly and get as much conclusive evidence needed for a potential conviction, if it came to that. That was my job. I needed to remain professional and get the facts.

I followed Tiff into the room.

The scent was a brick wall. It was so thick I could hear it.

My stomach heaved, and I swallowed down the coffee that threatened to decorate the inside of my mask. Tiff failed to hide her smile, if she tried at all. "Told ya it was bad. He smells worse than usual. Must have been hot in his house. I'm shocked there's any tissue left. He must have popped weeks ago."

Popped. The word echoed around the tiled room, invoking a respective image that undulated like my very consciousness. I searched my pocket for the ammonia.

Oh God. I chose the wrong fucking career. Again.

"Any—" I gulped air and swallowed down the saliva that pooled in my mouth. "Anything notable yet? On the..." *hiccup* "... exterior?" I asked. Maybe if I maintained my professional composure, asked the right questions, got a useful piece of information, I'd hold down my breakfast: black coffee on a hungover stomach. I'd planned badly.

"Umm... that's really up to the doc's discretion." Tiff looked nonplussed. "Skin's too discolored to see any marks. I don't really know if I should—"

The door swung open. A woman, presumably Dr. Smythe, backed in, tying her surgical mask over her blue hair bonnet and lifting her own face shield from a hook on the wall.

"Have you finished photographing, Tiffany?" The doc asked her tech. I turned to the sink behind me, mentally resisting the pulsing of my stomach. I braced against the stainless steel countertop and lowered my head between my hands. Then, fuck it. I ripped the smelling salts off the wall and cracked it open, taking a whiff of the ammonia before turning around again.

At least Reyes wasn't laughing. He actually looked concerned. The ammonia made my eyes water, but it didn't help the nausea. Too bad it wasn't the sight that got to me. That was gruesome enough, but as a former prosecutor, I'd viewed close-ups of the most horrific murder scenes with routine nonchalance.

Photographs were different. They didn't smell.

For the sake of decency, or a moment's relief, I could look away when my eyes had had enough. Here, there could be no turning away, because the smell followed you. There was no decency, no brief respite. With every inhale, my lungs filled with more putrefying death molecules. There was no escaping it.

I heard a smile in Tiff's voice as she answered the doctor's questions.

"Doc, this is Detective Wells," she said, a bit louder. I took a shallow breath and righted myself, turning to face the diminutive doctor. I started to reach out my hand before I realized she was elbow deep in gore and holding the arms of a giant pair of gardening shears, prying open the chest cavity of the victim. Her eyes flicked up to meet mine and images of last night flooded my brain. It was her. *Soula.*

Then... a sickening chunk, the sound of the tree pruners crunch-cutting through a rib reverberated through the ceased chatter.

The only sound—other than the exhaust of the malfunctioning down draft vent—was the spatter of my stomach contents hitting the linoleum at my feet. The last thing I remembered before my head hit the floor were Soula's frightened eyes looking up at me behind dark lashes and a plastic shield.

chapter eight

Soula—Now

THE CHEAP GIFT SHOP mug burned my hands.

I eased into my swivel chair, trying to avoid its usual squeaking complaint so it wouldn't rouse my living patient. It had been years since I'd checked anyone for concussion. Not since internship rounds in the ER.

Wells was concussed, but not badly. It was better for him to rest. Reyes had an interview at noon and left his new partner in my care.

Fine. This was completely fine.

I'd do some explaining. He'd probably agree that it was entirely natural for me to lie about my job after experiencing all this. Thenceforth, all future conversation would proceed in typical doctor/patient protocol. It was fortunate, for me anyway, that he fainted. It threw a clinical blanket over this whole, potentially awkward mess.

I set the mug on my desk and leaned back in my chair, looking at the room as if seeing it through his eyes. I never really took much stock in my office. It was a room for phone calls and paperwork. The files were the interesting part of my job, not the décor on the walls around me.

The only "decorating" I had done was removing the overhead fluorescent bulbs and adding an incandescent desk lamp to cut down on the headache-inducing blue light. I had to convince the maintenance guys that there was nothing wrong with the circuit, that I had simply taken out the bulbs so my colleagues wouldn't automatically flick the lights on when they came in for a meeting.

Now that I was really looking at my office for the first time, it was so... brown. The nondescript bluish industrial carpet was stained. Not with body fluids, but with numerous beverages through the years and rubbed in by too many cleaning solvents so that it appeared an even more nondescript brown-blue, as if those colors were the same. The walls were the tan of a peanut and I hadn't thought to enliven them with art. Not even a puppy calendar. My desk was a dark brown, wood-grain plastic laminate mass, a mess of paper files, crime reports, notes that I was still working on, and a laptop that I mostly used at home once my notes were complete.

The only thing about my office that didn't stink of commercial/industrial boredom was my plaid loveseat and its dozing occupant: one Detective Waylon Wells.

His eyes were shut, freeing me to study him in his slumbering form. The 70s polyester plaid couch cozily offset his blue button-down. The boyishness of his face was enhanced by hair that had gone awry at his temples. Tufts curled slightly around the ice pack on his forehead. I'd forgotten how handsome he was.

He grimaced slightly in his sleep. I suspected his headache was still there, lurking in the background of his unconscious state. His body held itself so tightly together, he looked like a mummy resting in a sarcophagus that was entirely too small. Indeed, the couch was not meant to provide a comfortable bed for a man over six feet tall. It was scratchy, too.

Suddenly, I was embarrassed by this space. Dr. Li's wife painted his office. He brought in his own desk and bookshelves. Antiques. Why hadn't I thought to do the same? I didn't even have a plant in here to break up the brown.

Wells sighed deeply. *He* broke up the brown. *He* enlivened the space much better than a plant ever could. Not just his human-ness, but his Wells-ness. There was something innately good in him. I could intuit his altruism. He was like the sun. Not the torturous summer sun. But the sun breaking through the clouds on a brisk October day, warming you just enough to burn off the damp chill and make you think of trick-or-treating and campfires. I wondered if he'd glow up my apartment as much as he did this room. Or did his shine only reach to the walls of this dim peanut can of a room.

What if I could keep him? Would it feel like October every day?

That was ridiculous. He'd never want me. No one that shiny ever wanted me. Only others as gloomy and morose as me wanted me around after they found out what I did for a living and that I had zero personality while doing it.

Well... this was a nice diversion, considering he was asleep. As soon as he woke, he'd...

No. Not asleep. Pretending. His eyebrows drew together.

"Should I leave, or...?" I asked. My voice sounded harsh after the long stretch of unbroken silence. One eye opened and shut again.

"I can smell it again." He winced.

"That's me. Sorry. Haven't showered yet. Before Reyes brought you in, I sprayed the room with lemon oil, though. I've heard it helps."

"You've heard?" He looked at me with narrowed eyes before closing them again. I could feel that icepick of a headache inside my own occipital lobe. I turned back to my laptop, finishing up my lab orders for the three autopsies I performed today. Wells has been here for much longer than planned.

"I don't really smell anything."

Wells made a sound in his throat. "That's nice for you."

"It's essential. I wouldn't be able to do my job if I had olfactory responses like yours."

"Meaning what? I can't handle my job?" He sat up and slowly pivoted his body toward me. I handed him a new ice pack as treaty terms.

"Meaning nothing. I don't mince words. We have different job requirements." I frowned and kicked my chair close to the loveseat. I leaned close to him and peered into his eyes, but he drew back. It was too dark in here to see his pupils, and God only knew where my penlight ended up after clinicals.

His hair was longer than I remembered from last night and his cheeks had a leanness that I found incredibly attractive. Also incredibly sad; knowing how often the trials of police work etched themselves upon the bodies of its participants. Midsections grew plumper, hair grew thinner, fine lines sunk into the corners of faces more quickly when working in homicide than, say, graphic design. Well's face already bore the early marks of premature aging of someone ten years his senior. He was less boyish awake, and it endeared me to him further. So far, I'd pinned him as a Huck Finn type. That good ole boy kind of player. All grown up, but still fishing in creeks. Baiting his hook to reel in women now, instead of crawfish.

Now I was re-working my theory. *This* Wells looked serious, astute, the kind of man I would choose out of a lineup if someone told me I could have any man I wanted based on looks and demeanor.

I remembered the mug of steaming tea, now cooled to a drinkable temperature. "This will help with the nausea."

His fingertips brushed the back of my hand as he took the cup from me. I resisted the urge to clench my hand from the unexpectedly thrilling connection.

He frowned into the Dolly Parton mug as I tucked my hands under my thighs. "What is it?"

"Ginger, peppermint, a bit of ashwaganda, and licorice root."

Inhaling the steam, his frown deepened.

"It's medicinal," I said. "It's not meant to be drunk with scones and watercress sandwiches. Sip it slowly and it'll relax the urge to vomit, if you still feel it."

"Only since you came in." I believe one tiny corner of his mouth quirked at me.

"Your cognitive function doesn't appear diminished. You're going to be fine, but I'll call Dr. Resovic to set up imaging." I ignored his comment, but it stung like nettles.

Wells looked like he was building the courage to stand, but after staring at the floor for several seconds, decided against it.

"No doctors," he grunted, obviously in need of a doctor.

"You're talking to a doctor."

His eyes shot to mine. "About that..."

"I didn't lie."

"You also didn't mention we work together. I presume you testify on these cases?"

The wheel of my chair slipped off the plastic mat thingy.

Unable to meet his laser gaze, I looked back at my screen. *Fuck.* I honestly didn't think about that angle. Or at least, not much. To me, nothing about a one-time social association could possibly present itself as a conflict of interest, but that's not how a jury could interpret it. Still, the only difference between Wells and, say, Reyes, wasn't the relationship itself, but the nature of the relationship. I was on *say-hello-when-you-see-each-other-at-the-Publix-sub-counter* terms with most of the detectives in the county. I bantered with them during postmortems. We laughed at inside jokes in the courthouse halls. Once, I was even invited to the station's holiday party. Not that I went.

I seriously doubted one sexual encounter would undermine my (or his) credibility in court, especially if that was the full extent of our social dealings.

Still, I needed to change the subject. "How severe is your dizziness?"

He leaned back and took a sip of his tea. He didn't try to stand. That answered that. "This isn't terrible," he sighed. He wasn't going to admit how bad I knew he felt.

"It's stupid how stoic you men become during the most ludicrous times."

"You think I'm being stoic?" He smirked.

"That was not a compliment." I handed him a paper I printed off. "Someone needs to stay with you for the next 48 hours, whether or not you see the neurologist. Monitor your headache. Take this home with you. If you label any of these symptoms greater than a three, you need to go to the ER."

"I'll be okay," he said. He took the paper and frowned down at it. "'*One, two, three, concussion?*' '*Tell a parent or guardian if you're feeling irritable?*' Soula, you gave me instructions for an eight-year-old."

I snatched the paper back. "Nevermind. You shouldn't be reading anyway. No thinking. No bright lights. No loud noises. No tv. No phones. No act—"

"No, no, no. How am I supposed to work? This is my first case. You can't take me off it now. His smell is burned into my nose for eternity. I didn't sacrifice my sense of smell or my cognitive function just for someone else to take over the lead."

"No driving. No physical activity. No NSAIDS. Nothing involving concentration," I continued, rattling off the list of forbidden stimuli. There had to be something that would catch his attention.

"I don't even know which ones are NSAIDS," he said, flustered. "I have interviews." He stood gingerly, depositing the mug and ice pack on my desk. He reached over for his suit jacket that was draped across the arm at the other end of the couch and he couldn't hide a wince.

I dialed Reyes's number on the office phone before he had fought his arms into his sleeves. It was ringing. I moved the receiver against my chin.

"Your sense of smell remains uncompromised. There is no evidence that putrescine and cadaverine destroy the olfactory receptors in the nose. Hey, Reyes."

"Great," Wells huffed sarcastically.

He ran his hands through his soft hair, and I lost my train of thought. "Uh, sorry, yeah. Wells is concussed. He needs 48 hours before resuming activity. You'll talk to Captain? Thanks. Oh, and who do I contact about babysitting him?... There's gotta be someone you can call, or... *ME?...* No. I'm not. But really, I'm the wor—"

I left the phone off the hook and ran to catch Wells before he escaped. I grabbed his arm and swung around in front of him. "You really don't have any family or friends who can look after you?"

I resumed speaking into the receiver. "This is really not in my wheelhouse, Reyes," I said before hanging up. I heard a chuckle from the corner of the room as he eased back down on the loveseat. He'd discerned what was happening.

I had agreed, out of necessity, to be Wells's babysitter for the weekend.

"Did you hang up on Reyes?"

"We had nothing more to say."

"Look, if you think I'm going to let you babysit me—"

"I don't think it." I clicked off my desk lamp and slipped my laptop into its sleeve. "That is exactly what's happening. And I don't like this any better than you."

"I have a case," he complained from his reclining position.

"And you look perfectly fit to solve it in your state." I glared at him. He glared at me. It was a standoff, and there was no way he was winning. Not when it came to healthcare. If I was willing to observe him for 48 hours, he would have to put up with me. But I could also see there was no way I could physically move him. I needed something better.

I hated giving out information before the case was written, but I made a concession this once. "Look, x-rays confirmed there was no metal in the body other than a faulty pacemaker, which means that gun you found at the scene wasn't a murder weapon, it was probably being cleaned. This is Tennessee after all. The tox screen won't be ready for weeks. *Your case* is pending the results of *my case* for the time being, and it looks like natural causes. You don't have any interviews, and Reyes knows it. He's just letting you have your fun little first case. Now let's go." I moved to the door, but he made no attempt to follow me. "Do I have to call for backup? I said, let's go."

"Okay, Warden." He stood, testing his sea legs. Six foot even. My visual assessments were usually spot-on. He took a few steps, gathered both of our mugs, which I always left for the cleaning crew, and followed me. I watched his feet for a few steps, ensuring they were steady and he didn't require assistance. Then I left him to hobble behind me.

chapter nine

Soula—Now

USUALLY, I CAME INTO the office on my days off.

The morgue was the only place I could manage some normalcy, unless there was a funeral happening in the Big House. Then, things got quiet. Even when my riotous brothers were small, they behaved like little old ladies during funerals.

When we had "company," i.e. a service or a viewing, we were allowed to read or watch tv in the attic. No fighting. No roughhousing. No quiet board games that would inevitably lead to fighting and roughhousing. The consequences involved a wooden spoon or house shoe to the behind, more shameful than physically painful, and confusingly followed by Mama dishing out an extra helping of dessert.

When there was no funeral, the house was a shrine to Chaos, the patron saint of adolescent boys. Deep in this meltdown-inducing pit of hell were the high-pitched wails of pranks-gone-wrong, stolen video game controllers, and the despair that someone else had eaten the last of the galaktoboureko. Life meant constantly being on guard for lurking brothers waiting to jump out from behind corners, being smack dab in the middle of the paths of boys throwing green beans at each other when Yia-Yiá wasn't looking and getting struck in the face by punches meant for others. It was the pungent smells of garlic or honey. Sometimes garlic and honey, complimenting the ever-present base note of formaldehyde drifting up from the embalming room.

I'd take the peace and quiet of the morgue any day.

Detective Wells awoke as my Tesla rumbled over the sparse gravel in his driveway. A black nose burst through a set of bent and broken miniblinds, though I couldn't yet hear the frenetic barking from inside the car.

"I'll just run in and get my things," he said drowsily as I shifted into park and unfastened my seat belt.

"For what?" I asked, one foot already on the gravel-dirt. We hadn't discussed a thing. Only that I wasn't letting him out of my sight this weekend. That was troubling enough, but I hadn't thought about housing. I assumed he'd want to recuperate in his own house.

I pivoted back into my seat. "You have somewhere else to go?"

He lowered his head back down into the car. "Well, we can't stay here. The floors." He shook his head. "It's not really guest-friendly at the moment. Just uh..." He glanced back toward the dog, furiously trying to decipher why her human was dawdling in a boring black sedan rather than throwing an object for her to fetch. "Just give me a few minutes to get some things. I'll call a kennel. See if they can take Kudzu for a few days."

His house was suddenly off limits? "I've seen the floors, Wells. They're fine. Eventually, they'll need re-sanding, maybe, but—"

"I started tearing them up last night."

"I was here last night."

"After you left." He squirmed.

"Okay. That's weird. Where do you propose we go?" I asked him.

He shrugged and looked at me like I was an idiot. "Your place."

"No." I looked straight ahead. It was impossible. Detective Wells above a mortuary hearse garage? I hadn't brought a guy onto Smythe Mortuary property since senior prom and that did not end well. Even worse was the idea of Detective Wells in such close proximity to my nosy, noisy family.

Wells smiled. "Don't tell me your house is a mess."

"We're not going to my house."

"You only have one bed and your spinster aunt wouldn't think it proper?" He was teasing me.

"This isn't a Christmas song." I did only have one bed, but I guess I could... "Not my house, please."

"Boyfriend?" He said it with a taunting smile, but his eyes lost a little of their sparkle awaiting my response. I should say yes. That'd probably be a convincing enough reason for him to drop the subject. But I hated lying. About anything but my job, that is.

"No boyfriend," I answered. His face didn't perk up. *Did I expect it to? Or want it to?*

"I can get us a hotel suite. A nice one, even. It would be like a vacation for you. Calm and relaxed."

"I hate to break it to you, but I've been a teenage boy. I've roomed with seven other dudes in college, too. I've lived through horrors worse than whatever you can bring, so don't think you can scare me away."

Scare him away? Away from what? Me?

A little chill ran down my spine. My cheeks were probably red, too. Part of me really did want to let him in. If anyone could handle the death part, it'd be a homicide detective. But the family part?

Maybe I could somehow sneak him in, spirit him into my coach house apartment. I could enlist Bethany's help. Or Dad's, or even Gus's, if he was around. He could be reasonable on occasion.

"You think on that," he said. "I'm going to let Kudzu out."

I nodded. This didn't have to be so bad. I wasn't in college anymore, trying to sneak a quickie in my apartment. This wasn't even sexual. It was medical. He was my patient and I had to look after him. It was against medical advice for him to be alone.

It's not like my family would have a problem with it, per se. It was the opposite I was worried about. They'd overwhelm him with unnecessary affection and food and questions. It was too much for him. He needed rest. From noise and activity and death.

I was still zoned out with my car door open when a cold, wet nose nudged its way between my hand and my thigh. I smiled at Kudzu and stroked her soft, golden-white head. She really had the sweetest eyes. I instantly wanted to sneak her treats behind her fur daddy's back. "Yeah, your human's hurt, huh? He'll be okay, but we have to take really good care of him. No loud barking, no jumping. You want to come stay at my apartment, Kudzu?"

Kudzu—that traitor—didn't even warn me that Wells was standing there, an odd smile playing on his lips.

"The kennel has room if you don't mind dropping her off." He looked at the leather interior and cringed. "I'll get a towel for the backseat. I just trimmed her nails. I promise."

"Waylon?" I called after him. "She's going to stay too. We talked about it."

"I appreciate it, but that's asking too much."

"You're not asking at all. In case you forgot, I'm the one telling you that you can't be alone this weekend. Now I'm telling you to bring the dog."

Two minutes later, he was layering towels on the backseat, and I was ordering takeout.

"What do you want from Puckett's?"

The dog hopped in, and Wells dropped his duffle bag into the trunk. "I'm sure I can make do with whatever you've got at home. I'm not picky."

"You can have the most accommodating pallet in Nashville and still not find a thing to eat in my apartment. Anyway, I'm placing the order now."

"I'd better not. I'm still not feeling great." He lay his hand flat against his stomach.

"That's probably because I still haven't taken a shower yet. You're not going to feel great for a few days, but you still need to eat. Come over here."

He leaned in, holding his breath, and I gestured for him to remove his sunglasses. His pupils were still equal. His eyes were still blue and brown and I was still mesmerized by their sunburst striations and dual colors. I could look at his eyes for hours, studying their bewitching, chimeric pattern. I shook my head to regain focus.

"Do you feel like you're going to vomit or just nauseated?"

"Just nauseated, I guess."

"How's the headache? Any better?"

"A little. The sunglasses help." I nodded. He let his sunglasses drop and sank deeper into the seat.

"When's the last time you've eaten?"

"Dinner last night at the Pig."

"You'll feel better with something in your stomach."

"Brisket Meat and Three then?" He pulled no punches when I told him food would help him feel better. "Mac and Cheese, coleslaw, green beans. Oh, and do you think you could get an order of the Pimento Cheese Bites?"

"Of course. It's a staple of my order."

"Awesome. I think I feel better already." He reached into his back pocket and retrieved his wallet.

"Oh no you don't." I pushed his credit card back on his side of the car.

"Next time, then."

Knowing it would take all of five minutes to get to the restaurant, I killed time by grabbing a sixpack of Honky Tonk's Blue Lemonade from the grocery.

"This any good?" Wells asked as I handed him the paper sack with the beer, a pound of dark roast, and a pint of cream for the morning.

"It's my favorite, but you aren't allowed alcohol." I threw the car in gear and prayed for street parking. I took too long at the grocery.

"This is gonna be fun," Wells deadpanned. I recognized the blatant sarcasm and couldn't agree more.

Curb parking. I got lucky. I ran into the restaurant to grab our to-go order, taking a minute to text a quick "911, but only if you're available. Meet me at the coach house in 5." to Bethany.

Wells, the BBQ restaurant, and my family home were all in the same general part of Franklin, five minutes from everywhere.

"God, this smells good." Wells inhaled the scents of woodsmoke and sweet, tangy brown sugar sauce.

"Best barbeque in Franklin," I said. Only a tiny part of me was thinking about how my car would smell like this deliciousness for days, perpetuating my never-ending lust for barbequed pork. I needed extra time at the club if I didn't start making some salads.

"Nah, the best barbeque in Franklin is that truck parked at the auto parts store."

"Which one?"

"On Columbia, near me."

"It's okay."

"Have you tried Big Jim's brisket? I could devour an entire plate heaped just with beef and come back two hours later for more."

"I'm not a fan of brisket," I lied. Really, you could take any meat, smoke it and slather it with a sweet-sour sauce and I was a diehard for it, but I was starting to discover that Wells and I agreed on too much as it was. I felt the need to be contrary.

I had to get through this weekend unaffected by my attraction to him. It was fortuitous then, that I had stellar practice being a cold-hearted bitch. Or so plenty of other men have assured me.

I put aside those thoughts and mentally planned my route. If I took Third home, I might be able to slip into the side of the property that didn't have any signage. Ignoring an industrial-looking, blonde brick cube of a crematorium behind the coach house, the property almost looked charming. Somewhere a normal, small-town family might live if they didn't incinerate corpses in their backyard.

Bethany stood in front of my garage bay door when I pulled up, her hands on her pencil-skirted hips. She was awash with a bright print, cluing me in that there were no clients. The stars had aligned. For various reasons, mourners arrived at all hours. To keep the bodies of their loved ones' company, they stayed for hours sometimes in the cold rooms downstairs. Sometimes, family members came to drop off a particularly beloved shade of grandma's lipstick or because they had forgotten to include shoes when they brought us their mom's funeral attire. We often had viewings that lasted late into the night. Such was the revolving-door of a family-run funeral home. Lovely for the clients, but damn-near impossible to have any sort of life outside other peoples' grief.

"You live here?" Wells looked around at the big white house, the multi-gabled coach house, the brick crematorium and when viewed through his eyes, it didn't seem as charming as I hoped he'd mistake it for. "Next to the cemetery?"

Oh. I'd forgotten about that.

"Yeah." I said it quickly and didn't elaborate, shutting off the engine and escaping the car.

"It's huge." He looked confused. Then he looked back at my Tesla as if it explained my masses of wealth—that didn't exist. I had one nice thing.

"No. I live up there." Pointing to the exterior stairs along the rear wall of the garage interior. Kudzu tumbled out from the back door and sniffed around the tires of the Cadillac XTC—my dad's pride and joy.

"I didn't realize Soula was bringing a guest. I'm not sure why she sent me the SOS." Bethany reached out a hand. "I'm Bethany."

"Just make sure Mom and George don't find out or they'll be up here in a second, putting him to work. He's just staying for the weekend. He fell. I have to watch him. He hit his head. And vomited. Actually, he vomited *then* fell. Then vomited again." Detective Wells's face was turning bright red. *Why am I flooding Bethany with information?*

"He's concussed." I said finally, as if that explained everything clearly. Since Bethany and I spoke the languages of Cause of Death and Anatomy, I sometimes forgot she was never trained in actually preventing death.

"Waylon Wells," he said, shaking his head and Bethany's hand.

"We didn't get to meet last night, but it's nice seeing you again," she smirked. I was trying to forget last night, but Bethany seemed eager to remind me.

"I'm going to let Kudzu do her business if it's okay with my keeper, here."

Bethany quirked her eyebrow at me. "I like the sound of that."

"Fine, just go around the other side of the garage where they can't see." I glared at Bethany as Waylon whistled for his dog to follow him.

"So? You're playing doctor this weekend?"

"I *am* a doctor *every* weekend," I reminded her.

"Yeah, but not with a repeat patient who looks like *that*."

My mind already wandered back to my patient. "He went the back way, right?" I didn't see him disappear around the corner.

"Think so, why?"

"I forgot about the cornerstone." I chased after him in the direction I thought he'd gone. Bethany hustled after me, running gracefully in her heels. I turned the corner and saw Wells, his attention glued to the bronze sign on the brick cube designating the building not only as the crematorium, but with my family name; Smythe.

"You didn't tell him he's staying at a funeral home? Don't you think he might be uncomfortable?" She whispered.

"Of course I didn't tell him." I hissed. "Just like I didn't tell him about my job until we came face to face across a decomp."

"And he puked," Bethany said on a sigh.

If that wasn't the most fitting image of my love life...

"Speaking of decomp...." Bethany trailed off.

"Let me guess, the family wants a viewing?" It always seemed to happen during the most extreme cases. Guilt about not finding their dead family member until it was too late.

"No, but they still want him embalmed, and guess who got roped in after I'd just promised Sofia I'd take her to the new Pixar movie tonight? Anyway, enough with the poor me, I better get to work, or he won't have an intact carotid. Text me if you need anything, and no, I didn't say anything to your Ma."

"Bethany?" I called after her. She turned back to me.

"There's no intact carotid." I winced with the message. It didn't really make her job harder, just more futile, since embalming was supposed to keep corpses from decomposing and this corpse was already the consistency of chicken soup.

She sighed.

"Whatever, freak," I teased her. "You live for this shit and you're fabulous at it."

"I know. I just like the solidarity of complaining." She winked and wiggled away to change back into her scrubs.

chapter ten

Waylon—Now

I NEVER REALIZED THE place where bodies were cremated was called a *crematorium*. It sounded too literal, too on-the-nose, and surprisingly morbid during a time when every word or phrase surrounding death had a preferred and impotent euphemism.

Most of the wakes I attended were now *celebrations of life*. Hearses were *coaches*, as if a team of horses drove them. Mortuaries were *funeral homes*, as if that made any kind of difference to the corpse being pumped full of shit and spray tanned. Even death itself was *passed on*.

It was ludicrous, now that I'd given it a moments' thought. So much so that the word *crematorium* emblazoned on the bricks in that Mad Men font was sort of refreshing. But only sort of, because I still knew what happened inside.

"I'm sorry," said a small voice behind me. I spun around. The spinning didn't stop with my body, but I ignored the sensation. I wasn't going to give Soula a reason to keep me any longer than necessary. If it *was* necessary. "Sorry for what?"

"You must be horrified. I should have told you where I live. I just..." She couldn't look me in the eye. Actually, she rarely made direct eye contact. She looked at me in her periphery. And when I wore sunglasses. Or when she thought I was sleeping. It made her seem small, somehow. Almost childlike. Except not, because that made me feel gross.

"I've had bad responses from men when they found out I live in a funeral home."

"That doesn't sound like a man you'd want to take home in the first place."

"That's true, I guess. I'm not a very good judge of character." She was still looking at the fine bladed grass, stunningly green under the dark clouds that were collecting. This whole little corner of the world was stunning. In the middle of a town, but also tucked into nature. The wind rushed through the heavy trees in the woods across the street and she shivered though the temperature hadn't dropped much.

"Soula," I stepped closer to her, reaching out, wanting to take that chill away. She looked up, stunned. Like I was a hunter, and she was the deer. I didn't move any farther, an attempt to lay down my proverbial shotgun. If we were stuck together because of me, I'd at least make her feel as comfortable as I could. And I sensed that meant a whopping dollop of honesty.

No games, no half-truths, no hiding anything. That was what we both needed.

"I didn't need a sign. I knew where we were as soon as we pulled in."

"You did?"

There was the eye contact I'd been wanting. My stomach dropped when her dark eyes let me in. For one too-short instant. All the weird shit I had felt when she was in my bed, when her legs were wrapped around my head, when I was deep inside her, it all came flooding back.

I had gone briefly insane with her once. I'd have to be careful or it would easily happen again.

"I'm a cop, remember? It's kind of our job to know where everything is. Besides, I've been to funerals here. It's not a big secret." I cringed, thinking of something my mom used to say. "Anyway, it's hard to keep secrets when you're a homer."

"Yes, well, whenever Kudzu's ready, we can..." She swung the take-out bag around her body. Sentences were rare with her. She spoke in starts and stops, making exaggerated hand gestures I suspected she might not have even noticed. Maybe she was hoarding her words deep inside her head, not yet trusting me with access to her thoughts.

But under her naïve and youthful façade, Soula reminded me of a general of an army, some Ancient Roman or Norse battalion. Cool and in command. Always quiet because words were unnecessary. Words were for the rabble, not plotting, brilliant tacticians like her. She was ten steps ahead of the enemy and had already won the siege in her mind.

I took a few more tentative steps, and she turned away from me. My fingers reached toward hers, wanting to be entwined with the heat from her hands, but something told me she wouldn't let this go anywhere. Not this weekend. Not in the state she needlessly assumed I was in. Instead of holding her hand, I loosened her fingers from the twisted paper cord holding our meals, relieving her of the food before she dropped it.

The dog and I followed Soula around the garage and up the set of stairs to her apartment, unsure of what to expect from her place. My imagination vacillated between bare drywall with a single mattress on the floor and a gothic castle.

"It's not much," she said. "I never intended to live here long. I need to start looking for other places."

I pinched the bridge of my nose. I hadn't thought about the ache in my head until now, as the throbbing returned. She read the pain on my face.

"Anyway, sorry about the mess. Let's get you fed and into bed." She blushed and her fingers froze on the knob for a second, but she didn't backtrack.

When she opened the door, I was struck by the glare of the coming storm streaming in from the wall of windows. She kicked off her doctor clogs and hung her bag on the only hook that wasn't already taken up by various blazers, suit jackets, and workout gear. She gave me a little smile.

"I'll clean this out for you."

Kudzu took off first, investigating her new surroundings. I smiled, then winced. The brightness made my headache worse, but ordinarily I would have appreciated it the airiness of the apartment. I stepped out of my oxfords and lined them up neatly next to the pile of Chuck Taylors and boots.

The apartment was open concept with a single hallway leading to the left. The kitchen, walls, and furnishings were all stark white, which made the small space look bigger but made me cringe, knowing how Kudzu would love jumping up and snuggling into the corner of that big sectional. Since it was usually just the two of us, I'd been a sucker and hadn't trained her to stay off furniture.

Other than books, the only décor came from outside those windows. They framed the verdant tree line so stunningly, I could see why Soula let the view speak for itself. We must be overlooking Harpeth River Park to the north. I couldn't see the river itself, since the trees were in full leaf, but there was no mistaking the circular-paved walking path below.

Soula stood behind a pristine kitchen island—cabinets and counter also white—awaiting my response, one way or another.

She'd seemed so out of her element at the Bunganut Pig. Was that only last night? Earlier today, I'd been barely able to register her presence before heaving my guts out and loathing my sheer existence for a few hours. Still, at the morgue, I got the sense that she was in control and in her element. The general. She was absolutely formidable in the those seconds before I was overcome with green, vomity, repulsion.

Just thinking about that feeling—the bile rising in my throat, saliva pooling in the crevices of my mouth—brought it back. I inhaled deeply through my mouth. Soula snapped into action, rushing toward me, slipping the overnight bag off my shoulder and physically moving me down the hallway, toward the bathroom.

What was my tell? That human version of what dogs looked like immediately before they vomited? The undulating, reverse-gulp alarm that sent you careening into the room to make sure they puked on the vinyl and not the carpet. I could only guess that's what my body was doing now. I was focused and determined to swallow it back down. I'd already puked in her morgue. I wasn't going to heave the few sips of that disgusting tea she made me drink on her hardwood.

She lifted the toilet seat and sat me down on the edge of her bathtub. "Deep breaths. It's okay if you feel nauseated. Just vomit. It'll make you feel better."

I liked Soula like this. In charge, soothing, pragmatic, and standing between my knees, her hand resting on my shoulder without consideration. An offering of care. She was less self-conscious when she felt needed.

Or maybe I wanted to like Soula like this. I wished she'd be more comfortable with me when I wasn't in immediate need of her medical attention, but maybe it was the only thing she knew.

The urge passed. I felt better, though still not as good as I pretended to feel. My eyes settled at her thigh, encased in hospital-issue green scrubs that stretched tightly over her muscles. I couldn't make out the line separating her strong quadriceps, but I remembered it was there. Her legs drove me crazy last night. If I just lifted my index finger ever so slightly against her knee, I'd feel her again.

She inched away. "I'm going to shower in the other bathroom. Stay here until I come back for you."

I was more than fine. Not just pretending to be. The nausea passed and I stood without a hitch, feeling only slightly like a naughty boy breaking the rules.

She came back with her hair wrapped in a towel wearing a stretched-out t-shirt and black leggings. It looked like something someone would clean their house in, and suddenly, this was my ultimate fantasy. Her in that thin, black t-shirt that looked so soft it begged to be touched and those prominent nipples that poked through what must have been a poorly functioning bra.

She handed me a glass of ice water and I sipped slowly, now trying to avoid her eye contact.

Why was she looking at me like that *now*? This woman drove me up a wall.

When she breathed in, her lips parted. Her shirt slipped off a shoulder, revealing flawless golden skin and no bra strap. My eyes darted to her breasts before I could stop them. Following their gaze, her cheeks reddened before she turned and closed the door, leaving me there in the bathroom, half-hard and holding a glass of ice water I'd rather plunge into than sip.

After splashing cold water on my face, I opened the door to Soula's round ass, tucking a hospital corner into the sheets.

Dear God, would there be no relief?

I craved the feeling of my hands around her waist; her ass pressing into me. Gliding my hands up the front. Under her shirt. Cupping her sweet little...

Shit. I was supposed to be here recuperating from a concussion, not dripping with desire for the doctor taking care of me. Even if it was unnecessary, my being here. These were doctor's orders and attraction would only make this weekend less productive. I'd read the writing on the wall last night. She wasn't open to any kind of romance between us. And I couldn't put myself through another no-strings night with her, so fuck desire.

"I changed the sheets. Obviously," she said, flumping pillows into cases. "Are you hungry?"

"Mmm... I kind of feel like smoked meat was a bad idea."

Soula looked stricken, but nodded. "I should have realized. I'm sorry. I, um... I'll give you a few minutes." She gestured to the hockey bag she'd brought into the room for me.

It didn't take me any time to change into a t-shirt and gym shorts and my nausea had eased. Soula said there was Tylenol in the kitchen, but I didn't feel like bothering with the pills. I'd sleep in a bit. Let oblivion resolve the pain. Right now, I was too hungry and curious to settle down.

I peeked around the door of the second bedroom that Soula used as a home office. Besides the blonde wood of the floors, the deep charcoal on the walls was the only splash of color in her apartment. Soula wasn't in the open kitchen/living room. Kudzu lifted her head briefly before letting it drop back down on the couch. *Of course she was on the couch.*

I was alone in Soula's most private space, and I was at odds with myself, both desperate to solve her like a case and determined to start building that wall Reyes talked about.

Besides the whiteness of the apartment, there were elements of hard, black, powder-coated steel—a coffee table just waiting to bruise your shins, a chest under the tv, matching the black steel casing of the windows. Besides that, there wasn't much personality to the space.

There were no framed beach photos with her friend Bethany, no giant quotes nailed to the walls, no modern art pieces. Maybe that was telling too, although I didn't know what story it told.

Maybe her life was so full, this dwelling was her inner sanctum, and she purposely kept it free from distraction. I wasn't taking that theory to the bank. The only thing breaking up the neutrality was the jungle of green foliage covering the bank of windows on one side of the open space. She didn't strike me as a plant person, but if Soula were to have a pet, I should have guessed it'd be inanimate.

It didn't surprise me to find her fridge just as blank as her walls, even lacking the typical plumber's magnets or Chinese takeout menus. I refilled my glass from the tap, trying not to think about the chemicals that probably got flushed down the drain at this property.

Soula had filled a large mixing bowl with water for Kudzu and the conscientious gesture stirred my sense of parental pride. I wondered if she'd ever had dogs before. Probably not if she grew up in the funeral home across the street. I'd have loved a dog running through a funeral service, barking at a UPS truck outside, but most grieving people would probably consider that uncouth.

The fridge was practically empty except for a drawer filled with tiny ketchup and soy sauce packets and a scattering of other to-go condiments. There wasn't a crumb or stray coffee ground on the counter, but she did have a top-of-the-line coffee maker that looked lived in. I'd die if this headache continued in the morning AND there was no coffee.

Enough snooping. Soula was bound to burst in and find me with my hand in her drawers and throw me out. On second thought, that could be for the best. I could go back to work. But then I would never solve the mystery of *her*. And my intuition was telling me I was right where I needed to be.

I had felt that same tug from my intuition the moment I saw Soula. I guess that was why I had gotten so carried away last night. It was easy for me to forget that some people didn't rely on instinct the way I did.

Or maybe Soula's instincts were driving her in the other direction. Maybe that's why she'd been gone for a while now.

Fuck it, I couldn't wait anymore. I opened the cupboards in search of Tylenol. I wasn't trying to sneak. Or notice the lack of food. Seriously. No ramen, no dusty cans of tomato soup, no five-pound brick of sugar. Nothing. I wasn't much of a cook, but damn, everyone had salt.

I gave up my search about the time I heard Soula come in, carrying a big bowl of something. Judging from the size of it, I wouldn't have been surprised if it was chunks of raw meat for the dog. That might account for why Kudzu was so taken with her, other than for the same reason I was so taken with her.

"Did you get much snooping done?" She sort of smiled. Or maybe I just imagined it. Her eyes looked even darker now that the sky was dark.

"Uh, yeah, actually. I was looking for Tylenol."

She shook a bottle of pills in her hand and tossed it to me. Then her bare feet stepped into the kitchen next to me.

"Spanakorizo. Greek comfort food from the big house," she said. "In case you don't want something heavy."

She lifted the cover off the bowl, and a sharp fragrance hit my nose. Soula grabbed a serving spoon from the drawer behind her and a plate from one of the cabinets—I must have missed the cabinet with actual contents. The dish looked like rice covered by some kind of pesto, except it smelled like pickles. I grimaced. It didn't look bad. It just looked... green.

"You don't have to eat it. You can stick with your meat and three. But now you have options."

Maybe my intuition was right about this weekend. Maybe there was even a reason I hit my head on the green linoleum morgue tiles and that my sister and I weren't currently on speaking terms so that I had to be nursed back to health—wink—by this mysterious, sexy, smart, quirky woman. And hopefully, if my intuition led me appropriately, I'd know what she needed from me in order to make sure she still felt comfortable around me.

This was the first step, I told my intuition. This was the building phase. No, more like the location-scouting phase. This wasn't the time to plan for a tire swing in the backyard.

chapter eleven

Soula—Then

IT WAS A TYPICAL, early spring day in the Smythe household.

The cool perfection wouldn't last long in middle Tennessee, but at that particular moment, all the windows that weren't warped shut with age had been flung open, the buttery scent of spanakopita drifting out into the lily garden.

Dad was soaping up the coach after it splattered through the cemetery mud during an early morning interment and my brothers and I raced down to the riverbank as soon as we tore off our church clothes.

It was our favorite place to play when we were little. We caught crawdads. I dissected them. My brothers tried to scare me with earthworms and potato bugs until they finally realized I was more comfortable with gross stuff than they were.

I liked to play Anne of Green Gables, imagining I had a bosom friend like Diana. Really, I'd just walk through the woods imagining myself in frothy layers of white gossamer cotton. Long skirts billowing behind me while my long dark hair flowed freely. I don't know what my brothers did, but I doubt it was as pensive.

I twirled around a flowering redbud tree and stopped short. My foot held aloft, frozen in place, lest I tramp directly through a ribcage. It was still meaty in parts, bleached white in other spots. A fawn. Long dead, and alone.

"Eww. Nasty." That was Gus. He was probably ten at the time, because he got really skinny that year, so I was probably eight or nine. He was also right. It was nasty. As kids, we didn't see many decomposed bodies. Animal or otherwise. Dad started us out in the business early, training us that the best way to deal with dying is to get comfortable with death. Since we lived with death, we got a running start. But he wasn't a monster. He still shielded us from the grimmest aspects of the trade.

From its skull down to its hooves, the carcass was mostly bones, but some of the characteristic white spotted fur remained on its rump. It was as if nature was playing a cruel joke, leaving behind this decaying remnant of a deer, while ensuring we knew it was a baby.

I didn't overly grieve the deaths of little people. Once, I went to the funeral of another kid in the second-grade class across the hall from mine. He died of a childhood cancer, and it was sad, but no more so than anyone else who cast a momentary pall over the household when a funeral was in session.

But that deer. That was different. I wanted to stroke his face but there was nothing there. I wondered how long his mother stood next to him, nudging him to wake up. What must it have felt like for her to walk away from her baby, in search of her next mouthful of grass or a lick of the muddy waters of the Harpeth.

My brothers were sad too, of course. They might have been on the naughty side, but they weren't psychopaths. It was a bummer on all counts. That tiny death stopped me in my tracks, though. Literally and figuratively. I started thinking about all those baby caskets we kept hidden in the storage room, ready for use at a moment's notice, out of sight of clients. I thought of all the little bodies my mom had lovingly prayed over and posed in their eternal satin beds, the security blankets and beloved books placed with toddlers when mourners came to kiss their tiny baby hands one last time. The whole backlog of those deaths hit me at once, and I couldn't let them go.

I couldn't let that deer go either. I hated him with every shuddering breath, yet I couldn't look away.

"Soula?" My brothers each grabbed an arm, steadying me, then sandwiching me between them in their arms. The strength to stand left me. My face was wet.

"Soula, let's go home. It's probably time for lunch anyway." That was the ever-practical George.

"You're crying." Gus said simply, holding my hand. He was ruled by emotion, but with me he always knew the simplest way of responding was the best.

I let the boys run ahead, assuring them I was fine. I *was* fine. I had regained control of myself. I told myself I wasn't a deer. My own future didn't lie in that bleak, gaping hole of a sunken eye socket. Barring injury or illness, I had a 99-point-something percent shot at aging into adulthood. I would decide my own fate.

Walking a little farther along the river before crossing Third, I took the path through the cemetery. The magnolias were in bloom. Who could feel disconsolate when the great big, cherry Chapstick-colored saucer magnolias were in bloom? Here, in Rest Haven Cemetery, I couldn't be Anne. I couldn't be Julie of the Wolves, or Kit Tyler from Blackbird Pond, or even any of the March sisters. I was Athanasía Smythe of Smythe & Sons Mortuary. And no matter what happened in my life, I was never EVER having children.

Soula—Now

"Soula, stay and eat. You never eat with the family anymore," Mama said. She shook her favorite knife at me: the eight-inch chef's knife with the broken-off tip and blade that's needed sharpening since 1995. That knife was barely a threat to chicken anymore, let alone her kids.

With a smidgen of guilt and a dollop of shame, I still lived ten feet from my mother, whose only hobby was force-feeding her children in the name of "love."

"Ma. The family never eats with the family anymore." George popped an olive in his mouth and leaned out the screen door to spit the pit in the boxwoods.

"We never have, really," I said, also taking an olive from the salad Ma was cutting. She whapped my knuckles with the flat of her blade. I carefully chewed the meat off the small stone in the center and placed it in the trash can like a human being. "We've been too busy. For the past ten years."

"And for the twenty years before that," Mama nodded. "Since I met your father, he hasn't taken more than a weekend off."

"Your honeymoon," I countered.

"Some honeymoon. Him meeting all the theas and cousins and Yia-Yiás and Pappoús. Everybody around us all the time, sleeping on the porch of your cousin's apartment because it was so hot. Georgíos, don't go to Greece on your honeymoon, Babymou. Go somewhere nobody knows you."

"Ma, I never will... again." George frowned. He'd sworn off women years ago, so Mama bringing it up at all was ludicrous. She still had high hopes that her oldest son would find happiness somewhere.

The rest of us didn't matter.

Anyway, if there would ever be another wedding among the Smythe kids, it would be Gus's, but he was almost as unlikely to marry as me.

In his early twenties, Gus had brought women here to "meet the family" for his traditional, post-sex dates—which turned into their traditional last dates, since the woman would take one look at the sign out front and break it off then and there. It worked well for him for a while; he came out looking like the good guy instead of the fuckboy he really was, and it got him out of a relationship he didn't want.

Then he straightened himself out, going a little too far in the other direction; he wasn't a fuckboy anymore. At least not while he was in seminary.

"When's dinner going to be ready?" I asked, anxious that I had left Wells alone for too long.

"Just a few more minutes for the rice to thicken. Then you can take the whole pot with you."

"Why do you need the whole pot?" George narrowed his eyes. He still wore his funeral director suit. The black matching his dark hair and the circles under his eyes perfectly. He pushed himself beyond reason, but he was kind of an asshole, so I didn't really care.

"Athanasía has a date," Ma explained—very, very incorrectly.

My mouth dropped. "What? How do you—"

George looked me over. "No way she has a date. She doesn't date. Look at her."

"Thea Soula, you have a date?" Bethany's daughter Sofia bounced in and Mama slid a small dish of feta over to her. *WTF, she gets her own plate?* The rest of us have to eat the good stuff from the Greek store on rations.

"I do not have a date. I'm babysitting a concussed detective for the weekend, and I just need some food to feed him so he won't throw up again."

"You go around hitting men over the head to get dates now? Smooth, sis."

"Georgíos! Eat some feta." Mama said.

I shook my head and glanced at Sofia, who momentarily looked like she wished she never stepped foot in the kitchen. Little did she know she fit in better than I ever did.

Sofia opened the lid to the pot on the stove, knowing to use the oven mitt because of the broken handle. I was pretty sure the mitt was so old it was made of asbestos and it was half burned full of holes, but she didn't scream out in pain. After only a few months of living here, she seemed right at home in this foreign kitchen. Another testament to how much my family preferred her to me. Not that I minded. At eleven, Sofia was sweet, funny, and a brilliant classical guitar prodigy. She deserved a family who loved her for all of that. It was just odd watching my Mom love anyone who wasn't Dad or George, her prized firstborn male.

I wished Gus was here to see this, but he wasn't due back from Massachusetts until May. In the meantime, I made a mental note to buy my mother some new cookware. And knives. And everything else that equipped a kitchen.

"Spanakorizo?" Sofia asked, smelling the dill from the rice pot.

"Bravaa, Koukla!" My mom stopped chopping to squeeze Sofia's cheeks between her still-knife-clad hands, congratulating her for her positive identification of the classic Greek dish of spinach, onion, dill, and rice.

Sofia was one hundred percent not-Greek, but since she and her mom moved into the apartment upstairs, she took more of an interest in the culture than I ever had and was one hundred percent adopted into Greekness by my family. She is the daughter my mother never had.

I grabbed my pot, forgetting the asbestos mitt, and burned my palm. Grabbing a bottle of acetaminophen, I kissed Sofia on the cheek and left. Out the screen door, George shouted warnings at me like I had "better keep my bra on" and that he was going to be around all weekend in case that detective thought he was going to take advantage of his sister. As if he ever cared about being brotherly before. I shifted the pot to my hip and flipped him off.

The bra thing wasn't going to happen. I knew it. George knew it. By then, I was sure even Detective Wells had *detected* my proclivity for going bra-less.

Wells was in the kitchen when I got upstairs. He looked bad. And guilty. He quickly closed the utensil drawer, color hinting at his cheeks.

"I don't care if you snoop," I told him. "But you'll probably get bored before you find anything. I don't have much of a life to snoop through." I didn't mean to say that out loud. Sometimes bits of too-much-honesty vomited out of me like... well, like Wells in a morgue.

I cleared my throat. That was always a good re-grouping tactic.

"You said it was messy," he said as I handed him the bottle of Tylenol.

"You probably know where the glasses are," I offered in response. He opened the correct cabinet door and brought down two glasses.

"Before we came upstairs, you apologized for the mess. It looks like someone smart cleaned up after a murder in here. There's no mess. I was kind of looking forward to seeing what your mess looked like." He smiled.

Why did he have to be so charming? Even passed out and puking up his morning coffee he was still adorable and sexy.

"You must not have checked the closets." I didn't have a lot of things. If I had stuff, it'd be out. Instead, the only thing I really had in abundance was clothes, or maybe swords, and those were both stuffed into closets.

He downed the pills and started rummaging through the takeout bag. Our food was probably cool by now, but I was used to eating on the run. It was the nature of a job in crime analysis. I'd bet money he also ate fast, with no concern for food temperature.

I lifted the lid off the pot and a pleasant, sour/savory, onion-scented steam rose to greet our nostrils. Wells stopped prying apart the aluminum containers and leaned over the stove.

"It's just spinach and rice with some seasonings. It's what my mom always made me when I didn't feel well. I texted her when you were in the bathroom and asked if she could make some for me. Usually, it takes a little longer but—"

Wells grabbed a spoon and dug right into the rice. It was still too hot to taste much like anything. "Oh, God," he gulped air into his mouth to get the bite to cool down. "Great. Now I can add *scalded tongue* to my list of symptoms."

I opened my pulled pork and started forking down my food. When I looked up after a few bites, Wells was staring at me. "Sorry," I said after swallowing carefully. "I'm just used to eating—"

"Fast?" He smiled. I didn't know if he was always amused or if he was just that way around me. Probably both. "I know. Me too."

"No really. I'm being a terrible host. We need to sit, at least. And you shouldn't talk too much." I grabbed our tins of barbeque—his with an additional helping of Ma's rice—and carried them to the coffee table.

"Tv?" He asked. I shook my head, getting up to grab a bottle of beer and swallowing down another forkful of macaroni and cheese mixed with pulled pork. "You shouldn't allow yourself to be stimulated by any media."

"What am I supposed to do with my life?"

"Eat. And sleep. Concussions are serious. You need cognitive rest."

"I hardly think the Property Brothers counts as cognitive activity."

"What's that?" I asked.

At last, it was his turn to be caught off guard. "Come on, everyone knows Drew and Jonathan Scott? The twins from Canada who flip people's houses and put in a bunch of fancy lights? HGTV?"

I shrugged. "I rarely turn on the tv. I never know what to watch. I feel like I'm starting in the middle of every story, and I'm lost."

"See, that's the great thing about home design shows. There's no plot. If you miss one, there's nothing to catch up on. You can turn it on whenever you can't fall asleep or need to work something out in your head and make fun of the people who can't get past that "the kitchen isn't open concept" even though they know Joanna Gaines is going to tear out all the walls anyway. Then—BAM—the idea comes to you, and you know who the killer is, or where they hid the murder weapon, or the cause of death, in your case." He gestured to me. "I mean, I'm exaggerating, but still. You get it."

He put a lot of faith in my non-existent skills to *get it*.

"Actually, that could never happen in my line of work. I need paperwork. Imaging. I can't determine cases by zoning out."

The light left his eyes and I realized I'd probably said something wrong. To use Wells's lingo, it was my M.O. Then I realized something else.

"You're feeling better!"

"Uh, yeah, I guess I am." He blinked. "Wait a minute." He shoved a forkful of barbeque in his mouth. "You don't have a thing that lets your mind wander while you're really focused on something else? Something important?" He asked around the bite of food in his mouth.

"If I have a case, I solve it in the morgue. In silence. Background noises are distracting. Sometimes it takes digging. Calls to a physician or family member to request medical history. Sometimes information doesn't come back for weeks, like with DNA or tox reports, but I solve it by focusing on it. I don't think I know how to turn my brain off enough to divide my concentration between two things simultaneously."

"That's the beauty of HGTV. It requires no concentration whatsoever."

I sighed. "Promise you won't abuse this." Passing him the remote, I continued, "If the Property Brothers are as boring as you say, I'll let this slide, but only for an hour."

"You are going to be so fucking bored, you'll wish you were waiting in line at Driver Services. Just wait. You'll love it."

Hours later, I woke up on the couch, house renovations still filling the screen, the volume turned low, and my head supported by a warm mass, rising and falling gently with each of Wells's breaths.

How did that happen? We were watching people buy houses after we finished dinner. He was excellent at guessing which one the couple on screen would choose and he turned it into a kind of game. It was not nearly as boring as he promised, and I made dangerous concessions allowing it.

After each commercial break, we found ourselves closer and closer together on the couch. At one point, he lifted my legs, draping them across his lap. He didn't say anything. Or look at me. When my hand found his, the game was over.

We watched the show. Silently. But both of us were paying more attention to each other than the screen.

Him breathing steadily, just a little deeper.

My own breaths becoming shallower.

Sometimes I forgot to breathe at all because of the nearness of him.

chapter twelve

Waylon—Now

I DIDN'T KNOW HOW long I'd been out, but I immediately registered where I was. Alone in a king-sized bed, propped up on several pillows and surrounded by darkness.

I reached over to the nightstand for the phone, but my fingers slid around the cool sides of a water glass instead. Soula had taken my phone. I forgot. She said she didn't trust me with it and if any important calls came in, she'd reroute them.

She was right not to trust me. I was only taking this concussion business lying down (literally) because I enjoyed following her instructions. And that urge to be connected to her had taken me so strongly that first night, I guess I had some sort of need to understand it. Without fucking with my head this time.

I didn't know how to be around her. Normally, I was the guy who wouldn't shut up. She didn't make me nervous, exactly. It was like the calmness in her brought out the calmness in me. Even Kudzu had been quiet.

What wasn't quiet was my phone. I heard the dings through the door Soula must have left ajar so she could better monitor me. I rose slowly, testing out my sea legs. No headache. Not yet at least. We'd have to see what would happen when I encountered daylight. I felt surprisingly lighter today.

Following the noise of the phone down the short hallway past Soula's office and into the open interior of the main space, I blinked in the streaming light and looked at the clock on the oven. 2:30. I had slept for approximately sixteen hours. I didn't want Soula to be right, medically speaking, but I couldn't deny I was probably worse off than I thought yesterday.

I didn't find Soula. Instead, a little blonde girl was tucked into the corner of the couch, holding my phone and my dog.

Kudzu's head lifted when I came in. The noises from the phone weren't notifications. They were the beeps and pings from a game I sometimes played to stay busy.

"How did you unlock that?" I asked, gruffly. My voice hadn't been used in a while.

The girl looked up, unafraid, and kept playing. "Don't worry. I didn't buy anything," she said.

"Answer my question," I said, forgetting that in gym shorts and an old bar t-shirt, my words had less authority than when I was Detective Hugo Boss.

"Your password was easy. It's your birth year."

"And how do you know that?"

"Your driver's license."

"Which you found where?" I said as intimidatingly as possible.

"Your wallet."

I sat in the armchair across from her but didn't ask her any more questions. Instead, I just waited for her to come clean. I knew she would, eventually. They all do.

"Okay," she rolled her eyes and put the phone down. "Thea Soula asked me to look after you while she went to practice. She said you'd probably sleep the whole time, which you almost did. Well...I had to look in your wallet, didn't I? What if you woke up and abducted me? Or killed me? At least I'd know your name and address."

"It wouldn't be very helpful to know my address if you're dead."

She rolled her eyes but smiled. "I like the name Waylon. It's like Waylon Jennings."

"That's what my mom thought, too," I said.

"My name's Sofia. I live in the big house with my mom and Thea Soula's family. I'm supposed to tell you there's a pot of coffee made, and Raynie made me bring over some cream and sugar even though Thea Soula said by the looks of your stomach contents, you drink it black. And George called you a malaka, but he won't tell me what it means. How did she see your stomach contents? Did you... oh." She must have realized. "You puked? That sucks. I hate it when I puke. Was that when you hit your head?"

I wasn't sure what to respond to first. I felt like I should be taking notes to improve my own interrogation tactics. Her brain was thinking so fast, her words spewed out before I had time to process.

"Who's Raynie?"

"Thea Soula's mom. Her real name's Ourania, which means Heaven, but she goes by Raynie. It's better for business. Did you know Thea Soula's real name is Athanasía? It means eternal life. It's kind of the opposite, considering what she does for a living—"

"Ironic."

"Ironic. Yeah. That's a good word. My name means wisdom and it's Greek, even though I'm Irish, German, Danish, English, and Polish. Have you taken a DNA test? What are you?"

"I don't know. Do they test for trailer trash?" I shrugged. "Do you always talk so much?"

"Uh huh, you can tell me to shut up and I will, though. Was it the body that made you puke?"

"Uh...yes. The smell in particular." I got up and headed to the coffee maker. Sofia followed me and sat on one of the stools at the island bar. Soula was right. I did drink it black, but I didn't like the idea that she had examined my "stomach contents" so I added a single, spiteful drop of cream in my cup and watched the colors bloom together.

"Yeah, you get used to the smell though. Mom doesn't really let me around the bad ones. But this one time, the babysitter didn't show up and I had to go with her for a pickup and it smelled so disgusting."

"Who's your mom?"

"Bethany." Everything this girl said was said in one long stream of monotone words. "I have a theory for dealing with the bodies. Wanna know what it is?"

"Lay it on me, kid." I took a sip of the dark rich roast. It was everything I always wanted, even if it came with a precocious, fast-talking whirlwind.

"There's cereal up there. But get two bowls. I'm not allowed to eat this at home." Sofia pointed to the cabinet next to the microwave. I probably shouldn't let her eat the cereal here either, but I did want to know her theory. Sort of.

I poured two bowls of chocolate cereal and splashed on some whole milk. Soula must have gone to the store this morning. There was actual food in the fridge.

Grabbing two spoons, I came around and sat on the empty stool next to Sofia.

"Most people die when they're old, right?" She said, chomping at the same time. I nodded. "That's like, what's supposed to happen. It's sad, but not really *that sad*. They have grown-up kids who buy them fancy caskets and tons of flowers and all their grandkids show up to their memorials and cry and you get to see them in their wedding pictures from the 60s and stuff. We usually get their bodies right away cause their families knew they died, or they were there, and the old dead people really do look like they're sleeping."

"I'm not hearing a theory here," I said.

"I'm getting there. Let me eat another bite before it goes soggy." She crunched down and drained the milk from the bowl. She was already done and she'd been talking the whole time. This girl's brain must go full speed all the damn time. She exhausted me, and I was kind of the same as her.

"Other times, we get a body and it's really old. Not old, like an elderly person, but someone who's been dead a long time before coming to us."

Us, she said. Like she was one of them. And she was, in a sense, growing up in a mortuary.

Was this how Soula grew up? Is this why she went into pathology? I'd looked it up. There weren't many board-certified forensic pathologists in the country. It was an extremely difficult and intense field of medicine, and she was still so young. She must have known from an early age that this was exactly what she wanted to do. I wish I had known young, rather than wasting a lot of years and too much money on a useless education.

Sofia watched me zone out, pausing her story until I re-focused on her.

"Continue," I said.

"Anyway, those bodies smell really bad sometimes. Mom doesn't let me around them, but I know anyway. Sometimes they're so bad they have to be cremated, even though the family didn't want that at first. Other times, there's just too much liquid and not enough body, they put the whole body bag into a casket, flood it with disinfectant—which stinks for another reason—and seal it up."

I pushed the rest of my cereal away from me. "Still not hearing a theory here, Sof."

"When that happens, I used to think it was super gross. Like, the most disgusting thing ever."

"Used to?"

"Well, then I learned that I can't be disgusted when I'm sad, so I really try to think of the dead guy as a human being, someone who died after something really mean happened to him. And if they weren't found right away, that probably means nobody loved them. And that's really sad, too. Maybe that could help you."

"I have a different job around dead bodies, though. I don't have to clean them up and pretend nothing happened to them. I have to find out if they've been killed. It's hard to do that if I let my emotions get in the way."

"It's probably hard to do that if you're puking, too."

"How old are you?"

"Eleven. But I've been dealing with this stuff a long time. My mom became a funeral director when I was six."

"Well, Sofia, I think you are living up to your name."

She grinned and hopped down. "Can I get some coffee now?"

"Nope."

"It was worth a shot."

I drained my coffee and refilled my cup. I told myself I really should eat something, but I kept thinking of liquefied bodies, and...maybe I'd wait a few hours.

"So, what do you do when it's already a really sad case?" Plenty of those, too. "Doesn't it make you even more sad?"

"Like kids and stuff? No. Then I pretend it's all rotten and disgusting. Or it's just an anatomy model. You can't be sad when you're grossed out."

"And you can't be grossed out when you're sad," I said. It made sense, in the most horrific way. It was a theory worth testing.

Kudzu jumped off the couch when the door opened. Soula came in carrying a long bag, almost as long as my hockey bag, though not as bulky. It was definitely designed to hold some sort of sporting equipment. Maybe she was a martial artist. That might explain her Zen ways. She dropped the bag and stepped out of her sneakers, straightening her messy ponytail.

"Hey, Thea Soula. Raynie was right. He did need cream."

"Hello, Girl Child," she said, giving the dog's head a good petting before making her way into the kitchen. "Maybe I need a refresher course on analysis." She poured herself a black coffee and took it to the couch, curling up in the opposite corner from where Sofia sank in.

The way she walked, her sock feet gliding over the floors, her low-slung sweatpants loose around her waist and her tight tank top bunching up to reveal the slender waist, she owned the world. She was beautiful before, in her scrubs and her work bun, but now, with her long ponytail, the post-workout outfit, no makeup, and red cheeks, I forgot to swallow.

I followed her to the couch. Still grounded from participating in life, I had nothing to do but act like my dog and follow her around the apartment. When I sat, she stood, not once looking my way, and padded back into the kitchen to mix up a protein shake. Then she disappeared into her office and closed the door.

Back to this again.

Last night, I thought maybe we were getting past this hot and cold shit. She was snuggling up to me on the couch, for God's sake. Now she wouldn't even look at me.

Well, I couldn't stand being around here with just my thoughts. I reached for the remote and turned on the tv, flipping the channels before settling on my favorite.

It was an episode of House Hunters I'd never seen before. Then again, I might have seen it three times. It didn't matter, really. I closed my eyes and dropped my head back. At least if I couldn't turn off my thoughts, I could close off one sense.

"Do you play the guitar?" Sofia asked.

"A bit." I said without opening my eyes. I'm glad she didn't take it as a hint that I didn't want to be bothered. I *did* want to be bothered. By Soula. By Sofia. This boredom of brain rest was awful.

"You must be from Nashville, then. Everyone from Nashville plays the guitar. Or sings. Even if they have regular jobs. Can you teach me something cool?"

I must have nodded out because when I opened my eyes next, she was standing in front of me with an acoustic guitar.

"Where'd that come from?" I wiped moisture from the corner of my mouth.

"I went home and got it while you were asleep. Please? I'd really like to learn something besides Bach."

"Where's Soula?"

"She's taking a nap. She watched you all night, but she doesn't sleep much at night anyway. Here," she thrust the guitar in my hands. It had been a while since I played and when I did it was mostly blues. I could always fiddle around a bit and make it sound good, but I couldn't think of any particular lesson to teach. I started with some mindless blues scales. It was the kind of run I played whenever I picked up an instrument. Same as anyone else who played. It's hard to stay quiet with a guitar in your hand.

"See, that's the kind of stuff I want to play. Where'd you learn it from? My teacher makes me read notes and play classical."

"YouTube's probably a better teacher than I could ever be. I just fiddle around with stuff. Same as anyone else from Nashville, as you pointed out. You like country?"

She shrugged. "Not really. The old stuff, yeah. I like Johnny Cash."

"Who doesn't?" I strummed a few bars, thinking of an easy song to teach her some chords. If she liked Johnny Cash, I guessed might as well introduce her to my namesake. I picked out the little intro. "Got a pick?"

"I only pick with my fingernails."

"Well, dang, Sof." She laughed. I liked this kid.

"Alright. This song is pretty easy." I strummed a D chord. "You sing, don't you?"

Her eyes got wide. I finally found her shut up button.

"Of course you do." I told her. "All guitarists have to sing, at least a little. You got to give your jam buddies the right cues. Pull up the lyrics to "That's What You Get for Lovin' Me" on your phone, er, my phone."

I started switching my fingers back and forth between D and G. "Can you do this?"

"I think so."

"Okay then, add an A real quick at the end of line two, then an E, A on line three, then back to D, G." I looked up but Sofia was shaking her head.

"I'll show you. Listen." I sang the lyrics slowly, nodding when she should change chords. The song was simple enough she could pick up the melody fast.

"Now you strum and I'll keep singing." I returned her little guitar to her. And her fingers went right to D major. "Good."

I sang the second verse, but I didn't get to finish the phrase.

Sofia didn't either. The E chord hung in the air while my words clashed into it. I looked over my shoulder at Soula standing in the hallway, looking villainous.

"We're caught," I winked.

Soula's eyes blazed as she strode into the room, looking at the tv once before clicking it off and moving my phone away from me, still without looking at me.

"Sofia, I asked you not to bother him."

"Okay. I've got homework anyway, before dinner," Sofia said, giving Kudzu a hug. "It was nice meeting you, Waylon."

"Detective Wells," Soula corrected her.

"Waylon is perfect," I corrected Soula, who averted her eyes from mine, to right between my legs.

Sofia bounced out of the room and hollered back. "Oh, and remember dinner tonight. Raynie says don't bring anything except yourselves, because the wine you pick is never good."

Sofia was gone and Soula's shoulders slumped. Because of the comment about the wine, or because now it was just the two of us? She had managed not to be alone with me, or even near me the whole day. But now it was just us, and I had to rely on her as my only entertainment.

"I liked that song," she said after a while. "I'm just worried about you. I don't want you to get overstimulated. You didn't go to the doctor, and—"

"Soula," I met her halfway down the hall and reached out a finger to playfully tap her elbow. Just one finger. It was safe and platonic enough. "I'm fine. I feel ninety percent better today. I'm just a little tired. That's it."

She looked up at me. I felt the buildup. She emboldened herself to look into my eyes. "Statistically speaking, I know you'll probably be fine, but you must realize... I don't see the 'fine' cases. I see the accidents that end up on my table." She said it in a breathy voice, exhaling all the air in her lungs with that statement. I inched closer. I didn't move my feet, just leaned in her direction. She didn't lean away.

She exhaled shakily, then pressed her lips into a thin line and swallowed. "But I respect your bodily autonomy. If you say you're feeling better, then I'll choose to believe it."

I had to give it to her; she was trying. It was obvious she had a hard time with me here. I was having a hard time here as well, for different reasons. But if she could respect my bodily autonomy, then I could respect that her tiny choices to relinquish control probably felt like giant, bounding leaps over the edge of a canyon. I'd do anything to reach out my hand so she didn't rip out her nails, clawing to gain purchase in the rock.

Right now, making it easier for her meant changing the subject. "What's this about dinner? I thought you were trying to hide me from your mom." I asked, looking at the striations in her eyes, the flyaway hairs around her face that curled a bit after the sweat dried from her workout. Her pillow-wrinkled cheeks from her nap. I didn't realize she had freckles before. I hadn't seen her this closely in the daylight. They belied her stony, doctor-y persona and something about that seemed so perfectly Soula.

Her eyes grew harder. It was almost imperceptible, the change. "It was futile. She knows everything that goes on around here."

My eyes dropped to her full lips, the top slightly wider, the bottom slightly wrinkled in a sexy scowl. I thought about pressing my thumb against her lips. Would it make her moan? Open her mouth? Would her eyes close? I was pretty sure that if I kissed her, she'd lift her chin and move closer. She'd open her lips and breathe against my mouth. How far would it go after that? To the bedroom, probably, if she had her way. She seemed to respond to my touch when it was sexual.

Then tomorrow morning, she wouldn't spare another glance in my direction. I respected my own *emotional* autonomy enough not to put myself through that again.

So I did nothing. And in another instant, she was gone, marching away from me.

"I'm going to take a shower." She said over her shoulder, pulling the elastic band from her ponytail and shaking her dark hair loose. I wondered if she knew exactly how much I wanted to reach out to her. And why I couldn't.

I was trying to avoid having that conversation. The *how do you feel about us* conversation. My object was to get through this weekend, maybe learn a little more about each other. If feelings developed, it would happen organically. If they didn't... oh, who was I kidding? I already had feelings for her. If I brought up the prospect of dating, I knew it would scare her away. But I couldn't leave it much longer, or the opportunity would pass us by. If she still felt nothing after tomorrow, I'd start building that wall.

chapter thirteen

Soula—Now

I WAS FUCKING BRAVE. I didn't understand it.

I didn't step away from Wells, even though he was so close I could smell his laundry detergent and see the fine lines and sun damage on the tops of his cheeks. I smiled at him. A little. At least, I thought I smiled. Sometimes my face didn't follow my brain's instructions. I even hazarded a peek into his soul and looked straight at his beautiful, weird eyes. I was perfectly clear, so... why didn't he kiss me?

Obviously, I was doing something wrong. This was why I always made my intentions crystal clear when I wanted sex. It was so much easier that way. There were no missteps, no mis-readings on my part or his.

I brushed my hair while the water warmed up but stepped into the shower prematurely anyway. The cold shock snapped me out of physically wanting Wells (for now), but it worsened my mood and served as an I-told-you-so to my already poor ability to read the room.

I scrubbed my scalp and let the water run down my face, fanning out my hair in a wide sheet. I made no attempt to tilt the water away from my nose to breathe easier. I wanted to block out everything but the feel of the scalding water and sulk in privacy.

This was why I couldn't have a romantic relationship, poor discernment.

I couldn't read a single person, much less a room. If men would just state their intentions, it would be so much easier. They disguise and play games and "see where things lead." Fuck that. I just wished someone would lay it out there from the start. Just be honest. Discuss and deliberate and then enter into an agreement. An outright, verbally-stated agreement. With labels and a clear map to our destination. If we ended up in a ditch on the side of the road, so be it. At least there'd be no confusion.

But as much as I might have wanted him to pull me close and kiss me, hear him tell me I'm smart and pretty and that he wants to go on that drive with me, I had to be honest with myself. Wells would never be in my car. I wasn't about to navigate my first romantic relationship with someone I was that enamored with.

I was inhibited enough with strangers, I couldn't begin to imagine that kind of intimacy with a man I really liked.

The image of a corpse on my autopsy table flashed before my eyes. Yep. That was about right. Stripped naked, having already dispensed with the external exam. Slashed from clavicles to sternum and then down to the symphysis pubis joint. That's what being with Wells was like. Bone-deep naked.

Thank God we had sex before I got to know him, before I knew he could play the guitar and that he liked 70s country. Before I heard that rich baritone throwback singing voice that he didn't take seriously enough. Before I made friends with his gentle, lazy dog. Now that I knew those things, I'd never be comfortable talking to him or asking him for what I wanted.

Intimacy was an act and I could only step on that stage with strangers.

But that didn't stop me from wanting it. With Wells, I craved more than just sex. I craved sharing takeout and watching his house renovation shows, listening to him absentmindedly fiddling around on the guitar and having deep conversations with children. I craved knowing him fully. And being known.

I turned off the water and wrang out my hair before drying hastily and wrapping the towel around my body. My fencing opponents were tough today, but it felt good. It felt even better to be clean and somewhat rested after a night of stealthy symptom tracking.

Wells was studying the bookshelves in my office when I walked in. He didn't turn and didn't apologize for invading my privacy. Not that I had anything private. His attitude and his low-key confidence were supremely attractive. I shook away the thought and swiveled into my chair to get some work done.

"You have a lot of medical books." He said, still looking over the titles on the shelves.

"You can't know everything. Sometimes you have to look it up," I said, closing a heavy book that was still lying open from a previous case. I wondered if I should feel insecure about the number of times each week I opened my old neuro path textbook.

"I kept a lot of my law textbooks too," he said.

"You went to law school?" I stopped straightening the things on my desk.

"Are you surprised?" He quickly glanced over his shoulder before picking up a model cranium that had been my friend since childhood.

"That depends. Did you throw that in so I'd know how smart you are?"

His face hardened. "No. I threw it in because I'm trying to talk to you. I was an assistant DA up in Davidson County first."

I went back to straightening. "Well, I am surprised. Not because that tells me how smart you are. I already knew that. I'm surprised that you'd just stop being a lawyer. Isn't that a huge backtrack, career-wise?"

"You don't pull your punches, do you?" He turned to me. "That side of the law wasn't what I thought it would be," he frowned. It made him look older for just a moment. "I went into it expecting to serve justice. I didn't like the man I was becoming."

"One would think you might have figured that out after your first year of law school. That's a big expense to forfeit your career like that."

"In more ways than one," he said. He sat on the office couch that was still in disarray after I tried to sleep there last night. "It's becoming more common, though; lawyers *backtracking*, as you say. There are a few of us in Williamson County and a few in Davidson, too. I was a cop first, when I thought I wanted a bigger, "more important" career. Then when I was actually doing that career, it didn't feel more important anymore. It made me feel worse about myself. Do you know how many cases are thrown out, pled, or don't go to trial due to investigator negligence?"

I nodded. "Yes." I wasn't following his logic.

He shrugged. He did a lot of that. "Yeah, of course you do. Well, I didn't know if I could spend an entire career in anger, with the wrong people behind bars, or the right people serving the wrong sentences. At least now I don't have to see it first-hand. I can do my due diligence and send it to the other guys."

I thought about it for a minute. "There's a margin of error in everything, you know," I said. "I sometimes consult forensic pathologists in other counties or states who don't draw the same conclusions as me on cause or even manner of death."

"So you're telling me I'm making a big deal out of nothing and objectivity is hopeless? Same line as I get from Reyes."

"It's not hopeless to consider that there's a bit of an art to what we do. It's not all science."

He rubbed his hand against the rough whiskers on his jaw. "That's surprising, coming from you."

"What do you mean?"

"I mean, you're a scientist. Not to mention you seem like the black and white type. Right down to your apartment."

"Oh... yeah." Maybe that was why I spent more time in my office than any other room. It was dark in here. Like my soul. "I guess it is sort of sterile. My friend, Decca decorated it. Anyway, it's wonderful you want to make the world a better place, stop crime in its tracks and all that, but you can't start by jumping on every death like it's a bad thing."

He looked up but his elbows were still on his knees, his hands cradling his temples. We stared each other down. Neither of us were angry, but this felt like an impasse. Then his face crumpled. Maybe it was something about his eyes that made him seem melted inside. I didn't know what to make of it.

"I'd like to believe you, but what do you mean not all death is bad?" He asked.

"I mean, *memento* fucking *mori*. Everyone dies. Sometimes it's sad, sometimes it's beautiful, but most of the time it just *is*, like your decomp yesterday."

His face hardened back up like Bethany had just injected formaldehyde solution under his skin. "What about the decomp? Are you saying you ruled on manner and cause? You didn't tell me?"

I shook my head. Wells could be really exasperating when he got hold of a bone. "I'm saying he was 82 years old. It was his time. The only thing tragic about it was that his children and grandchildren didn't call him sooner to find the body. That doesn't make him a victim of some atrocity, regardless of the state you found him in."

"You're saying it's natural causes." He leaned back against the couch. "This case isn't even a case."

"Manner is most likely natural, yes." I nodded. "But I haven't ruled on cause. I'm waiting for labs, but unless they find some trace of Iocane powder...." I trailed off, holding up my hands in surrender.

"Was that a joke, Soula?" He smirked. "Did you just make a Princess Bride joke?"

"I joke. Occasionally. Anyway, you'll have plenty of other cases. I see good stuff every week, so don't worry about that."

He got up from the couch in a rush. My eyes didn't follow him. I was now focused on his quads draped in soft athletic shorts, one leg hitched up a little higher, stuck on the cotton fibers of his boxer briefs, probably.

"That's what you think of me?" He asked. His angry tone shocked me out of my unfocused state. "You really think I'm disappointed that my 'first big case'—which this isn't by a long shot—might turn out to be an old man dying in his sleep in his La-Z-Boy?"

He shook his head and let out a rough breath.

How did we get here? What step did I miss?

He started to leave but stopped abruptly, his hand on the doorframe propelling him around to the front of my desk. "I just want the result, Soula. I don't care what that result is so long as it tells me the next step in the procedure. I thought you'd understand that. You know, you...." He closed his eyes. "You must have a really bad taste in your mouth about people. How can you, of all people, distrust someone so much? How can you think so poorly of anyone? Of me? You let me in once. Why did you bother?"

The sting of his phrase hung in the air as I tried to make sense of it.

"I can't answer those questions." I answered truthfully. "I never thought of myself as distrustful, but... I *don't* know if I can name one person I trust implicitly. But I bet a lot more people would admit the same if they were honest with themselves. Is trust really such a big deal?"

Logically, it seemed wise not to trust another human. We're all fallible and emotions ran too hot in most. Sometimes even in myself. Given enough time, we'd all disappoint each other somehow.

"You really think you're one hundred percent honest?" He laughed and ran his hands through his hair.

"Of course I'm honest." Now I was angry, too. "That's the biggest thing about me. I'm nothing if not my authentic self. I ask for what I want, and I don't make promises I can't uphold."

"You ask for what you want? Really?" He was visibly upset. This wasn't good for his condition. He was on my side of the desk in three strides. His face hovered above mine. I could feel his breath in my hair. He jerked my chin up to face him. His eyes were fiery, even his cheeks had gone red.

"Back in the hall. You wanted to kiss me. Didn't you? I felt it from you. Tell me I'm wrong. I fucking dare you."

His face was so close to mine now, but not tender like it was a few minutes ago. Now it was hard and forceful. "I didn't want it," I whispered.

Great. That was super convincing, Soula.

"Just like I thought. Real honest," he huffed, telling me the same thing I just told myself. His lips still sneering with contempt I wasn't sure was entirely placed on me. His ringed, mismatched eyes darkening into a look that was dangerous and enticing. But he didn't drift away.

Why was he pushing so hard? Feelings bubbled inside me, burning my chest like a cremation chamber retort aimed at center mass. I swiveled away from his viscerally angry stare and continued my task of aligning shit on my desk. A task that didn't matter."No one can be honest about what they *want* all the time. We'd all be in too much trouble. I'm honest about my needs."

"Okay, I get it. It's all just biological, right?" He looked at me, waiting for an answer. When I couldn't give it to him—I didn't even know what *it* was—he regrouped, remembering himself and taking a step back.

It was too far, that step. I *wanted* him back. *Wanted* him close. Even closer. I *wanted* to crawl into his lap and rip off my clothes, tear out my heart and offer it to him to weigh and dissect and examine under a microscope. With his one step backward, with his eyes dulling, recognizing who I truly was, something else was being torn away. First breath, then hope, then the feeling that this was all too good to be true snuck inside where my heart should be. This was why I couldn't be honest about my wants. They ran counter to reality.

He shook his head and ran his hands through his hair again. It was long enough that it stuck up in funny ways when he disrupted the side part. "People die, you deal with it. You always have. You say it can be beautiful, but I don't believe you. I think nothing is sacred for you. Has any death mattered to you?"

"In terms of?"

He softened. "Have you had someone close to you die?"

Besides Bethany and Decca, I'd never had anyone close to me, period.

"No," was all I said.

"When it happens, it'll crush you. It won't be a matter of paperwork and science. It'll be personal and it will break your heart." His eyes got a faraway look. I didn't understand what was happening any longer. Maybe I never understood what was happening.

I eased back in the chair, feeling the spring support the heavy wood for a minute before recoiling. My gaze trained on Wells's knees until I lost focus and I couldn't make out any defining characteristics. They were just knees. And then they were gone.

"Oh, and Soula?"

I looked up at the door where he'd disappeared to.

"I wanted to kiss you, too."

chapter fourteen

Soula—Now

Oh God. Pappoú's Buick was in the driveway.

I guess I should have expected my grandparents to be here. Except that it was Saturday night and barring weddings, funerals, and Greek Easter, Yia-Yiá and Pappoú were never anywhere but the bingo.

Me bringing a man to dinner, regardless of the current state of our non-relationship—un-communicative—was unheard of, evidently something the whole family had to see in the flesh like I was some kind of sideshow attraction.

So what if I'd never brought a man to meet my family? Why would I when I didn't even let men catch sight of where I lived? It wasn't any death pall that made the place uncomfortable. On the contrary, the house buzzed at too high of a frequency with its overpowering scents and flavors, insults and complaints tossed across the dining room table, and a symphony of loud chewing. My family home was a sensory nightmare.

I took a deep breath before clicking the latch on the screen door.

"Jesus, you don't look so good," spotted Wells. "Do they hate me that much already? Is it because I'm not Greek?"

I shook my head. "My dad's not Greek. It's okay. Let's just rip this band-aid off." I gestured for him to go ahead of me.

Mama attacked him as soon as we walked through the door. "Waylon, I'm so glad you could come to dinner. Soula didn't tell me how handsome you are," she exclaimed after leaving a pink lipstick smear on his unsuspecting cheek and giving me the evil eye.

"No, I don't suppose she would have." Wells smiled smugly in my direction.

"You like Greek food?" She asked.

"I liked that green rice you made. Thank you, by the way."

She held his elbow, navigating him sharply through the kitchen. Like me, Mama was at least a foot shorter than him, but her commandeering nature belied that bird-boned skeleton under her skin.

I'd performed so many autopsies on bodies that closely resembled my mother's. I used to beg her to eat more calcium and lift weights. It was like the woman was determined to break a hip. Then again, if anyone could will themselves into a long, contented life of complaining and nagging, Mama would be the one.

"Yes, Athanasía never keeps anything in her kitchen, so someone had to make sure you were well fed."

Wells didn't know where to look. At me, being called by my real name, at my mom looking up at him adoringly, or at George, who was stomping around the corner wearing his non-funeral-director uniform of jeans, a button-down, and a scowl.

"Waylon, this is my eldest son, George." Mama took over introductions, leading him further into the cramped kitchen. Bethany and Sofia came down right after George.

Bethany looked at me with wide eyes before her eyes moved to the back of George's head. So, that explained the look on George's face. My brother and my best friend now owned an equal share of the company. Although he had seniority as well as the family name, they were co-funeral directors and both were excellent at their jobs. They also had opposing philosophies about practically everything and could barely stay in the same room together for five minutes.

"I hope this won't be too torturous for you," George said, stretching out his hand with a crooked smile. He liked to pretend to the public that he was the reasonable one in the family. In reality, he was broken, burned, and took it out on everyone. I finally managed to tug Wells away from my mother into the living room to introduce him to my grandparents.

"I thought this was going to be rough. Your family seems welcoming, so far."

"Yeah, they'll be fine to you. It's me they don't like." I didn't give him a chance to say anything. "Yia-Yiá, this is Waylon," I raised my voice so she could hear over Wheel of Fortune.

Her face smiled like the sun coming out when we came into the room. "Élla ethó, koúkla," she said.

I came closer and kissed her cheek. She stretched out a paper thin, satin-skinned hand to Wells and he grasped it, she smiled up at him so warmly it seemed to still the ambient noise that made the house *too much.*

"It's nice to meet my Soula's friend," she said in her trippingly light Cretan accent. "Sit down and talk to me. Tell me what you do." He did as he was told. Yia-Yiá was nice enough, but she was a Greek woman and they had powerful ways to get what they wanted.

Pappoú sat in his recliner in the corner. I kissed his cheek, cringing at the feel of his dewy skin against my lips. "Páre mou mia bírra, Soula," he said to me, leaving off the parakaló. As usual. I rolled my eyes but went back into the kitchen to grab him a Bud Light anyway. After that, I could ignore him for the rest of the night. I didn't exactly dislike my grandfather, but he'd only ever been the man in the recliner to me. I'd always been his vending machine.

Bethany stood in the doorway, leaning against the dark walnut trim with her arms crossed, listening to the conversation between my grandmother and Wells. I squeezed by her, noticing but not fully understanding the twinkle in her eye. A strange smile played on her lips.

After a minute, she joined my grandmother and Wells on the sofa, amplifying the anxious feeling that my worlds were colliding. "I thought you could handle a familiar face," she said to Wells. "My daughter's been raving about you all afternoon. Said you even got her to sing along with her guitar."

"It was nothing. Literally four chords. The only thing any musician needs is someone who knows the tricks. That and practice." He shrugged. I handed him a Bud Light after my grandfather and took a sip of my own. It was vile.

"Are you sure?" He asked.

He needed something to take the edge off my family. "It's basically water."

"For what I'm paying her guitar teacher, he'd better be teaching her more than just tricks. He's supposed to be preparing her for her Nashville Youth Orchestra audition."

"She's that good? I'm impressed. I'd love to hear her play sometime. But I still bet she could stand to learn a couple Johnny Cash songs from time to time."

"Soula, he doesn't sympathize with my efforts to get Sofia a full ride to Julliard," Bethany stood up. "What are we going to do with him?" She smiled and pulled me into the kitchen to help Ma with dinner.

"What can we do, Raynie?" Bethany asked, knowing my mom wouldn't trust her with the important tasks.

"Take these plates into the dining room." Bethany gave me a look with her eyebrows as she turned around with a stack of china. For Greek-Americans, giving someone the task of setting the table was the equivalent of a Southerner saying "*bless your heart.*" The ultimate message of incompetence.

"Soula, crumble the feta into the salad then pour the oil."

I was grateful. Squishing briny cheese between my fingers was the extent of my cooking skills. "You want some cut for the plates?" I asked as Ma hoisted a restaurant-sized pastitzio out of one of the ovens in the wall.

"I already did that, Soula. It's on the plate with the olives and peppers. Tell Bethany she can bring that out next."

"I heard," Bethany deadpanned as she walked into her next task. Bethany was a decent cook, even if her talents were strictly Southern US and not the Southern islands of Greece. She had Sofia really young and had no help, so when we roomed together during college, she used to cook family dinners, always inviting Decca and I to share in her cheap but nutritious meals. Unless Decca had a shift at the body farm or I had study group, we joined them. It was one of the small ways Bethany tried to cultivate a sense of normalcy to Sofia's very non-normal childhood and part of what bonded the four of us as our own morbid little family.

"I think these are done, Raynie." Sofia stood stirring a pot of long-simmering green beans with tomato, garlic, and dill. It was one of my mom's favorite dishes and she'd started teaching Sofia how to cook. Specifically, cook in the Greek style. From this non-cook's perspective, that meant dumping in heaps more garlic, lemon juice, and olive oil than necessary, but it worked.

Like all other things Eleniká, Sofia took a shine to food. Bethany mostly rolled her eyes and reminded her daughter that she was an Appalachian hillbilly by blood, and that the banjo, not the bouzouki were the sounds of her people. Deep down, I thought Bethany liked being part of the family too, even if that meant learning to love this new culture and dealing with my idiot brothers.

"Hey, Sou," Gus said, coming in through the screen. He'd just returned home yesterday. I hadn't seen him since Christmas.

"How was your semester?" I asked.

My brother rubbed his face and hid his drained eyes behind a shrugging smile. "Most of the ancient shit's over, thank God. Now, I just have to get through my thesis about how the ecumenical patriarchate is fucked up while disguising it well enough for them to ordain me into it. Remind me why I wanted even more college instead of a stake in the family biz?"

"Because you can't stand the heat of the cremation retort?" Bethany offered.

"That's right. I knew it wasn't the study of Byzantine music. Besides, the women are, shall we say, healthier? Stronger heartbeat?" Gus smiled.

"Am I allowed to be offended by that statement?" Bethany teased.

"Not if it makes me picture you with my brother." I shook my head.

George looked up, scowling extra hard from across the room before returning his attention to his phone, but for once, he decided to let it go. He chugged his beer instead of picking at old wounds.

"I mean, I can *picture* her—"

"Gus," George reprimanded, still looking at his screen before slipping his phone into his back pocket. Sofia needed a dish from a high cupboard, and he brought it down.

"George, you know it's not like that anymore," Gus said. George didn't even look up to catch Gus's plaintive expression.

"Don't you have a date tonight?" George said, stepping forward with his arms crossed over his chest.

"Oh, George, lighten up," Bethany prodded him in the breastbone. He looked down at her hand and his nostrils flared like a spider had landed on his chest.

"He can't, Bethany. George is at war with everyone," Gus said.

Bethany's eyes locked on George's in a stalemate. They were deeply engaged in a territory war and sometimes, it really did seem like George's main goal was to make Bethany's life as miserable as possible. Bethany reciprocated in small ways whenever she could, but she was still new here and wanted to make a good impression. The two clashed about everything possible, both in funeral care and in their personal lives. If it wasn't embalming or casket suppliers, it was nights off and what takeout Bethany ordered for dinner on really late nights.

There was one thing that kept them civil: Sofia.

For some reason she had chosen George as a stand-in father figure and he had surprised everyone by stepping into the role gracefully, treating Bethany's daughter with an uncanny humor and almost sweet tenderness. I suspected that was the other reason Bethany didn't squash him like a bug.

Bethany's hand slid off George's chest and his Adam's apple bobbed. Something even greater was underlying this reaction. The two buzzed like electrical wires.

George turned back to Sofia, holding the serving bowl for her while she filled it with beans. He even laughed when some of the tomato sauce splattered on his plaid shirt, telling her it was no big deal. I took the bowl from him and watched his smile fade into a sneer.

"What?" He asked, like it was impertinent for me to smile at my oldest brother when it almost looked like his stony surface might be starting to crack. I shook my head in response as he dropped the bowl into my hands.

He hated me. I didn't take it personally. I knew why.

I was there when he turned to stone in the first place.

By the time I checked on Wells, he was still sitting on the fancy sofa, listening to Yia-Yiá's stories of her childhood in Greece and that time when her father had to sell her favorite milk goats to pay for her to come to America to work as a nanny in Athens, Georgia, which was not one little bit like Athens, Greece and she didn't know English or anyone else, but since at least there was a Greek church, she was able to meet a kind family who became closer to her than her real family who tutored her in English and politely explained that Americans don't normally think it's appropriate for their children to be running around barefoot outside all day OR soothe teething pain and colic with Metáxa in their milk.

Yia-Yiá usually cried when she recounted her youth.

Pappoú turned the channel to a baseball game.

I thought Wells would be asleep, but he wasn't even stifling yawns.

I was seriously impressed. Instead, he was asking questions, probing deeper into her history. Our family history. "What's a koumbára?" "You're *who's* nouná?" "So Soula's name is really Athanasía, which I think I already knew and, by the way, sounds nothing like *Soula*—and she's named after you?"

As I eavesdropped on the same old stories, it was like revisiting my entire experience of knowing Yia-Yiá. I'd heard her life story so many times, it didn't even register any more. They were just words. The emotion behind them didn't matter, nor the fact that they were in fact, an oral history of post-WWII Southern Europe. The words had tarnished, obscuring the beauty of their original gleaming brass. Yia-Yiá's life, I was ashamed to think, had become rote to the point of callousness.

I stood behind her, humbled. I kept listening. Not to her words this time, but to the hard-fought battles behind them. The heartache she felt when she left her father in Greece, never to see him again because of his untimely death only a few years after she came to America. The massive undertaking of having to adopt a language, country, and culture that was overwhelming and alien. The desperation with which she latched on to her husband, my Pappoú, when he provided a life that looked just familiar enough for her to willingly submit to a marriage of convenience. I perched on the arm of the sofa behind her, and she automatically reached for my hand to squeeze it.

"S'agapó polý, koúkla," her warm eyes glowed up at me. *Doll*, she had called me. It didn't fit. I'd never been anyone's doll, but it had been so long since I'd been called any term of endearment, I appreciated the gesture.

"I love you, too, Yia-Yiá," I said, meaning it for the first time in too long.

Wells smiled at me. I wouldn't have put it past him if he orchestrated this whole thing to accomplish exactly this. This renewal of generational bonds. He was tough to figure out. He came across as so nice and accommodating (if a little pushy). But was he using his powers for good? Or for the dark side? Maybe he was in fact, such a heartless bastard, his true motives lay coiled among the tall grass, waiting for the rest of us to lower our guard?

Then he yawned and I knew. He wasn't faking. He really was that good.

chapter fifteen

Waylon—Now

THE SCENT OF DINNER hit me as soon as Soula opened the door to the funeral home.

Or her parent's house. It was hard to put a finger on the right thing to call the big white house where a big family lived big raucous lives upstairs while the dead slept in their basement.

I never could train my nose to recognize the individual scents of things being cooked together in a pot. Then again, I wasn't raised with any kind of cuisine that had any real scent or flavor. The way I grew up, food didn't make up for unexpressed love. Sometimes mom cooked. Hot dogs, mac and cheese from a box, casseroles made from condensed soups. The rest of the time, I supplemented whatever was still good in the refrigerator with peanut butter and saltine sandwiches for my sisters and me. I was angry about it for a long time. Through college, at least. Especially when my sister, Loretta graduated from high school and didn't use her full ride to Tennessee and even more so when Patsy didn't graduate at all because there was no one left to look after her.

Stepping into Soula's house was like stepping into a dream childhood. The childhood I only witnessed when I was invited for team meals or dinners at friends' houses. The noise of the place screamed *family* to me, no matter how differently Soula painted her ethnic heritage.

Her family finagled Soula and I into adjacent seats once we convened in the dining room. I stole glances at her as her head dropped. Eyes in her lap, she shredded her paper napkin. Her overly-protective brother sat across from me. He didn't say anything but the way he kept glancing between Soula and I, I could tell he wanted to. I glared right back and held eye contact for longer. *Ha. He looked away.*

"Bethany, did you make the reservations yet?" The brother asked.

"I'm waiting until airfares drop."

"You keep waiting much longer and the rates will rise again. I put it in your Google calendar for a reason. I don't want to wait until the last minute. I already booked the conference tickets."

"Last minute? It's six months away. We had Mr. Chaconis' funeral this morning. Plus, the late-night pickup. Just when did you schedule me time to hunt for airfares?"

He checked his phone. "Ah, yes. The Chaconis funeral, that you drastically undersold. That man had a large family. He deserved a casket of appropriate grandeur. Here it is, from three forty-five to four o'clock. An hour after we came back from the burial. I even helped you clean up."

"I don't consider it help when you criticize every little thing I do. And that's when I was going to the Greek store for feta for your mom. Then I was helping Sofia with her science project. I'll get our tickets tonight, but I'm warning you now, I fly first class."

"Ma," Gus said. "You can't send Bethany to run your errands. She owns your house now."

"Gus, for the love of God...." George said through gritted teeth.

"Someone needs to be on her side," Gus said.

"No one needs *you* on their side," George said.

I had no idea what was going on, so I stayed out of it, and took a bite of that pasta dish that had my mouth watering. It smelled meaty, I could tell that much, and the lasagna-like square was capped with a deliciously-cheesy-looking layer. It tasted like... well, maybe I wasn't a big fan of Greek food after all. It wasn't spit-into-your-napkin bad—I could swallow just about anything—and it *was* meaty, but it also tasted faintly of dessert. But the biggest rip-off was that creamy layer. It wasn't cheesy at all. It tasted like nothing. It was disappointingly *meh*, so I did what any grateful southern man would do. I gobbled it down and requested a second helping.

"She doesn't own the house, she owns the business and only half of it," Soula's mom said, dishing me out another giant piece of the stuff. "Soula, eat something. Sit up straight."

Soula looked up at me once, blankly, her eyes giving me absolutely no information to read her situation. She wasn't my cold, calculating, decisive Soula here, in this house, twenty steps away from her own apartment. She was no longer a Greek goddess made of marble, ruling with an icy heart. In her apartment, I bet even her houseplants grew from intimidation alone.

Here, she was smaller. Not physically, though. Yeah, that too, but more childlike, overtaken by the dominant egos of those who shared her DNA. Her mom seemed to crave attention, judging from her deafening voice and near-constant humble bragging. George, the eldest brother, seemed to have better ideas than anyone at the table—leaving not only his own family rolling their eyes, but Bethany looking like she was about to rip out her sleek blonde beehive. Gus had filled his plate, scarfed down his lasagna-like stuff, and left for a date approximately two minutes after the weirdness with George. The dad, who I finally met, seemed to be the source of Soula's personality, and therefore barely present at dinner. Pappoú was still watching the baseball game, and Yia-Yiá didn't seem to be hearing any of this.

I played my role of detective, aloof and polite, gathering details and making sense of snippets of conversation. I had reserved judgement when Soula claimed her family didn't like her, but after that dinner, I was starting to see she was wrong. It wasn't just her. No one in her family seemed to like *each other*. I'd never wanted to leave a room faster. So, why did Soula stay?

"STAY HERE," SOULA INSTRUCTED before bounding up the garage steps into her apartment. She returned a minute later with my dog on her leash. Kudzu rushed to greet me, licking the remnants of whatever meat sauce or cheese remained on my fingers. Soula and Kudzu walked off, slowly, stopping on a grassy divider in the parking lot for the dog to urinate. "Coming?" She asked me.

I smiled. I needed air. I guess she did, too. I forgot that was what families can do to you. Both the good and the bad. They can deprive you of the space to breathe.

We ambled across Third Avenue and sought respite in the woods that flanked the park pathway. A quarter-mile, circular-paved sidewalk, surrounded by pretty perennials. There was little to no reason for Franklin's city planners to design such a beautifully landscaped place here, where it didn't get much foot traffic, but at the moment, I was overwhelmed with gladness for its existence. It was like someone designed a tiny, woodland kingdom just to give my dog a beautiful place to poop.

"So, are they always like that?" I asked. I figured I might as well get down to it, since the walk was her idea.

She nodded. Then shrugged. "Gus is alright. George was too... until he wasn't. Now Bethany gets the brunt of it, but that only adds fuel to the fire. Both are just as stubborn as the other and I think it makes the rest of us tired and cranky. Is it wrong to say I hate my family?"

I wanted to laugh but she looked so sincere. "I don't have an answer for that." She didn't hate her family. She just hated living twenty feet away from them. Probably.

We reached the edge of the woods, and I heard the rippling of the Harpeth River. I didn't realize we were so close. Not that the sound was deafening. Spring had been drier than usual, so the river looked more like a creek. The sun was down but the sky was still purple and orange up ahead. The backlit trees loomed above us, ancient and ominous, their shivering leaves in dialogue with the river. Soula was at home here. At the end of the day, in the place between the human world and the forest wall. Her eyes dark but shining, and she didn't step back from me when I stepped forward. She wasn't the least bit shy or cold.

Kud yanked her leash and tugged me aside. Soula laughed and the sound caught me unawares. It was magical, just like Soula in the twilight.

I blamed the concussion for my infatuation with her. I didn't know what to blame for our communication breakdown earlier.

"You ate a lot," she said. I suspected that was her attempt at a question.

"Yep."

"Are you feeling any nausea? Lightheadedness? Should we go back to the apartment?" Soula's eyebrows wrinkled and she lifted her hand as if ready to palpate... something. I was impressed. She actually looked concerned.

There were very few people I couldn't read. In detective work, people lied about the dumbest shit more often than not. People shot off at the mouth and in their interest of trying to appear one hundred percent innocent, or cover something up for someone they knew was guilty, they dug themselves into trenches. It didn't take a master of intuition to know these types were trying to be helpful in their ways, but I really wished there was some way of issuing a press release to all people everywhere that when questioned by homicide, please, just answer in as few words as possible.

Now I had met my match and *this one* was entirely *too* economical with her verbiage. I wondered what would happen if I employed the same tactics with Soula that I used to question witnesses that were less forthcoming. Did she appreciate a direct approach? I tried it out on something innocuous.

"Where are your grandparents from, exactly?" I asked as I let Kudzu off her leash to hurl the stick I had just finished ripping the bark off of. Third Avenue bisected the Smythe family property and the small park, but at this hour, there was no traffic. The park was essentially an extension of Smythe land. It was peaceful here, even with a dog racing back and forth.

"Heraklia, on the island of Crete and Athens. Both Greek." She added unnecessarily. She answered promptly and without second-guessing. I tried again.

"And your parents? Your dad's not Greek, but your mom is. Was she born in Greece?"

"No. She's from Athens, but the Athens in Georgia. It's not the same at all, in case you were wondering."

"Maybe, just a different type of Greek life?" I tried out a joke.

"What do you mean?" She looked worried. The joke bombed.

"Nevermind. How did they meet?" Direct again.

"My parents?" She laughed but it was more like a huff. "How do you think? On the job. Same as any other deathcare worker." She looked at me, ready for another question but when I gestured for her to continue, she sighed. "My mom's family came here for the funeral of one of their cousins. Dad was doing the funeral and Ma came up to him saying she could have done a much better job with the makeup and that Thea Barbara looked too old. He didn't take any offense and offered to let her help with the next one. He was surprised when she took him up on his offer. She ended up moving here, marrying Dad, and going to mortuary school and taking over the desairology, the mortuary makeup aspect of body prep. I sometimes wonder if Dad ever regretted asking her to help. I guess he expected to shake her loose eventually, but she latched on like a boa constrictor and her whole culture descended with her."

"*Her* culture?" Had I picked up on a disconnect somewhere?

"The Greekness. The family. The church. The smells. The guilt. The everythingness of it. It's oppressive sometimes."

"I can relate," I relented. "My family, what's left of them anyway, aren't Greek. They're just trashy rednecks. But talk about an oppressive culture." She looked at me. I had forgotten my directness. "Let's just say it was a struggle for them, my being on this side of the law."

"Is that why you didn't have anyone to take care of you this weekend?"

It seemed Soula preferred the direct approach herself. "Yeah. I had a big falling out with my sister after my mom died. She was probably the last of them. My friends close by are all cops or they have young families. I couldn't bother them."

"Does that bother *you*?"

"Which part? The lack of family or the lack of family?" I hoped it didn't come out bitter. I looked at her for confirmation, but her face gave nothing away. "Not most days. I figured one day, it'll be time to start my own family and they'll make up for my lack of background family."

"I guess we're the different polarities, then." Her eyes twinkled as she turned her body a little more in my direction while we strolled. "I had always planned to remain childless. To break the Greek streak. It seems I have too much background family. It's stifling. I don't want to be stifled on the other side as well."

"You still feel that way?" I wasn't surprised. Nothing about her was maternal. Or nurturing, unless you counted her plants. But you never knew.

"Absolutely. I wouldn't want to bring a child into this world. Not after what I... what *we* see every day."

"Oh, no way will I agree with you on that front. I have a whole treatise on why today is, hands down, the best time to procreate."

She laughed. "How can you possibly say that? Our government is breaking down. There is way too much violence, even in our little city. Plus, the environment—"

"Number one, child labor laws. Those exist now." I listed on my fingers. "Number two, child safety restraints. Babies aren't flying through windshields anymore—"

"Well, I hate to burst your theory bubble—"

"Number three," I ignored her. "Free and reduced school meals, and that's just the start. I could go on and on, but the fact that kids aren't filling their lungs with coal while working in the mines at age seven is a big perk."

"Not here anyway," she said.

"Here's all I'm talking about." I was breathing hard. This topic got me worked up. "Did you know that historians consider the year 500-something to be the worst year in history? 500. I'm not saying life today isn't difficult. It's a fucking battle sometimes. But relatively, it's more possible to stay alive, safe, educated, fed, and clothed now versus any other time in history. I'm sorry. I just... probably listen to too many history podcasts. I just don't love the whole 'not bringing a child into today's world' reason. I call bullshit on that. Be childless for other reasons; totally fine. I respect it." It totally didn't sound like I respected her decision, because of how wound up I was. *Damn it Tides of History.*

"I really do respect your decision." I said after a few quiet steps.

"You make it sound like it's a decision I'm actively making."

I felt even more stupid when she put it like that. *Why were we even discussing this? And like it was anything we needed to agree on.*

We were quiet for a while after that. "Thanks," she said, finally.

"For what?"

"For showing me a different perspective. I hadn't thought of that."

"So now you want kids?"

"Not really. But maybe there are other options I hadn't considered. I don't like to be shoehorned into the black or the white. The world is nuanced." She walked ahead of me, her eyes drawn together at the brows. She didn't speak for minutes. Once again, it was like she'd completely forgotten I was there. I was starting to realize that was her way and I decided to stop taking offense.

Whatever our relationship was, was unusual, but I'd be lying if I didn't admit it wasn't a relief to bypass the typical college stories and rehashed family backgrounds that were abbreviated into inconsequence over the obligatory series of drinks and dinners. Soula and I seemed to be saving our words up for when they mattered. Or she was. I was simply following her lead.

I attached Kud to her leash and followed Soula back home. She was still walking aimlessly ahead. That was where her brain needed to be. I gave her space.

The rest of the evening, and essentially, the rest of the long, excruciating weekend passed much in the same way. Soula thinking in her office. Soula thinking while watering her plants. Soula thinking while we watched Netflix. Me and the dog simply existing alongside her. It wasn't necessarily uncomfortable, the silence, but I was unsure what she wanted. Space? Someone to draw her out of her shell? Sex?

Okay, it drove me a little bit crazy that she took her bra off as soon as she entered the apartment. It wasn't like her breasts were inconspicuous, either. They were set on her chest like two perfect teardrops with highly expressive peaks—always peaked. It was really fucking hard to look away from her eyes, but it was even harder to tear my attention away from her perfect-for-me breasts. It was like a train wreck. Or one of those adorable kitten TikToks that go viral on social media and you really just wanted to reach out and stroke the kittens' thick fur and dream that you weren't recuperating from a stupid concussion in the wake of a very unfortunate first day on the job, hadn't thoroughly embarrassed yourself by fainting at a gruesome sight, and that those taut nipples were made ever more taut by their desire to be bitten.

It was hard, alright.

Soula got a text Sunday evening as we watched House Hunters reruns. I pretended my balls weren't aching when she passed the phone for me to look. It was from Reyes. He concluded the interviews, looked again at all the evidence we bagged for the Rogers case, or as I thought of him, Mr. Pukey. There was nothing. No evidence of foul play, at least. Plenty of evidence he was dead.

"I thought I wasn't allowed to look at devices."

"I thought it would ease your mind. You seem preoccupied." She tossed the phone next to her on the couch.

"*I* seem preoccupied?" I mean, only when I looked to my right, at the stunning woman cuddling my dog instead of me, but... I wasn't allowed to occupy my mind with literally anything else.

"Yes. You were sighing a lot and breathing heavy," she said. "Look, I know it's boring here. I'm not the most exciting person in Nashville. But that's kind of the point. You're not supposed to be excited by anything right now. The longer you can essentially stay bored to death, the less risk of stroke or TIA." She physically retreated into herself after her medical speech. Maybe this was what drove her to combat sports during her off hours.

"I'm not preoccupied," I said. "Unless you count the many ways I'd love a repeat of that night after The Pig. You're the one who's off somewhere in that giant brain of yours."

"No. People often think so. It's flattering, but I may as well let you know that my mind is never anywhere my physical body isn't. It's the opposite of a superpower."

"I don't follow."

"Okay." She paused to choose her words. I was already familiar with her speech patterns. How she curated language to fit the shape of her thoughts, pulling words out of the air as they floated by her. I could see her eyes light up when the exact word came into view. Or maybe I was glamorizing my way into her patterns because I wanted to be part of them. "You know how Oprah and those types have picked apart little bits of Buddhism—the meditation, the mindfulness, the presence?" I nodded, though I didn't have a fucking clue what she was talking about. "Well, I'm sort of constantly in that state of mindfulness. But without intending to be, or without any spiritual purpose. I try to think of my cases as we're watching House Hunters, but really and truly, all I can think about is that man's awful shirt, and why is this couple forgetting that they started the show convincing us that they absolutely needed a fourth bedroom, but because this house is 'cute' the need no longer exists, and lastly, why are there only three houses for sale in all of Santa Fe?"

"That sounds like a superpower to me. I'd love to be able to zone out on one thing."

Soula scooched closer to me, moving Kudzu's head off her lap. "I'm not zoning out. That's the problem. I can't zone out. I'm hyper-focusing on one idiotic thing at a time. I always wanted to be one of those people who could study with music on, or read a novel while waiting for a phone call. Can I just tell you how hard conversation is, especially with my family's chaos?" She stood up, apparently too agitated to be sedentary. "God, they're awful. So loud and there's so much jostling and teasing and crying and hugging. It's overkill.

That's why I'm so happy you're here. You,... you're like a thick, glossy-leaved Monstera deliciosa. It's wonderful."

"That's a plant, right? You just complimented me by calling me a plant?"

"Yes." She nodded but didn't elaborate. Instead, she started spooning tablespoons of dark roast into the basket of the coffee maker.

"I'm flattered, I think. But you're going to have to explain exactly how that's a compliment."

She continued counting spoonfuls and filling the water reservoir. When she pressed the brew button, she leaned a hip against the counter with her hands braced widely, her shirt pressed tight against her breasts, making me want to die at present.

"Okay, the third one from the right." She pointed. "That big one on the floor. That's the Monstera."

I turned around and looked where she pointed and saw a plant. One of many plants that all looked green and pretty much the same. I wondered why she picked that plant rather than say, a dandelion.

"Everyone says the Monstera is difficult to grow. It likes a certain soil moisture and pH, you can't over water it so that the roots rot, but you can't let it dry out either, since it grows wild in the tropics. But I guess I've never had to think much about it. I just sort of *intuitively* know what it needs and how to care for it."

"I'm still waiting for the part where I'm the plant."

"I'm getting there. I don't quite mean that I can intuit your needs, but I think you're the only person that I've managed to come close with. There's something about you that I inherently know. Like my body is aware of yours and our minds are synched together." She looked at me like she just woke up from a dream and couldn't decode what was real and what wasn't. Then she shook her head as if to re-collect her thoughts. "Anyway, the leaf shape is one of my favorites. It's interesting without being too showy. They are a luscious, shiny, dark green just like under the rainforest canopy where they grow and they don't just revel in their own beauty, their own sense of importance, they reflect the light onto others. Only a truly beautiful plant can serve as a mirror and a stage for others to shine. I think that also describes you, Wells." She stopped gesticulating with her arms and looked at me. "I think you're a very good person."

I could have fainted again. Soula showed her honest-to-God hand. I was almost too stunned to react, but I also needed her openness. That compliment aside, her speech almost validated the amount of time I spent thinking of her and that pull I felt toward her without knowing much about her.

"Which of these plants are you?" I asked, wondering what exotic selection she'd refer to. It was altogether possible that I was developing a warmth toward horticulture.

"Oh, none of these. I'd say I'm a Venus flytrap."

"Maneater, are you?" I smiled. That didn't fit the profile of my weekend caretaker.

"No. Because I look very interesting, but once I'm home, I'm essentially a dud. The plants almost always die immediately unless they have the exact proper acidity, moisture level, sunlight. It's the houseplant that's the easiest to kill. Even I can't keep one alive."

It was now past twilight and the sky was an awesome shade of teal. I moved closer to the wall of glass, admiring the various shades of green that popped against the night sky. It was dark enough now the glass also perfectly reflected Soula, who stood biting a nail and looking up at me from under her rainforest of vines.

"And you don't think there's anyone out there who is capable of keeping a Venus flytrap alive?" I asked, still not turning to her. She did better when we both pretended we weren't talking in metaphors.

"Well, the plant can be found quite readily, so obviously nurseries can grow it, ship it to plant stores. Botanical gardens always have an abundance of carnivorous plants, it's the casual buyer that brings it home, thinking it's going to be fun to have a Venus flytrap who ends up with a black-leaved thing rotting on a windowsill until it finally winds up in the garbage."

"Are you speaking from experience?" I stepped closer to examine the Monstera whose shiny, bold leaves were being stroked by Soula's hands; a surgeon's delicate, strong hands.

"Oh, plenty of times. I... wait... are we talking about plants now, or me?"

"What do you think?"

"Alright." She dropped her hand to her side. "I guess, I have experience with people thinking I'm something I'm not."

"Do you think that might have something to do with your lying to people on a first date?" I asked.

"My lying is a direct result of people thinking they can pick me off the shelf and I'll be normal. Like a Pothos. They think they can forget to water me. Or they overwater me. Not provide enough drainage. Or grow me in peat moss. Whatever. The expectation is that I can take whatever anyone gives me and still function. But I'm not a Pothos. I'm too weird." Soula slouched until her whole body shrunk. I wanted to reach out to her, be her touchpoint. It ached inside my own body that she felt like this—whatever this strange articulation of plant needs actually meant to her. I did stretch my fingers, willing her to acknowledge *my need* to meet *her needs* and throw me a bone.

"What do you want, Soula? What *is* your appropriate water level?"

"What do you mean?" Her eyes narrowed. "You can't possibly want to water me?"

"But I do," I assured her and goddamnit I closed the gap between us, reaching up and holding her arms. "I think I can keep that Venus flytrap alive if you give me the chance. No, I *know* I can. Because I'll try everything. And I pay attention."

"But I... just thought you'd like something a little less...." she trailed off and looked everywhere but my eyes.

"Less what?" I whispered, almost afraid that if I spoke too loudly or moved too abruptly, she'd startle and retreat from me again.

"Less scary. You know what I do. You know my annoying family and what they do. My friends, too. We are surrounded by death. That doesn't make you want to run away from me?"

"Soula, look at me, please. Look in my eyes and breathe with me." When she did and her black eyes met mine, the fear in them lessened. I wanted to smile. I wanted to breathe in the scent of honey-sweet skin and dog fur and coffee that wafted from her lithe bare neck. But more than anything, I wanted to make her trust me. Her lips parted and mine followed but I didn't dare. Not yet.

"Don't doubt this, Soula. I'm choosing you. I've been choosing you since I saw you across the bar. Since our eyes met over the corpse of my first homicide that isn't a homicide. Please, for the love of God, tell me how to water you right."

chapter sixteen

Soula—Then

My brothers couldn't believe it, but when I was a junior in high school, I was asked to prom.

By a senior. The attractive, semi-sporty/semi-smart, generally nice enough Josh Hampstead asked me during lunchtime in the library—where the cool kids hung out, obviously. Our paths had never really crossed before, although I had seen his face around the hallways and lockers. It was a pleasant face. Clear skin and a strong jawline.

The librarian had just stepped away from the center desk and I bent down to sneak a bite of my peanut butter and honey sandwich from my backpack. Then he slid into the chair next to mine, like I was an acquaintance or a chum he could just as easily slide into conversation with.

"This lady on lunch or something?" Josh said. It's not that I memorized his words or anything, but I trust my memory enough to approximate his tone and the surprising intimacy it created between us. For a girl who lived in a mortuary, intimacy with my peers didn't happen.

"Do you need help?" I plucked up my courage, took a giant leap of faith and spoke real human words to him, albeit words sticky with peanut butter. "I pretty much know where everything is in here. I could help you find a book if that's what you're looking for. I'm also very good at Boolean searches if you need help with research."

"Boolean searches?"

When he smiled, only one corner of his mouth moved up, making him look like a rake from one of Yia-Yiá's books (if there were rakes in Franklin High School, circa 2010). But I was quite partial to rakish heroes and after considering for a minute, I decided they must start somewhere. Why not start with me? I could totally be that one woman who *done him so wrong* he landed himself in rakedom. Of course, that required a few milliliters more courage than I knew I could screw up, and many more human words than I was willing to part with.

Something caught the corner of his eye, and he did a double take before hopping out of his seat without another word. *Nevermind*, I thought to myself. I probably didn't have it in me to be the girl who destroyed his soul anyway. I finished my sandwich and tucked the baggie in the front pocket of my backpack before marking the page I needed to return to in my calc textbook. I didn't have time or mental energy to dwell on the rake with the light brown hair who floated into and back out of my life for a whopping total of sixty seconds. It was almost time for Spanish, and I had to screw up my courage for something else: braving the spawning salmon of the hallways between periods.

I felt, more than heard, the heavy thud of books landing on the library table above my head. "Hey," said the rake. His cheeks were pinkish now, making him decidedly less rake-like and more boy-next-door-like. Still, he was handsome. I tucked my hair behind my ear.

"You're name's Athanasía, right? I'm Josh." He didn't reach out a hand for me to shake, but it was high school and not a board meeting.

"That's my school roster name. People call me Soula." I clarified. He sat up a little straighter and looked briefly stunned, as if my name actually meant something to him. I didn't know what it could possibly be. He probably didn't either, because that look on his face was gone almost immediately.

"Yeah, that's right." He said politely. The school was too big of a pond, and I was too small—a sandflea, more than a fish—for him to know that. "I've seen you around and I know of you, but I don't actually know you."

I nodded. But he paused to let me talk. "I've seen you around too. I just didn't know you had a name. Or, that it was... is... Josh."

Josh smiled his rake smile again and opened his mouth before looking at my face in earnest. "Are you seeing anybody right now?" He asked.

This was one of those moments when I legitimately wanted to look behind my shoulders to check if anyone had walked up. I resisted the urge, but that didn't help me come up with what whatever witty quip was warranted here. If I was really a rake's temptress, I'd have some sly yet brutal comeback for his mockery. It would make him fall in love with me instantly, quit his rakedom, and vow to protect me for the next 300 pages.

Instead, I said, "No?"

"Me either," he laughed. "Actually, I'm going to Vandy in the fall and I'm not trying to get attached to anyone before then. I just don't think it's fair to start college in an old relationship."

I couldn't decide if that was extra-rakish of him or refreshingly honest and wise. Either way, I agreed with him. "I understand completely. I'd do the same if I were graduating this year."

"You would?" he seemed surprised. Rakeish then.

I nodded. "You're just looking for non-committal sex. I find that very practical."

His non-rakish cheeks flamed pink, and he bit his lip. "Uh, actually... I was just looking for a date to prom."

"Oh. Well, good luck, then." *Was the bell late?*

"I mean, are... *you* just looking for that? Sex, I mean? I didn't think someone like you would be into that." He wasn't looking at me anymore. He was looking at the table.

"Well...." I deliberated. "It's a little earlier than I had in mind. I didn't plan to have sex until college. But I guess it might be good to get it out of the way now so I can completely commit to my studies, so I suppose... yes. I am."

The bell rang. Neither of us moved. It was a high noon standoff. Literally, because 5th period began at 12:05. But I no longer cared about the crowds, getting to my locker in time, or even making it to Spanish class at all, because I had found a rake of my very own who might or might not be willing to give me my own romance novel experience before I went on to pursue more serious, sciencey stuff. My mind buzzed with excitement. When I told him it was early, it wasn't because I wasn't ready. It was because I assumed no one would *see* me before college. But someone had. Josh had seen me.

Josh looked petrified. "What the fuck just happened?"

"Get moving kids," the librarian yelled, disturbing the quiet of the library and my moment of decision. "The bell rang three minutes ago."

I started to move, but Josh grabbed my wrist. *What rakishness.* I smiled. He'd do really well. I was already imagining it. "Well," I explained. "You need a date to prom. By your own admission, someone who won't harass you afterward about being your girlfriend. I would like sex—at least I think I would, and I imagine the same is true for you, so I think it's a very good thing you came into the library today."

Still, he didn't move. I stood, slinging my backpack over my shoulder. "Are you coming?"

"Uh... I think I need a minute," he said. I shrugged. It was more important not to be late to Spanish than to remain here with indecisive Josh Hampstead. I made it just in time.

The next day, Josh ate lunch with me in the library. It was a major disruption to my distraction-free study time, but it allowed us to finalize some of the details of our arrangement. He'd take me to prom. We'd go to his house afterward and I'd learn how to give a blow job. With a goofy smile, he asked if he could go down on me—which made me pause.

I assumed from watching tv that guys preferred women sans pubic hair, but I didn't know how to make the hair removal appointment. Or where to go. Or if I even wanted to, because wasn't that kind of *porny*? Finally, I decided the hair removal wouldn't be worth it since I barely had much hair there anyway, but the issue itself required tabling for later discussion. Then, he'd don a condom and we'd do penetrative sex. He said he'd be gentle. I said I'd probably stab him in the dick with my sabre if he wasn't.

Once terms were arranged, he pulled out a sandwich and an apple from his bag. "What are you doing?" I asked, horrified.

"Eating."

"You can't eat here," I said. "This is my table. Find another one."

"You can't share a table with me but you're going to suck my dick in two weeks?"

"Exactly. That's happening in two weeks. I have a research paper, a photography project, and two finals before then."

He rolled his eyes but moved to another table in the library. "This is all your idea, you know," he said as he moved one table away. Still in full view. He joined me in the library for the next nine days before the Saturday of prom.

Then came the fiasco.

I found a dress. That was no problem. The vintage clothing stores in Nashville were still stocked with fluffy, 1950s chiffon cupcakes. I chose a light blue one to offset my olive skin and the death pall that typically surrounded me.

It was late for renting a limo, so dad said we could take the family coach. I was only slightly squeamish, knowing our vehicular choice was normally used to shuttle crying, grieving immediate family members between churches and graveyards, but of course I didn't tell Josh why my family owned a brand-new Cadillac limousine.

Josh even procured dinner reservations and matching corsages, even if the latter sounded a little too boyfriend/girlfriend for my tastes. Josh said it was foreplay.

I refused to let him meet my parents or pick me up from my home. It was untraditional, but everything about tonight was untraditional. I would be chauffeured by one of our drivers to his house where his mom would take pictures of her "baby all grown up" before spending a girl's weekend in Nashville with her friends—thus leaving Josh's house free of parental interference.

It was the perfect plan.

Until it wasn't.

Josh didn't mention my name to his mother when he told her he found a date to prom. She thought my picking him from his house in the limo was an act of independence, one to be applauded, even if only in lip service. When Fred, our usual driver opened the door for me and I stepped out, Ms. Josh's Mom was already crying just a little, like a faucet had a drip. One tear dropping every second sigh as she snapped photos of Josh under the crepe myrtle, Josh and I on their staircase, Josh slipping his corsage onto my wrist with a knowing smile.

"Josh, look here. Look at me, Josh," she directed the photo shoot between tears. "You, dear—what's your name?—Sue? Can you just step out of the shot for this next one? I want to get another one of my son by the trellis."

When the camera was finally put down and Josh was stepping into the limo, I thought Josh's mother was going to follow us to prom. He hadn't needed to ask me to prom after all. His mother would happily have been his date. Before I stepped in, I turned and thanked Mrs. Hampstead. This was the woman who spawned my intended virginity recipient, after all. Not that I was going to thank her for that. Even I wasn't that blunt.

"What's your name again, honey?" When she smiled and cocked her head, her helmet of blond hair jiggled slightly.

"Soula Smythe." I reached my hand out to shake her hand, embarrassed that I hadn't introduced myself as soon as I got there. She took my hand but instead of shaking, her fingers went as limp as the freshly dead. Her smile faltered. She looked at the car before looking back at me.

"Smythe." She said, closing off her nasal passages as though my name was a bad smell she didn't want to breathe in. "As in Smythe Mortuary?"

She hadn't quite released my hand yet, either. I had to tug a bit before I could take a step back from the woman who was now standing practically on top of me. "Oh," I laughed nervously. "Yep. That's my family. I didn't think my name was an issue." More nervous laughter. Fred, always so adept at maintaining a stony face and blending into the background took a step forward, his eyes darting to mine. "Okay, well. I guess we'd better be off, or we'll miss our dinner reservation."

Mrs. Hampstead bypassed me and reached an arm blindly into the car, waving it around until she found her son's polyester tuxedoed shoulder.

"Josh." Her wild eyes were still trained on me. "Josh! Get your ass out of that disgusting car right this very minute. You can NOT go to the senior high school prom with no girl who lives in a funeral home."

"Funeral home?" Josh didn't move except to look at me, still standing by the curb. "Soula, what is she talking about? Mom, no one lives in a funeral home."

"Well, this one does. They probably just pulled a poor dead body right outta that car you're sittin' in. Lord knows what kinda smells are in there."

Josh looked at me wide-eyed. Like he was the last girl, and I was the slasher in a bad horror film. He slid out gingerly, not letting his hand touch the seat.

"It's not a hearse." I said, plainly.

"I don't care what it is. It's got bad vibes. And you, Little Missy, wanted to take advantage of my son, thinking you could show up here in your fancy car and your goody two shoes dress. But I know your type. You like to charm the mommas, thinking they'll give you more leeway. Nuh-uh, girl. Not this momma." She was beating her chest now.

I rolled my eyes and turned to Josh. I knew he'd see reason. "Decedents don't ride in a limo. A casket wouldn't even fit. There's no back door. There's nothing tainted about it. It's *just* a limo."

Josh said nothing. Nor did his eyes give anything away.

"You remember when Gramma Denise passed on? God only knows why, but I had the hospital brung her to *her people*," the woman pointed at me. Not just at me, right in my face. "They *said* they'd take real good care of her. But remember when I wanted to see her one last time? I called and called and no one picked up. I was desperate to see my mother just one more time before she was nothing but ashes. But no. They burned her before I had the chance to say goodbye to my momma." The faucet turned on again. This time it was more than a drip. It was a flood, smearing black makeup onto her cheeks and creating rivulets of red where her chalky foundation melted down her face.

It reminded me of a thing morticians call "seepage," which often happens after a person died with a lot of excess fluid in their bodies, like if they were on an IV. After death, there's nothing to prevent that fluid from coming out. And when it does, it comes out everywhere. Mrs. Hampstead's tears seemed to be pouring out of every orifice in her body, making her wet and dirty with her tear-stained guilt.

There's no way my family would have ever let a phone ring. We've had a 24-hour, 365-day two-ring answer policy since the day the first Edison telephone was installed in the home. Besides that, every mortician and funeral director I knew, my family especially, bent over backwards to prevent such an occurrence. It's such a common theme—the bereaved family suddenly wanting a viewing before cremation—it's not only allowed; it's expected.

But with death comes guilt. Especially after the death of a mother. I knew this from an early age. Well enough to know that this woman was making me and my family her scapegoat for whatever she felt so guilty about now.

Even if Josh wanted to oppose his mother, gently or otherwise, her crying, her *seeping*, her renting her garments and ripping her hair out was too much for a teenage son to have to deal with. I knew the situation well enough to realize I was *not* going to prom that night. And my virginity was going to remain intact after all.

Fred opened the door and closed it gently behind me, turning his back on a still shouting woman. I didn't intentionally look out the window as we pulled away, but I couldn't help it. Josh was still standing on the curb, watching us drive away with a defeated look.

I slunk down in the seat and rested my head against the back. It was frustrating. It was confusing. It was a fucking drag. If guys were so fickle they couldn't look past the fact that a willing and mostly attractive person lived two stories above a refrigerator full of corpses, I'd just have to lie to them. I was prepared to live my life without romantic attachment, but not without sex.

chapter seventeen

Soula—Now

"I'M GOING TO KILL him."

Bethany gulped her wine before pouring two more glasses and topping off her own. "Soula, I know he's your brother, but I'm going to need your help getting rid of the body."

"Leave her out of it. One of us needs to keep our job to pay for the defense attorney, and you know I was born to find creative ways to make bodies disappear," Decca said as she dug around in her bottomless pit of a purse until she produced three small boxes.

Bethany sighed but brought her takeout noodles to the coffee table and sat cross-legged on the floor. "Decca, seriously? Not tonight."

"The energy in this room is dichotomous and frankly, a little Tower-y. And I don't just think it's you, Beth. I brought all our decks. We need to just sit in our energy and let our intuitions speak through the cards."

"You know I think this is bullshit, right?" Bethany said. She was still glum over her last fight with George. But he did buy a new gaming system "for the house", which we all knew was really for Sofia, who'd been begging for one. Maybe that's the real reason Bethany was pissed.

"Yeah," Decca said in a long-suffering voice. "You only tell me that on a weekly basis." She opened the first deck, the one she considered "mine" since the cards were patterned with anatomical drawings. I didn't believe much in anything intuitive, but the art was cool.

"Anyway, I don't put down your spirituality." Decca acted hurt, but I knew she wasn't.

"What spirituality?" I asked. I'd never known Bethany to have any metaphysical leanings.

"Atheism can be just as dogmatic as any world religion, and I don't yuck your yum." Decca said to Bethany.

"You're right, Dec. And I'm sorry. I'm in a really foul mood and I can't seem to shake it." Bethany sipped her wine and held her glass tight against her chest.

"I think Decca's right." I told her. "You do need your cards read."

"Oh, way to encourage her, Soula. You don't believe in this anymore than I do."

I shrugged. Bethany was right. I was religious, meaning I awkwardly participated in the rituals of my religion, but it was more for the sake of my family. My brother was a year away from becoming a Greek Orthodox priest. I went to church to support him. But true spirituality of any kind wasn't really a thing for me.

Decca continued shuffling between bites of tofu and rice. When it was time to start pulling cards, I knew my part. I cut the deck once, Decca shuffled, and I cut again, trying as hard as I could to send my energy—whatever that was—into the cards so Decca would feel good about her reading. My eyes met Bethany's as she tilted the last of her wine down her throat with a slight shake of her head. Decca threw a bean sprout at her before shutting herself off to whatever ghosts were in the room with us. After a few minutes of silence, she broke herself out of her meditative state.

"We need a candle or something. Soula?"

"I think someone in the office gave me a candle once, let me see if I can find it."

"Hmm. I'll take anything. Hair, a toothbrush, that old ugly t-shirt you wear all the time. Anything that's like, *yours* yours. You know what I mean?"

"Uh...." I had no idea what she meant, but I'd see what I could do. I looked at Bethany as I stood up from the floor. Her expression had softened from annoyance to curiosity. Decca did spreads for us all the time. We never took much stock in them, but honestly, Decca didn't really either. It was all in good fun. This time, she was serious about it, and she hadn't even laid out the first card.

I headed toward my bedroom to get my favorite t-shirt but instead I paused before my open office door. Maybe a neurology textbook would suffice? I flicked on the light and scanned the shelves. I didn't see anything that screamed *mine* mine. Not until my eyes hit on something smooth and white. The cheap plastic medical cranium my dad got me for my twelfth birthday. It was my entrée into a world of more-than-death. The teaching model was embossed with the names of the bones that made up the skull and I pored over that head like my young life depended on it.

I hadn't remembered it existed on my bookcase until that day Wells picked it up, examining it, moving his thumb over the words burned into the plastic, familiarizing himself with my work and my life and my home. *Temporal, Zygomatic, Frontal.*

I didn't need to think about it any longer. I nestled it in my arm and shut off the light. Decca didn't say anything when I handed her the skull. Neither did Bethany. I always knew how lucky I was that I had found these two women who loved me and my odd ways, but sometimes, moments like these, where nothing big happened, just quiet acceptance, were enough to let me know everything was going to be okay. No matter what else happened in my life.

I sat back down and as Decca returned to a trancelike state, Bethany and I watched her solemnly pull cards. I took a bite of my Pad Thai and Bethany opened a second bottle of wine. It was easier to let Decca do her thing and pretend that whatever the cards told her was also meaningful to us.

"Ten cards?" I asked, when she broke free of whatever spell she was under. "You normally do three."

"Normally, I ask the cards a quick question and that's that. Times like these call for a complete reading."

I rolled my eyes at Bethany and took the skull back, cradling it in my arms as if it was soft and fluffy.

Decca gasped as she turned the first card over. The rest, she turned over in quick succession.

"No," she said. "No fucking way this can be right. Maybe Bethany's vibes are overtaking..." she was talking to herself more than us. Bethany and I looked at each other nervously now. Decca had never gone spooky before and this was...spooky.

Decca looked at me with fevered eyes. "Soula." She said, pausing before saying anything else. "I'm sorry. This isn't the usual Big Soula Energy I've come to expect from you. I mean...you're the Two of Swords. You're not...I mean, the Two of Swords is there, but..."

She wasn't making any sense. They were just cards. I glanced at the one in the middle. The one she flipped over first. "The Empress?" I asked. I didn't know what the big deal was, but the card crossing that was The Tower, and I knew that one meant catastrophe.

"What about that one?" I asked, pointing to the tower.

"The Tower's one of my birth cards. It's not always bad. It just means your life is in upheaval." Decca explained. She took a sip of her wine and was starting to calm down.

"I don't want my life in upheaval. I like my life."

"But what if it could get even better?" Decca asked. I think she was even hinting at something but whatever it was, was beyond me. "Holy shit, there are so many major arcana cards here. This is big time, Soula. Something's happening with you."

I couldn't say anything. It felt big time, alright. Big time in the wrong direction. Was I going to lose my job? Get the wrong person convicted of a crime? I took a long swallow of my wine. I took another. Then I took a deep breath to remind myself that these were tarot cards. Open to interpretation. Decca's interpretation. She could have everything wrong. Just because she was freaking out didn't mean I had to follow suit.

"Well, why don't you lay it all out for me?" I asked. "Maybe you're still feeding off Bethany's bad juju."

"Energy." Decca said. "And I don't think I am." She took a deep breath and started from the top. "Okay, card one represents you. I've pulled the Two of Swords so many times for you, it's just what I've come to expect at this point."

"Yeah, that sounds familiar," I said. Decca glared at me. Evidently, I should have been paying more attention. She continued, "I just pulled The Empress." She looked at me and Bethany like that meant anything at all. Then she fished into her bag and brought out a tarot book. I didn't know she still required a tarot book. "Birth, abundance, motherhood, creativity, femininity." She closed the book.

"Ew," I said. "That's not me." I breathed a little easier. "Your cards probably got stuck together from the Thai food or something."

"I would never let food touch your cards." Decca looked appalled.

"Maybe the cards lost their allegiance to me."

"They're not Harry Potter wands."

"Look Decca. I'm trying to think of a way to reconcile what is obviously not my reading with whatever's going on in your head" I tried to reassure her. "All that divine feminine... we all know that's the opposite of me."

"Soula." She clasped my hands in her own. "I know this reading is right for you. I'm sorry to throw you for a loop, but I see so many good things coming your way. There's going to be brilliance in your life like you've never known. I mean, The Sun alone.... Seven of Swords, Four of Wands... It couldn't happen to a better person. Just, please, promise me...whatever happens, try to remain open."

"It kind of sounds like you hit the jackpot, Sou. Do me next, Decca," Bethany said, probably a little drunk.

Decca took a second bite of food. It had to be cold by now and I offered to heat it up in the microwave. I needed a moment to myself anyway, after the weirdness bomb that was just dropped on me.

"What if he accidentally falls asleep on the gurney and the button gets pressed to load him into the retort. Then, boom, he's cremated alive. That happens, right?" I heard Decca already plotting George's "accidental" death.

"That does *not* happen, Decca." Bethany said. "Anyway, how would I ever convince him to take a nap on the retort? He's not an idiot. He's... smart, as much as it pains me to say."

I handed Decca her food. She'd already cleared the cards away after taking a picture of the spread and was now shuffling Bethany's deck. I, however, was still focused on my reading, as much as I hated to admit it. I *wanted* to believe my life was going to change for the better, but it was too hard. My career was static. I'd already reached the pinnacle in record time and unless Dr. Li retired, or I moved to another county, there was no possible upward trajectory. The only thing in my life that had any room to grow was... well, my love life. And that ship had sailed once Wells left.

I didn't want to dwell on that. Wells left. Of course he did. He had to. I was only ever going to be his weekend babysitter. But he took that last piece of my hope with him. Because it was just hope. I was never going to do anything about it except yearn from afar.

I knew I'd see him again. Our paths were sure to cross at work at some point. But the feeling that I'd somehow missed the chance of a lifetime was surging inside, turning me into a weepy mess of emotions and longing.

"Soula, listen to this," Bethany said. Decca's so off her game tonight. "My Big Bethany Energy is the King of Swords. Just think about all that career motivation when I was really hoping she'd pull The Lovers."

Decca put away her cards. "For two people so determined not to let the tarot speak for them, you both sure are placing a lot of stock in your readings tonight."

"It's because it started out so creepy. It made me a believer, Decca, it really did." Bethany said.

"Oh, shut up. *You* don't have to believe. I believe. You just have to wait and see."

chapter eighteen

Waylon—Now

I PUSHED THE BUTTON to retrieve my target, allowing my eyes to lose focus as the two-dimensional outline of a body flew up-range.

I already knew I'd shot a tight group right where the zombie's heart would be, but seeing it this closely on paper was a nice little reward. A careening whistle told me Reyes was on my side of the divider.

"Nice." He inched his ear protectors off one ear so we could talk. "About done?"

I nodded. I had spent a fortune in ammo today from my service weapon alone.

It's not that I necessarily needed the practice. I'd never fail to re-qualify for handgun course-of-fire. And knock-on-wood, I'd probably never see the need to fire my Beretta in the line of duty. Franklin was a small enough town that, as detectives, we spent most of our time in our cubicles or loaned out to surrounding counties to help with everyone's backlogs of cold cases. No, getting to the range was a necessity of a different kind: self-care.

I was reluctant, at first. You would have thought since I grew up in the south, I'd have been born with a shotgun in my hand, but no.

Not me anyway. Any guns my family might have owned would have been pawned for drugs long before they were bequeathed to me. Or confiscated by the police and held in some storage room somewhere.

Maybe if my uncles and my deadbeat dad had gone to the range and sought proficiency in shooting, rather than using each other for target practice, all our lives would have turned out a little more like a Southern Living article and less like a Breaking Bad episode. There was nothing like using a tool to vent your frustrations, and for that I'd never found better tools than a gun and a range.

I removed the target from the track, balled it up and missed a three-pointer into the trashcan behind the shooter station. After running a rag down the inside of the barrel, piecing my gun back together, reloading and racking the slide, I re-holstered it under my jacket.

The cleaning and reassembling had long ago become ritual. Something I could do without thinking. My hands knew every sharp angle and smooth, gun-oiled surface of that cold steel well enough that it was just as integral to the range experience as the shooting itself. And it was just as vital; the time and care spent afterward.

I grabbed my range bag, much lighter now, without twenty pounds of lead weighing it down, and met Reyes by the car.

"You want to eat first or after?" He studied my face. He was legitimately asking about my needs. Because they'd soon become his needs if I chose poorly.

I blew out a breath as I considered. "I think, first. It's better not to fly on an empty stomach. Maybe the same applies to dead bodies."

"We still have an hour or so before we need to be there. Izzy's?" Reyes and I both checked our phones before he started the SUV. No calls. Nothing new to look into. No pressing investigations, except the one I was currently dreading, and there was no text from the morgue letting us know that the autopsy we were scheduled to witness today was being postponed or canceled.

"Stop it with the leg, man," Reyes said. "You're shaking the car."

"Sorry." I put my heel flat on the floorboard, willing myself not to start jiggling again. "Stop by my house on the way. I want to let the dog out." *And swallow that Zofran tablet I had left over from my bout of food poisoning last year.*

Reyes gave me the side eye. "You're going to be fine this time. Last time, the guy was...." He shook his head and exhaled forcefully "Real bad. This won't be like that. It can't be. It's statistically impossible."

If even my stoic and seasoned partner thought that last body, the one that brought me entirely out of commission for three days, was hard to dredge up again, it made me feel a little better.

He continued, "You were fine at the scene. You did everything according to protocol. You completed the investigation. You helped the medicolegal investigators.... It was just the autopsy you couldn't handle. That's nothing."

"It's not the body. Well, not just the body." I finally admitted to my partner.

"Yeah, I know. It's who else is at the morgue." He was quiet for a while, focused on driving. "Still haven't talked to her?"

"Not for lack of trying. She won't call me back. No texts. I'd say she didn't care, but if that was true, she'd make some kind of effort to be polite, right?" God, it was stifling in this car.

"I don't know, man. From what Tiff says, Soula's real hard to read."

"It's stupid. We had a connection. And I know she felt it."

"She felt *it* huh?" He smirked. "How many times?"

"Let's just discontinue this discussion until after lunch, okay?" I cracked the window and let in the hot air that was too humid to offer any relief.

We arrived at Izzy's, the lunch place that was way too good to only cater to cops even though its location right across from the station certainly attracted a large number of them. I ran in and only waited a few minutes, huffing the delicious, smoky and rich scents of bacon and flame-broiled burgers before the server handed me a brown paper bag loaded with two ahi tuna salads. There was no way I was going to spend the next few hours vomiting up a bacon cheeseburger. Maybe my salad would digest quickly enough by one o'clock, when I needed to be at my least favorite place on earth.

Even the thought of seeing Soula again after... what was it? Six weeks? Six pathetic fucking weeks of thinking about her long past her moratorium on communication.

Shit, that was another part of the reason I wasn't looking forward to this. I still wanted to see her again after she ghosted me. I wanted to ask her what happened. If I was truly being honest with myself—which I was, to a fault—I craved her presence. But not under the operating room lights of the sterile, green-tiled morgue. Sterile, that is, but for the corpse in the room.

The dead really knew how to set a mood.

Reyes attacked his salad as I let Kudzu out the back door to sniff around a bit. I tore through my bathroom looking for that orange bottle with the little white tablet inside it. Success! Peeling back the foil, I let the anti-nausea medicine dissolve under my tongue. I was determined not to be a bomb that the rest of the morgue crowd had to gingerly sidestep. I would be as seasoned a professional as anyone else in the room. I hoped.

chapter nineteen

Soula—Now

"YOU FINISH IMAGING?" I shot the question to Tiffany as I tied my plastic gown over my blue smock.

I was exhausted from the effort it took to get from my office to the ground floor. I had to be coming down with something. Everything had been so fatiguing the past few days. Weeks? I wasn't sure how long it had been. Maybe I needed more B12 in my diet. Or vitamin D.

"Yep. You're good. I think we're just waiting on Ewen, as usual." Tiffany was lining up the last of the tools we used to dismember bodies after their ghosts left them for other realms.

Most of my implements were surgical in origin, but a few were acquired from local garden centers and kitchen stores. Ratcheting pruning loppers, for instance. They made easier work of removing the chest plate than the oscillating bone saw that not only had the potential to destroy soft tissues, and therefore evidence, but wafted an unnecessary cloud of bone dust around the decomp room. The clicking sounds of the ratcheting action also helped disguise the crunch of the ribs. Especially useful on days like today, when we had an audience.

When you spent half of your waking hours in the morgue, little things gave you joy.

I took my place next to the decedent and Tiffany phoned the receptionist to buzz our guests into the autopsy suite. I hated being watched while I worked. Not because I felt self-conscious or put on the spot, although there was an element of that. It was mostly because it was the last place on Earth anyone but me and Tiffany (my usual team) had any desire to be. I had a strong stomach and a desire to serve the public. My need to find answers, along with a willingness to deal with gory situations that, in retrospect, were never a big deal, kept me transfixed by my work. No matter how "gross" the rest of the world thought my career was.

Tiffany had a strong stomach and a fascination for gore—not that her predilection for dark shit made her any less of a professional. She was the best autopsy tech I'd ever worked with.

As for the cops, DA, Sheriff, and crowd of others who were about to step inside my office, I knew to expect the worst. Today perhaps, even more so.

This had not been a good death. I could tell by the scent of gas and charred adipose tissue—not unlike the smell of bacon. I hated for the layperson to look on, but Ewen Cameron, the DA, and OSHA insisted. Wells would be here, too, and my experience taught me he had the weakest stomach that had ever digested food. Hopefully, he knew to stand toward the back. I had Tiffany bring in a few folding chairs, in case anyone... felt faint.

Wells would be here. The thought knocked the wind out of me. No wonder I was dragging my feet today. It hadn't fully hit me that I'd be seeing him until now. I'd let weeks slip by without contacting him. I wanted to. My fingers itched to text him back. Last week after a particularly grueling bout at my fencing club, I stepped outside and the warm breeze felt like satin on my damp skin. It lifted the hair off the back of my neck so gently, like a lover's touch. The jasmine-fragranced night air was charged with magic, and I wanted to share it with someone.

No. Not someone. *Wells.* I wanted him to experience the dreaminess with me. I envisioned looking over at his delighted face, our eyes recognizing the energy of the summer night.

But I didn't know how to do it. He left on terms that felt hopeful, but I succeeded in killing that hope. Really curb-stomping it unrecognizably. I couldn't trust that I was reading him right. How could I read anyone right when I spent my days at the helm of death, wielding a scalpel and pruning loppers over a charred corpse with a determined look in my eye? He couldn't possibly be romantically attracted to me after seeing me like this.

Romance was not for me, regardless of Decca's cards.

That didn't mean my heart didn't seize up when I saw what little I could see of his face under the PPE I insisted my guests wear. He stared me down.

Oh, God. He wanted an explanation. I broke eye contact and looked down at the blue sheet covering my patient. I felt a little roll of nausea in my belly. I hadn't eaten yet. I was too tired to make anything this morning and my nervousness about seeing Waylon prevented me from ordering lunch from Izzy's today. Gus brought home gyros last night. All that grease oozing its way along my digestive track wasn't helping much.

Tiffany lifted the drape and slowly peeled it completely off the decedent. We usually didn't bother with a drape at all, but I specifically asked her to place it over the body today. It wasn't easy to see such charred human remains. Not all at one time. The smell was bad enough, but to be hit with the sight as soon as the door opened was the stuff of nightmares. The decedent's identity was not in question, since his co-workers were at the scene of his death. Nevertheless, this was a workplace accident. A complete autopsy was necessary.

Our group was entirely men, as was often the case. While they pretended not to grimace and gag, Tiffany and I got to work. She'd already performed an external exam, but in high profile cases where I'd be called to testify, I needed to double-check everything.

There wasn't much of an *external* to examine, but when a case had this many legal ramifications, I needed to personally document everything.

"Identification is known. Decedent is Steven Richard Claybrooks. Pronounced dead at 16:13 by paramedics who responded to the emergency call at Williamson Grinding and Manufacturing Company, Inc."

I proceeded with my usual observations, calling out my notes to Tiffany, who stood at the lectern with my laptop, checking my notes against her own. The soft tissue and even some of the bone on the extremities was mostly gone, as was common in such a high-temperature burn. I noted the position of the limbs. The decedent was driving the forklift in the coating shop when, presumably, something in the engine ignited during a propylene gas leak. The body remained in a seated position. This wasn't something you'd see on an ER-type show.

Not only was it a *death*—that filthy word that most people in Western cultures liked to pretend doesn't exist—this couldn't even be an open casket death, and I'd seen my mother and father and George work absolute fucking miracles allowing families to see their loved ones one last time.

"Have you seen the video?" The DA asked me, poking around on his iPad, I presumed, in an effort to avoid watching the show in front of him. I had, and although it appeared to be a hellish death, regardless of how it happened, video footage didn't matter to me. It interfered with my own investigation. After the completion of any postmortem exam, I had enough information that I could visualize exactly how *the mortem* transpired.

"Why should she see the video? What difference does it make?" Someone snapped.

"To help determine manner." Cameron shot behind him. Nevertheless, he shut the cover of his iPad and paced around me. He hated this. All of them did. I couldn't blame them today. I didn't love the smell of burn victims. It was too similar to the scent of my favorite food, barbeque. The idea was enough to turn even my stainless steel stomach.

"You don't have a lot of faith in your ME if you think Dr. Smythe needs video footage to determine manner." I couldn't help but pay attention to that voice. I had been trying to forget that laid-back drawl for the past five weeks. Or was it six? I'd finally stopped mentally keeping track of the days since I'd seen him. When Wells spoke, it was softer, less emphatic than the others, but he commanded the room. Cameron barely looked at him and I knew the DA didn't really care. Picking a fight was a way to release the pressure.

"I'm going to open using a Y-incision and eviscerate. I'm just mentally preparing you boys." Tiffany had to hold the decedent upright so that I could make the cut from one collarbone to the bottom of the sternum and down to the pubic bone. The problem when your patients are essentially cooked is the tissues don't slice like they're supposed to. They cut like, well... meat. And cooked meat—or, in this case, very, very overcooked meat—isn't easy to dissect.

My stomach wasn't as steely as usual, and I was hit with the first wave of nausea. I looked up at Tiffany. "You okay, boss?"

"Of course." I swallowed down the saliva pooling under my tongue. There wasn't much skin, and the ribs were softer under the circumstances, so I was able to cut through what was left of the chest plate with just a #22 blade.

Inside looked like a stew left on the stove so long, it had burned into the skillet.

Once again, that imagery met with a sense of *wrongness*. I took a moment to readjust my spine and crack my neck, but the nausea grew stronger. Tiffany glanced to the crowd and back at me, raising her eyebrows questioningly. "I think you might need to get Dr. Li to finish up. I'm not feeling very well." I said quietly.

"Of course." She nodded. "Now?" She panicked when I just stood there, stone-faced, trying not to breathe or move lest I pull a "Waylon" and puke into the floor drain in front of four law enforcement officers, the DA, and an OSHA investigator.

"Javi," she asked for her husband, although she was still looking at me with eyes wide. "Can you come here and... hold this?" She referred to the portions of the right arm and leg that she was using to position the corpse. He stepped up, already gloved and gowned, and assisted. I stepped back and ripped off my three layers of gloves, lowering my respirator to suck in mouthfuls of BBQ-ed corpse air. The scent wasn't worse without the mask, but it was a lot easier to envision the particulates—no matter *how* particulate—entering my lungs. The whole, swirling sensory mess sent me running for the red biohazard bin, vomiting up my morning coffee in front of a room full of people.

This wasn't supposed to happen.

I didn't feel listless or feverish. That was good. Once that initial purge was over, my stomach stopped spasming. Hopefully the nausea would leave as fast as it came. I stood slowly, waiting for another sign to reach for the lid.

I didn't want to turn around, knowing there'd be seven sets of eyes on me. There were squeaky footsteps and the swish of plastic gowning, and I knew my boss arrived to relieve me of completing the procedure. He spoke to the voice recorder. "This is Dr. Chen Li, resuming the procedure for Dr. Smythe." I felt the room's attention return to the gurney. Only one person had his eyes on me and a second later, he was there.

"What happened?" Waylon's hand hovered behind my back. Was he afraid to touch me because he was afraid to get sick or because he was afraid of me? The question shouldn't have mattered. Especially not now. But I still thought it.

"Uh... I don't know. I was fine and then I wasn't. I think...." I lifted my hands, the layers of latex still coated in the grease from melted adipose tissue. A few red smears marked my smock.

Blood.

I had just started the internal exam before I'd made a scene of my own. I had barely registered the fact that the peritoneal cavity contained quite a lot of blood. It wasn't altogether unusual for a burn victim, even one with such extensive damage as this case, but it was a relief. The ability to draw blood would tell us without a doubt whether or not he was alive at the moment of the initial explosion. I looked at Waylon, his face admirably worried. So much came flooding back to me, seeing his face. He felt safe and thrilling and suddenly I didn't want to hold myself back from him any longer.

"Soula?" His brown-blue eyes searched my face.

I had so much to tell him I was practically giddy. But I couldn't get the right words out. "I... I think I have to finish."

I rushed from Waylon's side back to the body, excited to find something that would tell us definitely. "There's enough blood in the heart to get a sample. I can do a blood draw and we can close."

Li, who hadn't hesitated a moment when I needed him, despite being in his "court suit" having just returned from witnessing, gave me a concerned but relieved look and a little nod. "You sure?"

I wasn't sure. Whatever virus I contracted might very well rear its ugly head again any second, but I'd already embarrassed myself once. I no longer cared if this group of suits saw me rush back to the bio bin once more. Besides, this wouldn't take long to finish now that I had a lead. Tiffany could even close what little tissue there was if she needed to. Her stitches were impeccable, and she was usually the one who completed the task. Again, if not for the audience.

Tiffany passed me the vial without being asked. Was there a National Autopsy Tech Appreciation Day? I owed this wonderful, competent assistant a really big gift—*Swiss cheese plant* big. She deserved a raise, but we were government employees. Her salary, like mine, was determined by the county.

I couldn't find much else that was useful, but I hadn't hallucinated that thick, blackish liquid. Good. Soon this day would be over.

With one vial of blood drawn directly from the pericardium, I would know whether the victim died from burns or smoke insulation, which was about as detailed a cause of death as I could get without the presence of lung tissue. It was possible the man died of a heart attack or stroke, but the brain had evaporated in the heat, and the heart was too cooked to show the telltale signs of a myocardial infarction. From witness reports and yes, the video, it was clear that even if Claybrooks had a one hundred percent occlusion in one of his coronary arteries, the explosion wouldn't have allowed a blood clot enough time to travel to his brain or kill off cells within his heart.

I stepped away from the body knowing I had sufficiently performed my role. "You can go," I told the group.

The men didn't move. They remained standing at attention, staring me down as if I hadn't followed protocol. I knew for a fact I had. I pulled off my gloves and grabbed my laptop. "Okay, well, *I'm* going to take my notes with me into my office. I'm pending the case until histology releases the results of the blood, which should be very soon." They already knew all that; it was the same protocol followed by any board-certified forensic pathologist in every state, but maybe if

I spelled out my next steps, they'd get the hint that they really were released.

"Dr. Smythe," Ewen Cameron sidestepped over to me while the rest of the men broke formation and resumed their normal lives. As usual, the DA wasn't wearing a plastic gown. It cramped his tailored, lean-legged style. He was absolutely correct as far as fashion was concerned, but he must spend a fortune on dry-cleaning. The plastic couldn't keep out all the yuck, but it certainly helped. "Are you feeling alright?"

His head bent close to mine, and he had that smirk on his face that he often got when he had when he was cross-examining witnesses. I had no idea why my first instinct was a glance in Waylon's direction. He was standing on the outskirts of the group, the farthest away from the corpse, talking to his partner, but just as my instincts told me, his eyes darted toward Ewen and I. His mouth might have even gotten a little firmer, more serious.

"I'm fine. It's just a virus or something."

"You need someone to drive you home? Cook you up a little chicken soup?"

"So I can vomit that into the biohazard bin, too? No, thanks." I had to duck under and away from him he was so close to me.

"Come on. When are you going to give me a chance? I'm a good guy." He shrugged and smiled in a country boy way that didn't fit his bespoke-suited image.

I frowned. "You're a good prosecutor. There's a difference." Then I played by his rules and took a tentative step back to him, leaning in close and slowly looking up from his lips to his denim blue eyes. "Besides," I whispered. "You and I both know you'd never make a move that would compromise the testimony of your favorite expert witness."

We laughed and he held up his hand for a high-five. He really was a good guy. That's how I could flirt with him so easily; there were no consequences.

Before I got in the elevator, I glanced again to Waylon, still in conversation with Reyes, though I was sure that could just as easily happen in their shared vehicle, office, or commute. He was purposefully lingering and for some reason, I felt caught.

chapter twenty

Waylon—Now

"I'LL MEET YOU BACK at the station," I told Reyes. I wasted enough time deliberating out in the parking lot.

"Of course. Go check on your woman." Reyes didn't say it to mock me. He said it because he was a married man and was keenly aware of the stakes when women were involved.

But the words felt wrong. Soula wasn't *my* woman. She wasn't mine to check on at all. Hadn't Ewen Cameron already done that? And sent her away with a laugh bigger than I'd ever been able to coax out of her. I couldn't believe Soula would go for an ass like Ewen Cameron. Were they together? Is that why she didn't call me back? Because she'd moved on to taller, fancier, better looking guys with bigger paychecks?

Well, only marginally better. Cameron still worked for Williamson County, same as me, but DAs didn't stay DAs their whole careers. Eventually they became defense attorneys. Very successful ones who charged hundreds of dollars per hour to crush the souls of newly-appointed, fresh-out-of-law-school DAs who'd taken his job when he moved on to greener pastures.

That would have been me, if I stayed on that path. Too bad it never suited. Not really, anyway. Not after seeing so many criminals end up in deals too good for their crimes, or getting off scot free because of a technicality or law enforcement negligence. Let the Camerons of the world take on that shit.

But something in me, something primal, didn't want him to have Soula, too.

I swung open the right-side glass door to head back inside, just as Cameron was leaving out of the left. "Hey, Wells. You think I might consult with you on a case of mine? I came across a case of yours over in Davidson involving precedent. I wanted to run something by you that my paralegal found out." *Dick.*

"Uh, I don't really—"

"Aw, come on. Just an email."

I paused, looking at the door ahead of me. "Yeah, sure." Anything to get away from this conversation with this guy that might be my rival. No, not rival. My *better.*

"Thanks, dude. Appreciate it." He swatted me on the back as he jogged down the stairs. Okay, so maybe he wasn't that bad. I'd begrudge him that favor. Maybe I'd need a favor one day.

I told the receptionist I was headed to Dr. Smythe's office.

"Floor three."

"Yes. I know," I barked at her.

Jesus Christ, I was tense. I punched the button twice for the third floor. The non-morgue floor where I didn't need anti-nausea medicine to visit, not that mine had worn off already.

I had only been to her office once, but I knew instinctively where to go, around the perimeter of the cubicle cluster in the center and over to the office with the chicken-wire glass windows.

It was dimly lit inside and, same as the last time I was here, the vertical blinds in the windows were drawn but I saw the warm glow through the partially opened door and heard voices.

"This is all fine, Doc. It could be great, even. Either way." It sounded like Tiff's voice.

"How could this happen?" Said a voice thick with emotion, and something. Despair seemed to drift through the crack in the door. It stopped me in my tracks. Something bad was happening.

"*You* went to med school, not us." Another woman laughed.

"You know that's not what I mean. I can't do this. I'm the worst..." Soula let out a sob and my chest physically hurt for her. I was eavesdropping on this very private situation. But she was hurting, and I wanted to scoop her up and protect her from whatever was making her hurt.

"Aw, you'll feel much better in a few months, honey."

I knocked and inched the door open enough to see Soula. She was in her chair, spinning in slow circles behind her desk, shoulders slumped forward and tissues crumpled in her hands. "Oh, God," she sobbed and lowered her head to the desk.

An older lady stood in one corner holding a folded sheet of paper. I recognized her as the usual receptionist. I looked over at Tiff, perched on the arm of the sofa Soula kept in her office. The one I was shuffled to when I passed out. I remembered the scratchy brown plaid upholstery, since it must have been the same model my grandfather had in his basement when I was a kid.

Tiff smiled at me. I didn't have to know her very well to realize I walked into the right place at the right time. "Well, well, well. If it isn't Detective Wells, himself." She stood and put a sympathetic hand on my shoulder before referring back to Soula. "She's your problem, now."

The receptionist left, dropping the paper on Soula's desk. Tiff followed her out, closing the door behind her. Soula picked her head up at the sound, but seeing my face instead of her assistant's, she dropped it back down with a groan.

"What's going on? Are you okay? I couldn't help but overhear at the door—"

"You heard?" She looked horrified and wrapped her hands around her waist protectively. Shielding herself... from me? "You weren't supposed to hear that. Not until... I can't think about it yet."

I wanted to reach for her. Pull her into my arms and stroke her hair. It was obvious she'd gotten some bad news and I felt impotent this far away from her. I took a few steps closer, taking Tiff's place on the couch. Soula's chair rolled another few inches away from me. That little unconscious gesture hurt more than if she kicked me out of her office. Especially since not fifteen minutes before, she'd been so chummy with Cameron, sliding up close to him without the effort she needed to make to be around me.

"Please. Tell me. Are you really okay? I won't stay. I can see I'm making things worse, but if you need anything—"

"You didn't hear much, did you?" She picked her head up and looked up at me, pathetically, like a puppy in a kennel who knew she'd be overlooked. In that position, with her tear-stained cheeks, red eyes, and swollen lips she looked so vulnerable. It was hot as fuck, and I was a piece of shit for thinking it.

She sighed and fished through her trash can, producing a white plastic stick and tossed it to me.

I caught it with one hand. Her face growing even more miserable. I looked down. I didn't know what I was looking at. No. I knew *what* I was looking at. I'd seen enough tv commercials in my life to recognize the use of the test. I just didn't know *why* I was looking at it.

"A pregnancy test." I was a brilliant detective.

She nodded, finally daring a glance up into my eyes. “It’s my urine.”

“I figured that part out myself.” I nodded.

“It’s your sperm.”

“Okay.” I was nodding. It was all I could do. I just kept nodding like an idiot, waiting for a reaction—*my* reaction—to come.

Soula sniffed and straightened her shoulders. She gathered up some of the other loose paperwork on her desk and tapped it into an even bundle, placing it in the corner before opening her laptop. She handed me the folded sheet of paper without looking at me. “This confirms it.”

“How long have you known?” I opened the paper and scrolled the data. Nothing really made sense.

“Since about twenty minutes ago.” She was logging into a program of some kind and tapping at the keyboard. I dropped my arms to my sides, staring in her direction more than looking at her in particular. In my head, I ran the information I knew in a loop.

Soula’s pregnant. The baby’s mine. Soula’s pregnant. The baby’s mine. Soula’s pregnant. The baby’s mine.

After that, nothing. I couldn’t even begin to feel anything until she started talking to me. And she and I both knew how painful that would be. I moved closer to her and glanced at her screen. She lifted her eyes but said nothing. I read Williamson County Morgue across the top. She was continuing her case?

“Soula. Talk to me,” I said, sitting across from her at her desk. “We used a condom.”

“I’m keeping it,” she said at the same time. She made a few more clicks then closed the screen on her laptop once more.

“What? No. You don’t want—” I said.

“Condoms fail,” she said at the same time.

“You’re on birth control,” I said, assuming.

“No. I don’t like the hormones,” she said it so matter-of-factly.

“Why did I think—"

"You don't have to worry. I have no expectations from you. I won't even put your name on the birth certificate, if it gets that far. Many pregnancies fail." She said it so plainly, so simply. Maybe talking right now was a bad idea. Maybe we were both shell-shocked.

"Maybe we should wait. Talk about this later, once we've digested this."

She didn't respond right away but I couldn't leave her like this. In limbo. Dealing with such a weighty thing. It was an out-of-body experience for me, just realizing that no matter how I/she/we proceeded, life was now altered. It was... bigger than ten minutes ago. But she was physically carrying the difference. Could she feel the difference already? Apart from the morning sickness, which I presumed was what accounted for before, even though it wasn't morning.

"I never wanted kids." She leaned back in her office chair, still looking at her laptop screen instead of me. "But...I feel something. About This one. I can't explain it. I feel like I found out weeks ago. Have you ever looked back on the minutes before you found out some monumental news and wondered how you couldn't have known it then, too? Because the moment was too big to fit into time?"

I nodded.

"Ugh. I'm turning into Decca. Don't pay attention to me. I'm getting way too metaphysical. Just... thank you, Waylon. I don't know what will ultimately happen, but please, I can't keep you attached to this."

I shook my head and laughed. "I'm already attached to this. There's no way you're shaking me loose."

"You are?"

I felt drunk. There were simply too many thoughts to have at once, so I started with fear. "Soula, the only reason I'm not acting more thrilled is that I'm scared of getting attached if you're not going to keep it. I am thrilled. You're carrying my child. Yeah, that's a lot of pressure but it's a lot of power. You hold all the cards, and I don't really know how to reckon with that at the moment. You think you want to keep it, but it's early. What if you change your mind next month?" Just thinking about the loss made me want to implode.

"I won't," she said sharply.

"I've known you for a collective three days. Granted you did a number on me in those three days, but I don't know your mind like you do."

"Then maybe... we get to know each other's minds," she said.

chapter twenty-one

Waylon—Then

THE FIRST TIME I became a cop was right after college.

I went from a criminal justice degree straight into the academy and from there, straight onto the streets for six months of probation. It was exciting at first. Then it sucked.

Nashville metro was nothing like what my degree prepared me for. There were the cliques and officer infighting. It was ridiculous. Not so much that they wouldn't come for backup if you called a 10-82, but the mean girl cafeteria shit got old real fast.

The phrase "I'm just playing around" was thrown around more often than I'd ever thought I'd hear as an adult.

And I could swear; if I was on duty, *I* was the officer called to every 10-64 within city limits. It must have been one of their initiation rites. Send the new guys out to all the deceased persons calls. You'd think that would have made me more comfortable around death, but no. It was the final straw that made me reconsider law school.

My first deceased person was the worst—not in terms or gore or decomp. The emotional backlash was just as horrific though. I was first on the scene after the paramedics. They had been called immediately once the family knew something was wrong. But it had taken them a while. The EMTs did their best to provide medical assistance when they arrived, but it was too late.

An elderly man choked to death on a piece of steak. It was a common enough death. Depending on the year, it could be as high as the fourth leading cause of death in the US. Always ranking in the top ten. A death that took you quickly. For this man, it was under three minutes from steak on a plate, to steak in his larynx, to dead. He looked peaceful.

It was the being there right after he died that was hell. His family was gathered around the table. When he stopped talking, no one looked up. *They didn't know*. Then, someone, the man's daughter screamed, "Dad's choking!" Chairs were overturned in the rush to get to him, to give him the Heimlich. The son-in-law got to him first, wrapping his arms around the man's firm midsection. He squeezed and shook. The grandson took over. He was a football player, so maybe his brawn would better dislodge the unchewed bite caught in his throat. That didn't work either.

In their shock, no one remembered to call 911 until twenty minutes later. *They didn't know.* Not how bad it was or how bad it could get. After they arrived, the paramedics had tried and failed (of course) to resuscitate the man. He'd been deprived of oxygen for too long. They explained to me, to the family, that the throat swells around the blockage and sometimes, the pressure of the Heimlich maneuver isn't enough to force it out.

Until the paramedics stopped, the family held on to hope and kept a grip on their emotions. *They didn't know.* But when the paramedics stopping working, stood, and came over to talk to me, deciding whether we should call the Medical Examiner's office or if they should just take the man to the hospital and have the M.E. pick him up from there, that was when the daughter lost it. She saw me and it pulled her trigger. I nodded to the paramedics, telling them to call the M.E. and went to talk to the family.

"I'm sorry," I started. I didn't get much farther. The football player had tears streaming down his face and his mom pulled his head down to her shoulder as they both shook with tears. The son-in-law covered both of them with his arms. He wasn't crying, but I got the sense he was being a champ, holding it together for his wife and son.

The dead man's wife was there. She wasn't crying either. She was leaning over the gurney, in denial, cupping the man's placid face, stroking his cheek and telling him everything would be alright. *For whom?* I wondered. Another woman, a second daughter, was there as well, her hands gripping her mother's arms as she looked over at me, frantic for some kind of help. *They didn't know.* They couldn't. None of them knew what to do or how to move or which way was forward. How did you go from a joyous family dinner where the only real concern was how the Titans were going to improve their chances for next season, to making arrangements with a funeral home for the very man who had just promised to watch his grandson's every home game this season?

I never had that kind of family. They called the wrong cop. I didn't know what to do. So, I did what I always did at my own house. I cleared the table.

I righted the chairs, I picked up fallen napkins. I stacked plates quietly so the family wouldn't be disturbed by the noise. I brought the salad, the broccoli casserole, the mac and cheese—it looked homemade—into the kitchen and looked for containers for the leftovers. I even started the dishwasher.

I knew they didn't need a cop. They didn't need me at all. But I made myself useful and scarce, knowing my presence (if they happened to look my way) would only increase their pain.

When I left, after the body and the paramedics and the death investigators, the family was still in the same state of unresponsiveness. They didn't even know. I pulled away from the curb and it felt wrong just going on with the rest of my shift. Like I'd left a piece of myself behind. But that's exactly what I had done. I'd left a piece of myself with that family. Now, *I knew*. That's what a life in deathcare really was. A constant cleaning up behind the scenes, leaving little pieces of you behind. *And no one knew.*

Waylon—Now

The nerves in my stomach were doing what nerves seemed to do best in my body—making me feel like I was adrift in a small boat on choppy waters rather than trudging my way up the concrete steps that led to Soula's parents' house.

"You look ill," Soula paused on the top step. "I'm already sick. You can't be sick, too." I turned to her and took one last deep, clean breath. It was what I did before court proceedings, eyewitness interviews, or anytime I came face-to-face with death. I thought I hid it pretty well. Apparently, not to Soula.

She, on the other hand, had nothing to hide. This was her family, her body, her pregnancy, and the most nerve-wracking part for me, her decision. She didn't need to feel as nervous as me. *Wasn't it normal to be nervous telling your family you're pregnant with that creep of a one-night stand? But, look. Here he is, conveniently eating your home-cooked food, right at your very own table.*

"You look confident." I was honest. "But you don't have anyone to impress. You're a grown woman with a great career—notwithstanding the fact that I can't be in the same room while you perform said career—and your family loves you."

"That's up for debate." She frowned and leaned back against the metal handrail.

I reached out and clasped her hand. She looked down as if something foul had brushed against her skin, but I gave it a squeeze anyway.

"Soula, hang on a minute." I took a step down to see her better. "This is so new. It's been, what? Five hours since you've been pregnant?"

"Six weeks."

"Since we've known, I mean. Let's not tell them. Not yet. Maybe not ever, depending on what you decide. *We've* barely talked and we're the only ones who matter."

Her eyes shot to mine and her jaw clenched. "*You're* the only one who matters," I rephrased, grudgingly.

Until she decided if she was indeed having this baby—and I knew she thought she's already decided, but that remained to be seen—I was in no man's land. I was ready, nay, enthusiastic about my role as a support person, but realistically, the best I could do was tell her how I felt. The rest was up to her and if she wanted to be committed to this accident—committed to *me*—for the next eighteen years.

"You wouldn't be here if I wasn't keeping it." She huffed and left me blindsided on the stoop as she blew through the door into her mother's kitchen.

So, her decision was made? Telling her family we were having a baby seemed like the point of no return. It was hard to believe she needed no further discussion than a few Spartan sentences in her office and in the car. It didn't seem like something someone like her—a scientist; a doctor—would do. Weeks of reading and agonizing and creating pro-and-con spreadsheets seemed more like it.

But no. She went from crying to full acceptance with the squaring of her shoulders and in the space of a few minutes.

I knew she was a weird one. I wanted her to be *my* weird one. But the light was starting to dawn on me, standing out there on that concrete stoop with the scent of beef wafting through the screen, I really had no idea what kind of force Soula was after all.

I grabbed the door handle and stilled. Something else was starting to dawn, too.

I was going to be a dad. We were going to be a family. A tiny, oddball family. We'd have to learn how to love each other, at least a little bit and even if only for practical purposes. I couldn't process sharing the most intimate part of someone, a DNA structure, if our paths only crossed at work and childcare pickups.

My nerves were gone. Instead, a warm glow replaced them. I was unconquerable. I was ready to face anything. I was ready to love these people with everything I had.

As if just eating dinner with Yia-Yiá wasn't a big enough adventure.

As soon as I stepped into the kitchen I was hit with the scent of raw garlic and an embarrassingly weak left hook to the jaw.

I was barely a step behind Soula. "I see you wasted no time in telling them the big news," I told her, holding my jaw. Her eyes were wide, but she didn't say anything.

"I thought you were cool," George's pointing finger was inches from jabbing me in the nose. It was a tough-guy move that looked ridiculous on a man in a business suit whose only brush with competitive sports was probably typing figures into an old school calculator.

"You've got the wrong guy, George." Bethany moved in and swatted his hand out of my face. "The only one who's not cool is you." He adjusted his suit jacket and backed off, giving Bethany a hateful glare as he turned.

"Nice to know the patriarchy is alive and well in the Smythe house." Bethany deadpanned, turning to me. "You sure you know what you're getting into?" She added under her breath.

"Not at all," I replied.

"I knew I liked you." She put her hand on my shoulder to get me to lower myself so she could kiss my cheek. "Congratulations, Daddy. And welcome to the family." She gestured to the circus around her.

I took another step into the scene unfolding in front of me, hesitating to get too close to the other brother, Gus, who stood opposite the Formica peninsula from Soula's mom who was yelling in Greek and slicing bread with such ferocity, I had to look away. A hand slapped my back.

"I don't know why I'm the only one in this house to see the beauty in this situation. Soula's going to be a mom. We never thought we'd see the day. And she's the first one of us to have a kid," Gus said.

"As far as you know. How do you know there aren't a few little *Gus*es running around out there somewhere?" Bethany added.

Gus ignored the indictment on his character and offered me a handshake. "And that means I get to truly fulfill the role I was made to play, Fun Uncle." I took his hand. If ever I needed an ally, it was tonight. God, this family really was tough.

"And dare I think, Nounó?" he said it to rile up their mom, but she slammed her knife down.

"You know that'll be Georgíos," she said.

"Sorry, dude. I tried. You know I'd make a better godfather," Gus told me.

"Well, I mean... don't Soula and I get some say? Maybe Gus has a shot, after all." I shrugged. Honestly, I didn't know what they were talking about, but I hated the thought of my baby's future grandmother calling the shots already.

My foot coming down—however gently—was met with a snicker, but finally, she met my eyes. "Kósta, put this on the table." She handed Gus the wooden bread board and turned her back to me.

Jesus Christ, how many names did these people have? Gus is Kósta, George is Georgíos—well, that one made sense, but I still couldn't pronounce it to save my life. Soula is short for Athanasoula, which is already short (long?) for Athanasía.

"Raynie," I said. "I want you to know I'm fully invested in raising my child. I know we haven't been together long, but I'm committed. To the baby and to Soula. To whatever extent she'll allow me." I said this all to her back as she loaded the dishwasher. I knew nothing was getting through. "I don't blame you for disliking me. I guess you'll just have to see."

"No. *You'll* see." She spun around, ripping the towel off the cabinet and dried her hands. She was a capable woman, used to being the spine of the family. It was even apparent in her economical movements, it was like she budgeted for the least amount of wasted energy while looking incredibly competent. Also, I wouldn't be surprised if she somehow harnessed energy itself and bent it to her will. Staring at her hands ringing that towel, practically tearing it to shreds, I saw Soula in her. I saw that feminine strength, the kind that cut through the shit to accomplish whatever was necessary and doing it without fanfare or acclaim.

She sighed. "You know nothing about each other. How can you be so calm? So confident that you can do this? How can she? You seem nice, but you don't know her. She doesn't care about anything or anyone. That's what you'll see."

Well, shit. I wasn't expecting that. "I thought you were mad at me. For being unwed. We'll get to know each other. The stakes are a little bit higher this time, but worse things have happened. We're both old enough to know what we're doing." That last part was a Hail Mary, but I made it sound convincing enough.

"She can't have this baby, Waylon. You must have seen enough to know that, at least. She's not cut out to be a mother." She alternated between looking at me and looking out the window over the sink with a pained expression. Her martyrdom wasn't going to work for me.

"You're wrong," I said. "Soula might not be a fluffy bunny, but she has other maternal qualities. Strength and intelligence, insight, determination. And I think she gets a lot of that from you. It's okay if you choose not to see it. I see it. I see *her*. I've already dealt with an unsupportive family in my life and I'd rather Soula not lose you, so please keep any negativity to yourself."

Her nostrils flared but she gave a tight nod, saying nothing.

"Now, what can I bring to the table?"

chapter twenty-two

Soula—Now

I THOUGHT THE SALAD and a skewer of souvlaki would be safe, but I could barely get a bite of the pork down before remembering the burn victim from today and gagging on the grilled meat.

I groaned and set down my fork. How was I ever going to get through the first trimester this way? Pregnancy had become an occupational hazard.

"Did you at least try the aloe-based arterial fluid I bought? You might love it." Bethany was arguing her usual case with George for more eco-friendly, non-carcinogenic preservation techniques.

"If Rose Chemical doesn't make it, I'm not going to waste any more money reinventing the wheel. We've always used Rose here and that's why we get more repeat business than any other mortuary in town. Pass the feta, Soula?"

"Repeat business?" Waylon tsked. "If it were me, I wouldn't let that get around, George."

"If it was just the family here, it would stay between us. Why don't you stick to protecting us from bad guys? Or are you incompetent at that, too?"

"What's that supposed to mean?" Waylon bit delicately into his bread, more curious than offended by my idiot brother's mocking.

"You quit the DA's office in Nashville after you lost that case that was so cut and dried one of our refrigerated occupants could have won it. Then you got my sister pregnant, which I can only think meant you failed the number one rule of one-night stands: protection."

"I'm not family and I'm here." Sofia's quiet voice cut in before Waylon could respond.

George closed his eyes. "Of course you're family, Sof," George told her. He had such a soft spot for Bethany's daughter. I hoped that could extend past her one day and he could stop being such a bastard to every other breathing human.

"Georgíos, that's enough," Raynie said. Her eyes flicked over to Waylon, but he didn't respond. He just kept chewing. Purposefully. Maybe that bread was his way of counting to ten. Of cooling off so he wouldn't say something he regretted.

I didn't know him well enough yet to know if he was internalizing the negativity like I often did, or if he had some kind of permanent oil cloth covering his back, letting the comments bead up and drip down to the floor. These were the kinds of things we had to learn about each other during the next eight months. Longer than that even. I put just the tops of my fingers on his thigh, resting them there in an uncharacteristic show of support.

Waylon swallowed hard and shifted his rear end in his seat. I released my hand, but he caught it and returned it to his thigh, squeezing it once before picking up his fork.

I gripped his leg; my rapt attention focused on the shape of his nicely developed quadriceps. My thumb grazed the line that separated the rectus femoris and the vastus lateralis. Such an underrated part of the anatomy. I gripped hard, working my way closer to that elegant sartorius muscle that snaked around the thigh from under the femoris to the inside of the upper leg. Waylon's hand clasped mine again, stilling its path. He cast me a chastising, sideways glance but the tiniest muscles in his cheek let me know my timing was the only thing off.

I squirmed in my seat. I might not have been hungry for dinner, but suddenly I was starving for Waylon. Could pregnancy make you extra... hungry? Was Waylon actually eating slower? We hadn't done much talking yet, but he did bring an overnight bag. Did that mean sex was implied? *How do the neurotypicals know these things?*

Waylon's napkin slipped and he clenched his thighs together to catch it before it hit the ground. We really needed that talk.

"Are you getting married Soula?" Sofia asked. Utensils dropped and all eyes shot to me, then Waylon, then me again.

"Haven't you always hated marriage, Soula?" George wasn't really asking. It was another accusation. For me or for Waylon. I wasn't sure.

"We thought she hated kids, too, but here she is." Gus winked.

"Don't be ridiculous," Mama said. "They just met. You can't expect Waylon to hitch his wagon to her. His cart to her? I'm not sure what the phrase is, but young people today can raise kids together without being together."

I hadn't even thought about Waylon not wanting to be with me. Or that he might not even want to try. The way he looked at me when he lowered his fork didn't give me any clues, either.

"I never said I didn't want to get married," I said. I'd never even thought about marriage.

Mama shrugged and went back to dishing out more of the potatoes that didn't hit the floor.

"You're having a baby, Thea Soula? I didn't know people with Autism have babies." Sofia smiled so wide her braces shone in the light. I slipped my hand off Waylon's thigh and wedged it under my own.

"Sofia!" Bethany gasped. "Oh my God, Soula. I'm so sorry." She lowered her head to whisper something into her daughter's ear.

Waylon lowered his fork and carefully finished chewing his potato. His face was carefully devoid of expression. I, however, was no longer invisible at the dinner table. The whole family was looking at me.

"Alright! You finally get a diagnosis, sis?" Gus smacked me on the back so hard I almost got whiplash, then took at huge bite out of his souvlaki pita.

Mom gave a sharp look at Bethany. "What is she talking about? *Autism*," she practically spat the word out. "That's ridiculous. There's nothing wrong with Soula. She's just—"

"Don't start, Ma. Not this time. And not with this," George said, meeting my grateful eyes before taking a sip of water.

"It's true. Dad knows," I confirmed. I said it quietly, looking down. I wasn't embarrassed, but I wasn't ready for this conversation. I hadn't been ready for this for the past three years, either. "I was diagnosed a few months after I started working with Tiff. Her middle daughter...." I shrugged in lieu of a lengthy explanation for what everyone at this table except my mom and *maybe* Waylon already knew. Something told me this news wasn't so revelatory to him either.

"So what if your autopsy tech says you have... it? That doesn't mean—"

"I went to a psychologist. I took a test. I'm not ashamed, Mama. There's nothing suddenly *wrong* with me just because my brain function patterns have a label. But I knew you would be ashamed, in spite of what I've achieved in my career. Or you'd deny it. Or downplay it somehow. But none of it matters right now." I finally realized that I'd said all that to the pattern of my jeans rather than my family. I looked up. Mama was trying hard to wipe the stricken look off her face. "And don't any of you dare treat me any differently than five minutes ago. This changes nothing."

Mama continued looking at me with those deepening worry lines between her brows. I could take any more of her martyrdom tonight.

"When's Dad coming home?" I asked, knowing he wouldn't try to decide my future in one evening. He was going to be thrilled to learn he would be a grandpa. Maybe he'd help get me more thrilled about it too.

I intuitively and immediately knew having this child was the right decision. I made it the same way I made all my decisions from going to med school, to which specialty I'd pursue, to which men I'd fuck. Intuitively and with precision. Maybe it was a neurodiverse trait. Or maybe it was just me. I never saw paths. I saw *my* path and that was the one I ran.

But even while I knew this was right for me, I knew it wouldn't be fun.

"Dad had a pickup about an hour away. He'll probably be a while. Volunteered himself. Said he needed some space," George said.

Didn't we all?

That was the considerate thing about dead people. They really knew how to give you the space you need. It was the one thing we all had in common, us Smythes; our need to be alone.

"I think I've had enough for one night." All eyes snapped to me. I rose slowly and brought my untouched plate into the kitchen, dumping the contents into the trash. Then I leaned back against the counter and waited for my heart to stop beating so fast. From the dining room, I heard Waylon excuse himself and follow my lead.

I grabbed his hand and pulled him out the back door and down the concrete steps. "I didn't mean for you—for everyone—to find out that way. I'm sorry if you think I hid it. Or that I misrepresented myself. I just don't like to just throw autism out there like it's an excuse for my weirdness. That felt cathartic, though, sticking up for myself," I said quietly.

The house was not well insulated and it would totally ruin my moment if they overheard us from outside the dining room window. "I know it wasn't much, but I never stand up for myself. I just take it and take it. Because their opinions about my life don't matter much to me, but this was different." I spun around and nearly skipped away, heading for the walking path instead of my apartment. "You're not saying anything."

He shrugged. "You said not to treat you any differently."

"That was for my brothers, mostly. So they won't tiptoe around me from now on. I know you must have something to say. Questions to ask?"

"You want me to tell you I'm shocked?" Waylon hadn't kept up with my erratic pace. He sidled along with his hands in the pockets of his jeans, looking casual and amused with his crooked grin. I stopped and turned back, admiring his lazy, confident gait, his rumpled good looks, his tall, lean body with those prominent quads. "I'm not shocked, Soula. And this changes nothing about the way I perceive you. If you want to talk about it, though, we can."

I blew out a breath of relief. We needed to talk. But about my pregnant body, not about my neurodivergent brain.

I removed my phone from my back pocket and pulled up the results from an earlier search. I closed out all the "how to tell your one-night stand you're pregnant" articles. He knew all of fifteen minutes after I came back from the bathroom holding the HCG strip, courtesy of Tiff and her prolific reproduction system. When I didn't believe the plastic strip, she personally drew blood and took it upstairs to the histology lab—a perk of working at a morgue that I'd never before considered.

"None of these are helpful." I complained to my phone as I scrolled past useless articles. Waylon had caught up with me, peering over my shoulder.

"Did you Google 'what to do if pregnant by a one-night stand?'" I think he tried to look suspicious, but his face still read as amused. A smirk seemed to be his default expression, like he was in on some joke that I wasn't hearing.

"Of course not." I slid my phone back into my jeans. "Yes."

"That's a bit insulting."

"I'm not great at talking to people. I never know the right thing to say, or when to say it. I just assumed I'd be bad at this."

"You're not bad at this," he said. I continued walking.

"Hey. Wait a minute." He grabbed my hand and wove his fingers through mine. "I mean it. You're not bad at this. This is an impossible situation to navigate expertly. I guarantee you, no one's good at this."

"Improbable. Not impossible. Ninety-eight percent improbable."

"Whatever. You know what I mean."

I nodded.

With his free hand, he threaded an errant lock of hair behind my ear. His fingers lingering on my cheek until he traced over my zygomatic arch and down to my jaw. He moved close. So close, bending down as his eyes skated over nose and lips. My own lips parted in anticipation. He smelled like garlic from dinner but it didn't even.... *Oh, no. It absolutely bothered me.*

My stomach heaved. I didn't even have time to turn away from him. My few bites of dinner and the soup I tried to ingest after the autopsy spilled out of my mouth and bubbled down the front of his t-shirt. I turned away just in time to vomit the rest into the grass.

"That was so disgusting," I garbled through a cough. "I'm so sorry, Waylon. I don't know what's wrong with me." I was still doubled over, afraid to stand straight or else I might vomit again, afraid to see his horrified face. I could deal with bodily fluids. Waylon could not.

Then I remembered exactly what was *wrong* with me and I'd never felt more stupid in my life.

I heard laughter behind me. I looked up, my hands still on my knees. "Hey, this is new," he said. "We've known about the baby for what? Five hours? I don't think that's enough time for it to truly sink in."

I stood, slowly stretching myself up and taking a step away from Waylon so the garlic that I was now hyperconscious of didn't waft my way. "Five hours was plenty of time for the news to sink in for you. Let's go home. I need another shower and so do you."

"Hey, good thing I took a Zofran today, right? Came in handy." He beamed. So that was why he was so composed at the morgue earlier.

"You won't be able to take a Zofran every day when the baby starts puking on you after every feeding."

"Maybe the baby won't be a puker, like you," He poked me gently in the side.

"Like *me*? No way. My stomach is Teflon under normal circumstances," I said.

"So, it's just me that brings out the vomitous side of you."

"That's not a word. And no, it seems to be raw garlic that brings out my vomitousness."

"You can use the non-word, but I can't?"

"I believe special concessions are supposed to be made for pregnant women." I stopped at the foot of the stairs leading up to my apartment. "Pregnant women." I repeated it slowly, still waiting for something to kick in. I didn't feel pregnant yet, even with the nausea and how tired I'd been for the past week.

Maybe that was why it was so easy to share the news. Because the news didn't feel real. Was that some kind of defense mechanism? Something evolutionary that aided newly pregnant Neanderthals so they wouldn't become so emotionally swaddled in cocooning baby-ness that they forgot to survive?

What did that say about me and my job? What if the nausea got worse and I couldn't perform my duty? What about the tiniest cases?

Would I be able to continue my job at nine months pregnant? What about once the baby came? Would I be able to deal with the children who passed through my morgue knowing I had a thriving child—fingers crossed—at home?

"What's wrong now?" Waylon asked. I was still paralyzed at the bottom steps. "You're...leaking."

"No, I'm not." I sniffed and pulled the tears back into my lacrimal glands. *Nope. That didn't work.* "I was just thinking about the kids. In the...in my job..."

His face suddenly lost his usual smirk. "Yeah. That was one of the first places my mind went, too. We see the most fucked up shit. It'll only get harder now. Not that there's a bright side, but at least we both know what it's like to deal with. You know what I mean?"

I nodded. The news didn't show half of our workload and for good reason. Seeing some of the horrors that Waylon and I saw would cause PTSD in most of the general population. I could deal with cases by dissociating, in a way. I could parse out the human sadness from my overarching goal of improving public health. But it was going to get really hard with a child of my own. Of our own. It was good that we both *knew*. That way, no one else had to.

We said nothing more but went upstairs. Kudzu met us at the door. I'd never been happier to see the loveable brown and gold beast. I gave her a big squeeze, running my fingers through her thick fur and letting her lick my face. Maybe this was how we'd deal with the tough cases.

By coming home. By sharing affection, which was something I never thought I'd need or even desire. It couldn't make up for the tragedies in life, but like the human body, living was essentially a self-righting machine. *We grieved when we lost someone or something and until then, we loved the shit out them.*

chapter twenty-three

Soula—Now

"I'M JUMPING IN THE shower." Waylon pointed to the bathroom as if I'd forgotten where it was.

Or maybe to give his hands something to do.

I wanted to bathe too, if only to wash away the morose cloud that was hanging over me.

He brushed his teeth before running the shower and when the glass door slid open, I smiled to myself, wondering what he'd do if I joined him. I never expected pregnancy to imbue me with confidence and sexuality, but a fire raged inside me. It seemed to bring out my most primal self. I'd have to remember to ask Decca about all that woo woo stuff. She'd know if that was a variation of normal or not. Moreover, she'd be thrilled. Probably bring over heaps of crystals, candles, and other crap that would smell up my apartment if I told her I was suddenly experiencing any changes of the metaphysical nature.

Before I lost my nerve, I unbuttoned my blouse and stripped out of my jeans on the way down the hall. Unlocking the bathroom door from the outside with my thumbnail, I stepped into the steamy room. I brushed my teeth quickly, unable to see my reflection the mirror had fogged so heavily. Waylon must've liked his showers scalding. I mentally filed the information away, along with all my other Waylon observations. Maybe I'd never need to access that file, but the way I saw it; we had a defined time period to get to know each other and I didn't yet know which details would be pertinent.

I thought opening the door and standing at the sink for two minutes would have been enough to alert him to my presence but after slipping out of my underthings and sliding the glass back, the shower stall revealed a man with his back turned to me. One hand reached above his head, leaning, his palm flattened against the tile wall. He bent his head low, letting the spray hit the back of his neck and run down his body.

I hadn't noticed his back before. How could I have? I'd only seen him naked that one time and I wasn't exactly trying to create a lasting image of someone who would never be mine. Waylon's back was wide and each muscle was well defined. Backs have long been underrated when it came to sexualizing the male anatomy, and as backs went, Waylon's was incredibly sexy.

Just when I thought he might not have heard me enter and I began to kick myself for interrupting his private time, his hand slid down the wall and he turned.

"You're shivering." He wrapped me in his arms and pulled me into the stream of water. I hadn't realized I was cold, standing there in the steam of his shower. I hadn't realized how long I'd been watching him. Or how long he'd let me, since there was no expression of shock on his face when he turned and saw me standing behind him, watching him like a creep. The water ran over my head but instead of turning my face into the stream, letting the rivulets run in the correct pattern down my face and scalp, I pressed my face into his chest.

Then, remembering what I was doing there, I looked up. He shifted us out of the direct stream of water and wiped the hair from my eyes. "I was thinking..." I started. But his erection that was already half hard when he had turned to face me had grown even harder as it pressed into my belly, the place where our child was growing—no, it was way too early for those thoughts.

I stopped thinking.

"Yes?" He stepped away as if to jostle my memory back into functionality and returned with a palm filled with shampoo that he started massaging into my hair. I spoke fast, getting my thoughts out before the soap ran into my mouth.

"Maybe, instead of sequentially hashing out every one of the hundreds of choices we have to make before—and after—thirty-two plus weeks from now..." The soap won. I rinsed my hair, then finished talking as I conditioned. "Maybe we could just... not."

"Not... talk?" He shampooed his own sandy hair under the stream of water as I grabbed the bar of soap. "Do you think that's a good idea? Thirty-two plus weeks isn't that long to make the decisions we need to make. That's assuming you'll even want my help making those decisions. I don't know if it even gets to be my kid really. You've told me nothing."

"I know. And I'm sorry. I'm very decisive and I'm not used to consulting. This is... not a position I ever thought I'd be in. I never wanted to be a mother. Until five hours ago. But I absolutely want you to be a part of everything. I can't imagine doing this without you."

He finished with his part of showering and considered leaving. He was probably desperate to leave. And he was right to be. This was no place to talk about heavy things. And yet, here we were, naked and in complete confusion. Sexytime this was not.

I sighed. "You're right, we'll talk. We have to. There's too much on the table just to leave it unsaid." I closed my eyes and tilted my head back to rinse my hair. But Waylon didn't leave. When I opened my eyes, he was with me again, physically and mentally. He was kissing me, letting the spray run down our faces and into our mouths as we broke apart and came back together again, lips suddenly desperate to gain more traction, drinking each other in with the cooling water.

He pressed my back to the wall, holding me in place with this chest. My hands moved over his forearms, but I was otherwise pinned as he pressed the full weight of his body against mine. At one point, he drew back. I thought he was going to stop. I waited for it. Waited for him to come to his senses and realize he shouldn't have any further dealings with the woman he knocked up, other than to get to know me in only the most businesslike fashion. He sucked in a breath and my body didn't listen to my head. I pressed forward into him, needing him to return the pressure of his body against mine. It felt so good to be up against the wall, crushed by the wet weight of him.

He didn't stop kissing me or sliding his hands over my skin. Instead, he changed the pace of his desire from frantic and needing to tender and sensual. His eyes followed his hands to my breasts, skirting around my stiff nipples to stroke the sensitive undersides. God, his hands must have some kind of electrical charge. He looked into my eyes. His expression hadn't really changed but somehow, a little piece of his smirk was returning.

I was at such a loss. I just wished I knew what everything meant. My world was spinning, and I needed to connect to the horizon. But I didn't know what that horizon was anymore.

He groaned when I grabbed his cock, pushing into my grip. It was my attempt at taking the bull by the horn. But the bull didn't want to be led. He moved my hand away and smiled, shaking his head. Then he knelt at my feet, kicking my legs wider and diving between my legs with his lips and tongue. My legs widened, which changed the direction of the stream of water and when I looked down, the rivulet ran down my bare mound and met my clit on his tongue.

"Oh, my God, Soula. You're so wet, I'm going to fucking drown on you." He made no attempt to change anything. I tried to squirm away, giggling. I didn't want to be his cause of death.

"What's so funny?" He looked up but his fingers continued slipping and sliding toward the deep end of the pool.

"I don't know how you say things like that without laughing. I'd feel silly."

"Do you feel silly hearing it? I'm just telling you what I'm thinking, but I can keep it to myself."

"Yeah, but I also feel... wanted."

"Do you want me to keep my thoughts to myself? I've never been very good at that, but if it makes you uncomfortable..." He stopped his exploration.

"No. Keep talking. Don't stop whatever it was that you were doing. Just be prepared that I might squeal in delight occasionally."

"I plan to make it more than just occasionally, then." He dove back under the stream of water running down my body and began a three-pronged attack. "I kind of wanted to ask you this the first night, but it felt weird and then you ran off. Do you have a thing against pubic hair?"

I blushed. I know I did, even under the hot stream of water. "Yeah, I hate it. Bethany turned me on to waxing in college and it felt so much better. I know it's kind of porn-y and it makes me self-conscious, but it eliminated a sensory nightmare I didn't know I had. Do you mind?"

He chuckled and petted my outer labia where hair should naturally be. "No. I don't mind. It's very pretty. And I can see all the good parts. I was just curious." He slid my feet farther apart and settled himself on his knees. The tile must have been killing him, but I wasn't going to last very long with this onslaught of sensation coming from every direction.

His long fingers spread my labia, exposing my clit to a tiny, perfectly placed stream from the showerhead tapping a rhythm that was weakening my knees. I was getting fucked by the showerhead. With his other hand, he slowly eased one finger, then another into my vagina and stroked my clit once through the front wall. He was still looking up at me, his hooded eyes and lazy smile telling me he was enjoying the whole process almost as much as I was.

But when he looked down and a groan escaped from some guttural place in his throat, I was already close to orgasm and desperate for something to grab on to.

“Grab my hair, Soula. Hold on to me. Ride my fingers.” His thumb pressed into my clit and circled the base of that tiny mountain while the water rained down from the front. God, it felt ... It was... “Oh, God. Oh my fucking God,” I screamed out. I never experienced an orgasm like this. It was obscene being this exposed, this on display. It was also sexy as fuck and I didn’t know how I was going to live after this.

“You’re a goddess, Soula. These hips that curve out from this tiny waist.” His hands were still occupied, still wringing out the last of my pleasure, so he gestured with his kisses and tongue instead. He drank the quickly cooling water from my belly and hips, lowering his mouth to my pussy.

"I think this might be my favorite way to hydrate.” I didn’t giggle that time. He wasn’t going to let this end yet. And fuck, I never wanted this shower to end either. I could be in here for days, finding new ways to fuck and just be seen by this man.

“I love you watching me,” I said, lifting the face he just buried between my legs. His eyes brightened. “You’re going to love me licking your pussy, too.” He didn’t break eye contact as he leaned in. I couldn’t help but arch my back when he started stroking the underside of my clit with his tongue.

With his other hand gripping my ass, he moved me so I was directly facing the water. The now-cold stream hit my breasts and made his mouth feel suddenly hotter. His fingers slowly pumped in and out and I couldn't help but rock my hips to meet his rhythm, bracing my hands against the wall. I was fucking his mouth and hand with an abandon I never would have expected to allow myself. But I'd also never expected to feel this level of intimacy with a man either.

When I came, I was snow blind. I gripped the back of his head, using him as my crutch so I wouldn't collapse. I don't know how long I was "out," but it felt like minutes had gone by. Waylon was standing now, kissing my mouth. I barely tasted myself on his tongue but I wouldn't have cared. He stroked himself once, twice, so slowly but not leering at me like the Big Bad Wolf. It was absentminded and adoring. With no expectations. But God, I wanted him to expect it. I was hungry for that cock.

"Waylon, can we forgo the condoms? I'm clean. I did an STI test when I sent my blood to the lab. Have you—"

He looked pained. "There hasn't been anyone besides you. Not for a long time. You shouldn't take my word for it, though. I could just be saying that."

"I don't think you'd say that if I couldn't trust you," I sucked his tongue into my mouth, desperate to be entwined with him everywhere. "Please, Waylon."

"You want to do this in the shower?" He moved away a little, but I held tight to the back of his neck. "It's getting kind of cold in here. And you're kind of... short."

"But I'm light and you're strong. Please? I need to make you feel as good as you made me feel and I decided I'm never leaving this shower."

My body was still writhing. It had a sexual mind separate from my own brain. It was an insatiable monster.

"Fuck," he groaned and lifted me from behind my knees. My head hit the back of the wall but there was no pain. I gripped his tanned and freckled shoulders to help support myself as he lowered me onto his cock. He groaned as he entered me. He pushed in, easing slowly back out, watching me adjust around him.

I didn't avoid his eyes. I never did when we did this. After a few more slow strokes, he began moving faster, harder, fucking me like a storm at sea. I was tossed under the water and rocked against waves of fury. With every thrust, it was harder to breathe. I was underwater and never wanted to come up for air. When I came down on his cock, it was hard, and we both panted and moaned in the shock of it. It was a good angle for me—maybe every angle with Waylon was a good angle—and I cried out again.

As my vagina pulsed around his cock, he slowed his pace to savor the new sensation, thrusting a final time before succumbing to his own powerful orgasm. "Soula." He leaned his forehead against my sternum for a long time before realizing he was still inside me.

"You better put me down before your arms start aching and you drop me." He let out a huff, dropping one knee first, then the other, ensuring both of my feet were solidly on the ground.

I didn't know how solid they were, though. I barely felt capable of supporting my own weight. If I could just make it to the bed, I'd be okay. And maybe in a little while—after a nap because I was utterly exhausted—we'd see if bed sex was just as good as shower sex. If I remembered correctly, I didn't think there would be any discrepancies.

chapter twenty-four

Waylon—Now

I NEVER EXPECTED MY quick shower to turn into sex of lifetime. But everything Soula did was a fucking delight.

Much less delightful, however, was the audience parked on her living room sofa when I stepped out of the bathroom with a towel wrapped around my waist. Bethany and the black-haired woman sitting on the couch weren't even trying to hide their smiles or pretend they didn't just hear the moaning and God-knows-what-else coming from the other side of what looked like a very thin wall. At least they didn't applaud like my cop buddies would have done.

"Ladies." I drew out the word, thinking it might help in the search for more words to follow. Only a sheepish grin widened over my face. Oh hell. If they weren't going to pretend this didn't just happen, I wouldn't either.

Soula turned the corner and snaked her hands around my waist. As she slipped under my left arm, unblocking her view of the room, she gave a yelp and ducked back behind me.

"So, this is the reason for that very un-Soula-like energy I got last time I was here. I think I found your Sun card. Good for you, Sou."

The other woman uncurled herself from the corner of the couch and tiptoed over to me. The fluidity of her movements reminded me of a cat. I'd never trusted cats. She stuck her hand out with a chuckle and I shook it, using my other hand to ensure the towel remained tucked in at my waist.

"I'm Decca. We haven't officially met, but I approve, Waylon Wells," she purred, twirling her pointer finger in the air following her finger with her eyes. "This whole vibe is very, very homey."

"I'm thrilled," I said, tucking the end of the towel tighter around my waist. Decca circled me and grabbed Soula's arm, "Bethany, you coming?"

"For fuck's sake, Decca. Give her a moment to get dressed before you start in on the questions." Bethany shook her head in an apology and rolled her eyes. "Ugh!" She groaned and rolled off the couch. "I had the day from hell. I don't need all this spiritual shit tonight," she griped to me. "Welcome to our world, Waylon." She patted my shoulder as she started down the hall and stopped again. "I think."

I got dressed in the bathroom and leashed the dog, figuring the friends needed girl talk, or to harass or interrogate Soula about us and everything they just witnessed, or whatever Soula and her friends did that required such extreme immediacy that Soula couldn't dress first.

I grabbed Kudzu's favorite football toy and by the time we got to the park, she was panting and hopping up and down. "I know, I know." My voice sounded like a doting dog dad as I scratched her neck. "We haven't had a lot of daddy-doggy time. Have we girl? Nooo, we haven't. And we're going to get even less time together once this baby comes, aren't we?"

I threw the ball and smiled as Kud missed it by a mile before that last statement really hit home. *Once this baby comes.* There was a baby coming. My baby. Soon I was going to have two girls to throw the ball around with. Or a boy. You could play catch with boys, too.

I'd always wanted a family. Even when it wasn't cool, and no other boys wanted to admit that they wanted to be dads one day. I thought it'd have happened already, I thought I'd be a dad several times over by my mid-thirties. But then my career left me in a black hole, there was that string of bad breakups, and my own rocky family of origin didn't help anything.

I hadn't thought much about that old dream in a few years. I didn't kill it outright, but the idea of "family" just dissipated. And when it vanished, it left nothing in its wake. Another empty black hole that I hadn't even considered until Soula and our baby came in and stitched up that wound. Or started to. We still had a long way to go.

And yet, I was outside while Soula was talking this shit out with her girlfriends, no doubt. Was that just bullshit or was that what she needed?

No. It was definitely bullshit. Soula and I were the only ones who needed to talk. Her friends just need to be there afterward. If we're going to try, or *try to* try to be a kind of a family, we need to give it a legitimate chance. I whistled to Kudzu and snapped her leash back on. Jogging back to the coach house, I nearly knocked down Soula's dad closing the garage. He was wearing a suit.

He chuckled. "You trying to send me to my own grave, son?"

"Sorry, sir. I was just trying to—"

"It's alright. Go on up to your girl." His shoulders were a little stooped. He was thinner than I remembered, his face more sallow. It was probably just the dark material against his pale skin. Some people started to look like their partners after decades of marriage. This man spent as much time with the dead as he did with his wife. I wondered if it might be an occupational hazard to start resembling a corpse after decades in this industry? Or maybe the news of his only daughter's unplanned pregnancy saddened him somehow?

Maybe he expected a type of aw-shucks-sir obsequious attitude from the guy who knocked up his daughter. He'd have to wait a long time before he got that from me. I abhorred anything that reeked of a father's implied ownership of his daughter. Nevertheless, this was an awkward moment between us.

"Soula called me while I was on my way home. I don't personally stand on ceremony so I might as well tell you, if she's happy, I'm happy." His face looked warmer, less waxen with his sincerity. Or maybe I had leapt to conclusions. Maybe the pregnancy hormones were affecting me. I was acting like an asshole.

"Well, thank you. Sir." I threw that in because he earned it. "But..." He'd already started walking away but he stopped and turned sideways, slowly, patiently, looking like he lived his life on a sigh. It was a look common in old investigators and detectives. In a lot of people who lived their lives around other people's incessant bullshit.

"You sure she's... you know... happy?"

"You're her boyfriend. You'd know better than I."

"But you know Soula." *Much* better than I. I didn't have to draw attention to that elephant.

He didn't say anything but he didn't leave, either. He looked across the parking lot and pocketed his hands. "Soula's decisive. She's a physician in every aspect of her life and she's the best at making good decisions quickly. I don't think she's learned how to slow down the process, or... process input from others, but...." he shrugged. "To be honest, this is probably the first time she's been in a position where she *should* let someone help her process. She's steered herself better than her mother or I ever could." He didn't quite smile, but his expression was warm. He reminded me a lot of Soula during this speech. I was starting to see her similarities to both of her parents. "You're sticking around, right, son?"

I nodded, not fully understanding exactly what he meant. But regardless, I was definitely sticking around.

"Then, yeah. She'll be happy. Not for nothing, but she needs more people to know her. Truly understand her. Hell, everyone does, right?" He chuckled and it set off a wheezing cough. "My lungs are about as non-functional as the bodies in the basement."

"Smoker?"

"Don't have to be. Embalming fluid does the job just the same. I came from a time when the chemicals were harsher and the masks were non-existent." He turned and headed off, throwing his hand up in what I guessed was a sort of wave without glancing back. I watched the enigmatic man walk away until he disappeared into the kitchen, then bounded up the steps to Soula's apartment.

I let Kudzu free, and she made a beeline for Soula, who was unloading the dishwasher in the kitchen.

"Sou, we need to talk, and we need to talk alone." After saying this, I realized how quiet the apartment was and I looked around the open layout for her company. "Where...?"

"That's exactly what I told Bethany and Decca when I asked them to leave. Bethany had to drag Decca out with a promise to attend the next Green Burial Council meeting, but yes, they left about five minutes ago." She refilled her water bottle and drank half. "I usually need alcohol for these kinds of 'talks' but this will have to do. It just might send me running for the toilet. So far, this pregnancy is a slow torture of excessive thirst compounded with an inability to keep fluids down."

She wasn't talking to me. Not really. She was speaking to the air around us, looking anywhere but my eyes. I closed the gap between us. "What can I do for you?" I asked her, solemnly.

"Start a central line?" Her mouth creased on one side. An attempt at humor. It was a good start. We'd had conversations before. We definitely weren't strangers. But any more than that and I was lost.

Whatever our relationship was or would become, right now it felt un-navigable. "You seem to be as uncomfortable as me." She noted. "Would *you* like alcohol?" Her eyes met mine, wide and innocent. They seemed to implore me to say yes. Perhaps it was just anything to delay the inevitable.

I shook my head slowly. She wasn't going to get away with it. "No way." She looked away again. Not thirty minutes ago, I was inside her, listening to her scream my name. Now we were back to this awkwardness again. The entire time I've known Soula, we've been reliving the same pattern. There was the sex. And there was the morning after. We were never deepening. Never taking real steps to close the emotional gap.

"Come here." I clasped her hand in mine and pulled her over to the couch. I sat down. "Sit on my lap."

"What?"

"You heard me. Wrap your legs around me. Straddle me."

She laughed. "Here? I thought you wanted to talk."

"I do want to talk. I want you to talk to me like we're about to fuck. That's when you get honest. That's when you're real. If we're touching, maybe it'll be easier."

"I'm real all the time." She bent her knees anyway to place them on either side of my hips.

"Then maybe this was just my trick to get you to seduce me again." I smirked.

"No. You're honest all the time. You'd just ask me to seduce you. Where do you want my hands?" Her palms faced me in a position of surrender. I did want her to seduce me again. I already knew it'd be impossible for me to get enough of her, but I craved the whole Soula, and for our whole selves to join, some type of verbal communication was needed. "You can put your hands anywhere. I'll keep mine to myself."

"That's a shame."

"There's my Soula coming out to play."

"I'm going along with this, but I feel ridiculous."

"That's okay. I'll start. Did you always know you wanted to chop up dead bodies for a living?"

Her eyes snapped to mine and her hands fell to her thighs with a smack. "God, that is the worst stereotype about my profession. I do not chop up dead bodies. I'm a doctor, not Jeffrey Dahmer. Why does everybody ask that?" She started to get up.

"Uh-uh. Stay here. We're talking, this is good."

"This isn't talking. This is arguing."

"Even better." I smiled.

She pursed her lips and softened her shoulders. "You asked that insipid question on purpose."

"Of course I did. Soula, I know what your job is. I've seen you do it. I may not like to watch you do your job, but I very much like the result."

"You mean cause and manner of death?"

"I mean criminals are behind bars because of you. We have answers to health questions because of you. Family mysteries are solved because of what you do." I sighed and held up my hand showing her before placing it on her arm. "First of all, as a cop, I'd never put down the importance of your work, but more importantly, as a man who cares for you, I'm in awe of you and your career competence. No matter how gross it is."

"Okay."

"Just like that? We're okay?"

"My turn," she said eagerly.

I chucked at her decisiveness. Wasn't that what her dad called it? I raised my eyebrows.

"When do you want me to meet your family?"

Soula—Now

His jaw clenched. His teeth even clicked together a few times.

"Next question." He looked over and reached out a hand to scratch a velvety pair of ears as if that was the bottom line.

"What do I get for skips?" I asked. I had to increase the stakes somehow. "If you don't want to introduce me to your family, there should be something in it for me if you don't want me to press the issue."

"It's not you, it's just..." He closed his eyes and dropped his head back.

"Oh, I know. I mean it's so early. Too early to be telling people, really. I think you're supposed to wait until twelve weeks, but I can't keep anything to myself." Waylon still wasn't looking at me. "I'm going to meet them right? Family is family. And your side is going to have a new, littlest family member in eight or so months. Eventually, you're going to have to bite the bullet."

"Not exactly." He wasn't just clenching his jaw. He was full-body grimacing now. Even his thighs were tense, unconsciously ejecting me off his lap.

"Oh no you don't. We can revisit the question at a later date, but you don't get to shut me out like this. Not after getting me on top of you."

He huffed out a breath and softened again, touching his hand briefly to my thigh. "I'm sorry. I don't mean to hurt you, I'm just not ready to rehash it all yet."

"Two questions," I commanded.

"Technically, *you* didn't even answer my first," He reminded me.

He was right. I went on a tirade against the same stupid question every ignorant son of a bitch asked as soon as he found out what I do. Was it any wonder I had to lie to get anyone in my bed? I mean wording it that way sounds really, really problematic, but still....

"I briefly considered emergency medicine. Does that surprise you?"

"Do you want me to be surprised?"

I shrugged. "It surprised everyone else when I applied for residencies. I loved my emergency med rotation. I had a great preceptor who challenged my thinking. He made me realize I wasn't only cut to fit the pathology mold. I started to think I might actually have a future among the living after all. That I could be a first responder rather than a last responder."

"Do you ever feel you made the wrong choice?"

"No."

He raised his eyebrows. If he were wearing spectacles, he'd be looking down his nose at me.

"I'm not saying I didn't love my pathology rotation, too. I even requested to do some clinicals in the morgue, which not all doctors opt for. The reason I became a doctor was to contribute to public health. The best way I could think of to do that is to objectively discover what finally takes away that last lick of health. That's why I get more excited about occluded arteries than gunshot wounds. Despite what everyone thinks of the job, I'm not a living, breathing true crime documentary."

"No, that's my job," he said.

"Exactly. Seventy-five percent of my cases are unsuspicious, natural causes deaths." I was getting worked up. "I'm sorry. I'll stop talking with my hands so much."

"Are you kidding? This is the part of you I was hoping to see."

"The wild medical examiner part?"

"The part that's devoted to something—a cause, a person, a career. That's how you really get to know a person." In the dim lamplight, his eyes looked even more dichotomous. One dark and one light. Sometimes his heterochromia gave him a suspicious, even sinister quality, because the blue, his left eye appeared larger. The brown-streaked right one appeared narrowed in comparison. Other times he looked cartoonishly insane, or like he'd experienced a blunt force injury resulting in hyphema. Right now, when the colors were at their most distinct it was just easy to get lost in them. I forgot how to process language, let alone my thoughts.

I shut my eyes tightly and thought back to those four frantic weeks during my clinical rotation in the Vanderbilt ED. "I think parts of my personality were suited to emergency. The extremes between downtime and full-moon rushes, the constant feeling of being in present tense—of stitching them up and getting them out the door. It was nice to solve surface-level problems efficiently. It made me feel like I was doing some good in the world.

But ultimately, that same non-comprehensive care made me turn back to the dead after my brief sojourn among living patients. I might not be able to heal patients in my current role, but the nature of my care is to leave no stone unturned, no cavity unexplored, no organ undissected if need be. And I can use those stories to help so many others in nearly as bad shape."

I removed myself from his lap. His exercise had served its purpose. It forced me to open up. He didn't force me to remain in place, so he must have felt it, too. I grabbed the throw blanket off the back of the couch and tucked it around me.

"I'm worried, Waylon." He rotated so our knees were touching and stretched the blanket across his own lap. "What if I can't do my job anymore?"

"The nausea? That goes away after the second trimester. I've heard. I'm sure—"

"No. Not just the nausea. I've gotten away with compartmentalizing my feelings. You know how much of a loner I am. What if I can no longer keep my feelings out of the morgue?"

"You mean when your *patients* are children?"

I nodded. "What if I can't check my grief at the door? What if the three-year old on the table looks like our three-year old at home? And that's if I carry the fetus to term."

"How does Dr. Li manage? He has kids, right?"

I nodded. "I don't know. I've never talked to him about anything personal."

"Start there then. And keep telling yourself why you're doing this. But ultimately... who cares if you can't hold back your grief and your anger? You think I'm not furious and sickened when I investigate those cases? Who cares if you cry all over the table or puke your guts out? There's a lot more to being capable than remaining unaffected. I think you got a first taste of that today."

I rolled my eyes. "Ugh. When I couldn't handle it."

"When you accepted Dr. Li's help, which he was happy to give."

"But how happy would he be if my growing incompetence made him step in more frequently?"

Waylon laughed. "You've heard that phrase, 'life has no guarantees,' right?

"That's what people tell themselves when they don't truly consider the potential consequences for their actions."

"I saw you go back and take blood out of that guy today after you'd been sick. You already proved that you can overcome the emotions to get the job done. I've never seen you stronger."

"You've *known* me for a grand total of about five days."

He smiled, remembering the line he gave me the last time we were in this room. "Yeah, well. We can talk about how much we don't know each other, or we can start getting to know each other. I already know you're made of cast iron. I don't need more than five days to see what's right in front of my face."

"That was maybe the nicest compliment I've ever gotten."

"I figured that would do the trick." His mismatched eyes crinkled in the corners.

"You hungry?" Waylon bent down to kiss my forehead.

I hovered my face over my phone until it recognized me. 9:15. "No. But I need to attempt the consumption of food regardless. Blegh."

"You are the strangest pregnant person I've ever met. Do you always think like that?"

"Literally, you mean? Only when thinking through a clinical problem. And even when I'm not pregnant, good nutrition is a problem. Now, when I can't keep anything down...."

I was looking forward to that magical second trimester everyone kept mentioning. I knew the placenta and my blood supplied all the necessary nutrients to the fetus, but I'd like for my own body to remain as strong and healthy as possible. Plus, this puking all the time could shove it.

Waylon stood up. "What do you have? Can I make you something? Eggs?"

I scrunched my face.

"Okay, how about... are you craving anything?"

Poor thing. He looked so excited. Like me craving pickles and ice cream was something akin to feeling a first kick. I shook my head.

"I'm craving everything. The problem is, once I smell it, I'm not craving it anymore.

"Okay..." he thought aloud. "What's something palatable, but bland enough that would give you calories without making your stomach explode? Or, you know... whatever the clinical definition for exploding stomach is."

"Pad Thai."

"Really? That doesn't seem bland." He looked horrified.

"Sour food seems palatable. I'm guessing you're not a Thai fan?"

"Not really. But this is all you. And the baby."

"Fetus."

"Oh, come on."

I sighed and focused on a spot on the sisal rug under the coffee table. I really didn't want to go there tonight.

"Do you know how many fetal cases I receive? Or how *normal* it is to miscarry? Are you familiar with the feeling of a ten blade slicing through ribs so tiny and translucent they don't even dull my blade? If I thought of every one of those cases as *babies*, I'd never be able to do my job. I couldn't find about the undetected genetic anomaly that occurred, or the brain that didn't develop." I shook my head, my eyes still looking at nothing, but seeing the countless faces of mournful parents. "I'd never be able to tell the mother it wasn't her fault."

I didn't have to look at him to know he looked stricken. It was the part of my job that was impossible to speak of. It was something I could only share with Bethany, Decca, and my colleagues and autopsy lab techs.

I breathed in and searched for the right words. "*You* see this pregnancy as scary because you'll have new responsibilities with me and a kid, but I think I'm right in that you also see the hope and the fun and the good times ahead." He nodded a little but let me go on.

"I see this pregnancy as scary, not for what might happen when the teen years arrive and I have to take a second mortgage out on my house to feed the monster, but because I only get to see the horrors that can accompany pregnancy. So... I'm scared as shit, okay. I'm scared I won't be able to do my job because of this pregnancy, and I'm scared *because* of my job, that this pregnancy might end in loss."

My eyes filled with tears. I hadn't even realized this was how I was feeling until I started saying all this. The tears spilled over. I wiped the wet off my cheek and sniffed. "Please. Don't equate my clinical mindset with coldness. I'm not being cold. I'm just... I'm using my brain according to how it was trained. I'm controlling things to the extent of which I'm capable even while knowing everything's totally out of my control." I looked him in the eye as I said the last thing. It was too important for me look at the rug.

"None of me-and-you can work unless you let me think how I *need* to think."

He didn't say anything or move an inch. Neither of us did. It was like the weight of grief filled the room and settled over us like a weighted blanket. I was used to the coziness of mourning. It pushed me deep into the softness of the couch. I welcomed the excuse to be still for a while and sit in the feelings.

Looking back, this was the usual spot I went to when I had a tough, or a too-young case. I would sit here mourning and praying in my own way, thinking over their charts, my notes, and whatever information their doctors and next of kin could provide, regurgitating each incision and dissection in my head to ensure my own peace of mind.

No matter what people said about me, I wasn't cold. Cold wasn't even a coping mechanism. Cold was what brought me to terms with loss, yes. But it also solved a hell of a lot of cases. It wasn't *my* lifeline.

It was theirs.

Waylon eased himself deeper into the coziness with me. He linked our fingers together and squeezed my hand, but he didn't say anything. What could he say? *I'm sorry?* He didn't choose my career path. And his wasn't much better. I saw more young deaths because most weren't suspicious. They didn't need investigation or police intervention. But the cases he saw were brutal and horrific. He watched people become monsters and responded to their attacks.

"It's my turn." He looked down at our hands but remained quiet for a long time.

"I'm not a practicing attorney anymore because of one case. I mean, it was cumulative, of course, and I had personal issues going on. I've seen rape kits go missing, and lack of investigation in certain neighborhoods leading to no arrests after obvious murders... But this one case was the final straw. Double murder. Man shot his fiancée and their four-year-old daughter. He confessed that night. He claimed he thought she was cheating and a lot of other crazy shit about angels that put him up to it."

"Meth?"

"Oh yeah. There were no other suspects. No one else had motive. But police were really rough with him that first night, focused more on their own anger, which was natural after seeing what they saw, but they should have been better than that. They took advantage of his mental state to get that confession out of him rather than sealing the crime scene and properly gathering evidence. The case didn't get thrown out, but I had nothing to stand on."

He didn't continue. I looked up at him, gathering up my knees and resting them against his leg. "What happened?"

"I lost. The man was only convicted of child endangerment and possession. By that point, I'd been a prosecutor for four years and I swear it took a year off my life every time something stupid like that happened. I love the law. I'm just not cut out to practice it. Not in that way. I couldn't be responsible for any more final results. I started to wonder how I could help from another angle and... I don't know." He took a deep breath and picked at a pill on the throw blanket.

"If I could help from another angle, knowing the kind of evidence that sunk or made a good case from the get-go, maybe that would be worth it. I know it's not a great use of a law degree and I've moved into a much shorter-lived career with much less earning potential, but I'm still in criminal justice and now I feel like I'm part of the solution rather than the reason a child killer walked free."

I didn't say anything.

"I'm sorry" wouldn't cut it with Waylon just like it wouldn't cut it with me. I didn't know if he felt that oppressive blanket start to lift at the same time I did, but when he finally turned to look at me, and I met

his eyes, things felt easier. I was being pulled toward those denim blues and the faint crinkles around them softened. His eyes were relieved by mine and mine by his. Maybe we were exactly right for each other. His honesty fortified me like an iron pill—which reminded me, I needed to take.

He brushed my hair back and raked his fingers through it. It felt so personal, like he really knew me now. I supposed he did. I shared more of myself with him than I had with anyone, including my family that lived fifty feet away. But instead of putting me on guard, our newfound emotional intimacy strengthened me. I knew I was diving in fast, but I hoped one day, I could be his strength, too, if he ever needed a second source.

"So... Pad Thai?" I asked.

Suddenly, I was ravenous.

chapter twenty-five

Soula—Now

WATCHING WAYLON DRESS WAS a thing to behold.

After he stepped out of his morning shower—his solo morning shower—he transformed before my very eyes from scruffy dog walker to clean cut and casually be-suited.

After two days without shaving, I'd forgotten how sharp his jawline was until he ducked his head around the corner as fog billowed out of the bathroom. He took a few steps closer. I was still cocooned under my thick comforter. He produced a long, clear bottle of snail mucin facial essence and held it up for me to examine with the most earnest expression in his crazy eyes.

"If this is what I think it is, half of me is disgusted and the other half wants to smear it all over my face just to see what it does."

I peeked out at him, hiding my own naked skin and unbrushed teeth in the soft white cotton. His golden skin was still damp from his shower and the towel around his waist showed a lot of it. I almost regretted not taking another of those really long, really relaxing showers like the one we shared last week when we both got so... clean.

"What are you smiling at behind there?" He crossed the room fully, perching on the edge of the bed next to me.

"How do you know I'm smiling?"

"Because I'm an incredible detective with otherworldly skills allowing me to intuit basic human facial expressions." He yanked the covers off my face. "Told you."

I pulled the comforter up to hide my whole head this time. "Am I still smiling?"

He didn't pull them back down again. "I don't know. I can't see your eyes."

"What do my eyes have to do with it?" I asked from inside the cocoon.

"Come on, Sou. Your whole face smiles when you smile. Your eyebrows raise up and your left eye kind of scrunches a tiny bit. Your family must have told you that before." I let him pull the sheet down again. This time, he didn't stop at my chin, but just below my nipples, his suspicious gaze following the trail. The warm cotton percale teased its way across my skin, luxurious and comforting.

"I shouldn't have done that. I just got clean." His eyelids drooped heavy as he delivered that comment to my chest.

"I shouldn't have slept naked." I wasn't sorry, though.

"It'll be the death of me." He thumbed the tender underside of my breast before leaning down and kissing and nuzzling into the soft skin. His touch was feather light. Almost as light as his breath. I wasn't ready for the shock of him sucking a tight, pert nipple into his mouth and I let out a yelp.

His eyes shot to mine. "I'm sorry. I thought you liked that. I wouldn't have—"

I stared at the ceiling. I was such a moron. "No, it's fine. I usually do. But my breasts have been so sensitive lately. Not to mention huge." He cupped my breasts like his hands were a bra, soothing them, weighing them, considering...

"Well, they're huge for me." I replaced his hands with my own. Shit. Overnight, it seemed like pregnancy hormones surged. My body didn't feel like my own anymore. And, really, it wasn't. But I still wasn't ready to fully accept my uterine occupant quite yet. I needed this time of sexy bliss, first. This little glimpse into coupledom. Normalcy. I was obsessed with it.

My eyes drifted back to Waylon. I hadn't noticed I'd been playing with my nipples, but he definitely had. His pupils were huge, and his towel was looser.

"Fuck. Soula. This is the prettiest view I've ever seen." He croaked, his voice thick with want.

I blushed and dropped my hands to his lap, but he moved back. "I can think of much prettier sights." I said.

"Can you tell me what feels good right now? Can you show me how to touch you?" He was studying me. But I wanted more, too.

"Not unless you let me touch you." He shook his head, hypnotized by the ripening abundance of my pregnant body. Or something.

On a whim I decided to abandon my own body for his and reached my hand out, seeking and then finding a long, rock-hard length of...

Snail mucin essence.

"Give me a little more credit than that." Waylon stood, readjusting his towel before snatching the bottle of skincare back, laughing. "Now, to goop this shit on as aftershave or not to goop?"

"Definitely goop. Your skin will smile."

After he gooped and dressed in his overly-expensive, light grey suit, which I assumed was a holdover from his attorney days, I was still in bed. Barring any mass casualty events or serious crime sprees, I didn't have any bodies to chop up on Saturdays. It was paperwork only for me, and I could do that from my office. Or even my bed if I was so inclined, although even I wasn't as keen on bringing postmortem notes to bed with me these days.

For now, as long as I stayed relatively still and horizontal, I didn't have to race to the toilet bowl.

Waylon was putzing around in the kitchen. I heard the cabinet doors thudding shut, the water filling his three-million-ounce bottle he carried with him in his car and finally, the coffee maker starting. My heart sank at the thought of another day fortified by only two hundred mils of caffeine.

"Here you go." Waylon strode into the bedroom, unwrapping a sleeve of saltines. "I read that if you have a few dry crackers before getting out of bed, it can help the nausea." He placed the sleeve on my nightstand before walking back down the hall. He came back with a tall glass of iced tea, with actual ice cubes. God only knew how bad they tasted considering I hadn't used my freezer since it briefly stored the top tier of George's wedding cake almost ten years ago. Come to think of it, that cake might still be there, frosted with more freezer burn than buttercream. That poor cake exponentially outlasted George's first marriage and there was no way a prick like my brother would ever need my freezer space again.

Waylon stood above me looking skittish and I realized I forgot to respond to his offerings. "It's ginger tea. Like you made for me that first day in the morgue. I made it last night so it could cool because it seemed more palatable that way."

"Did you make the ice cubes, too?" I smirked.

"Yes."

He said it matter-of-factly, without bravado or an *I made ice cubes, what are you going to do for me* attitude. It was so simple. He had anticipated my need—a potential need, at that—and acted in advance to meet it. But that simplicity meant everything to me. I was used to being an annoyance. I assumed pregnant-me would be even more of an annoyance to everyone except my best friends. But Waylon cared enough to think about me. To remember that my stomach wasn't so great in the mornings. Or afternoons. Or ever.

My eyes burned. Again with the fucking tears. This was maybe the worst pregnancy symptom of all. Over-emotionality. Waylon looked at the tea, then back down at me. Stricken was the word that crossed my mind. Twice in as many days. I wanted to ease his mind. He did good. I should tell him.

Tell him, you idiot!

He took a deep breath and checked his watch.

What was wrong with me?

"I'd better go."

"Where is your interview?"

"Salemtown. I should be back early. In time for your appointment."

"What appointment?"

"With the midwife. Decca said—"

"Decca made me an appointment with a midwife?"

"I take it this wasn't your idea?"

"I haven't had time to have any ideas. I mean, no but... It's fine. What time is it?"

"Twelve forty-five?" He drew out the words. "But that's what Decca said. Now I'm second guessing everything she told me."

I sat up, ignoring the lightheadedness that accompanied my sudden movement. "What is this *everything* she told you? When did you talk to Decca?"

"She called on Thursday with her list of demands. Then she emailed me a reading list. She didn't tell you? Not even about the appointment? Do you want to cancel?"

I shoved a cracker in my mouth. It immediately absorbed all my saliva and turned to sawdust, but I kept chewing. Kept thinking. "Umm." *Real intelligent, Sou.* Plus, some cracker flew out of my mouth. "No. It's fine. I'll keep the appointment. No use in prolonging the inevitable. Where is it?"

"Here."

"What do you mean *here*? Doesn't she do an ultrasound or something? Bloodwork? Urinalysis? Is she just going to take my word for it that I'm pregnant?"

Waylon backed up with his hands in the air. "Don't look at me. She's your friend. I'm just along for the ride." He was talking about Decca, who was known to do things—and push people to do things—in the most outside-the-box ways possible. But Decca was also cryptically brilliant and if she trusted a person, it meant that person was empirically trustworthy. Besides, if it meant I didn't have to sit on a paper-covered exam table under sterile fluorescent lighting that too-closely resembled my own morgue, I was almost happy to relent.

"Ugh. Okay. Now for more important questions: Are you taking 31 home?"

"Wasn't planning on it."

"Re-phrasing: *Could* you take 31 home?"

"I'm guessing there's a certain eatery along that route that you'd like me to stop by."

"You already know everything about me. Yes. Arnold's. In the Gulch."

"The line will be long today."

"No kidding. It's fried chicken day, but I never get there for lunch and dinner's not the same. It'll be worth it. I promise."

"You think I can convince Reyes to make an hour-long diversion for Arnold's." He looked doubtful.

"I *know* you can. He loves the trout. He can take enough orders of fried trout home for his whole family. I'm paying. Take my card with you."

"I'm not going to do that."

"No, seriously. I'm a single doctor with a very mediocre salary who's only indulgence is excellent takeout. Take the card."

"Did you forget I was a single lawyer for years, also with a very mediocre salary whose only indulgence is... you? I'm buying dinner."

He kissed me on the head and walked over to the chest of drawers where his badge, wallet, and gun laid. I watched him lengthen his body by bending forward slightly to slip his wallet into his back pocket, then he turned toward me again, rather absentmindedly, as he snapped his gun into a waistband holster near his kidney and clipped his badge on the front of his slacks.

I met him when he was wearing this suit. The same tie that brought out the blue in his one blue eye. It wasn't that long ago, but now everything had changed. He was in contact with my friends, researching ways to help me feel better, bringing me iced ginger tea with sink-to-table ice cubes. He was attending this baby appointment for his fetus that was growing inside me.

All that felt... okay. I was still trying to convince myself this wasn't trickery, but an honest-to-God relationship. But this... this watching him dress, operating with leisure around me and my apartment, felt solid and purposeful. And real.

It was the *getting ready for the day* that I liked.

No. It was the *getting ready for the day* that I *loved.*

Waylon caught me staring and quirked his head to the side like a Rottweiler. I shook my head. He understood. Our silent methods of communication were just another thing that secretly thrilled me about us. He put a hand next to my hip as he leaned down and kissed me. I felt tears stinging at my eyes again. He felt so good, so... *home*, it hurt. I deepened the kiss. I needed more of this, reassurance or whatever it was. The nape of his neck was prickly as I grabbed his collar and pressed him into mine.

I felt a rumbling in his belly and then he broke the kiss, laughing. "I'll be home by noon. Can you wait until then?"

"It's not about sex. It's just... I'm so..."

"What, Sou?" His happiness-drunk eyes searched my face, desperate to latch on to whatever words I would give him. But I didn't know what to give me. I didn't have the procedure manual for this.

"It's... fried chicken day at Arnolds."

chapter twenty-six

Soula—Now

I TOOK A FEW tentative steps toward the bathroom after consuming my prescribed hardtack one dusty bite at a time. So far; so good. Maybe there was something to this theory. Pulling on a pair of leggings and a t-shirt that felt like a cocoon, I padded into my office—my sanctuary of purified air and knowledge from the abundant greenery and bookshelves overstuffed with medical texts and stacks of journals. After a week of being smashed up next to Waylon—not that I minded—I finally had time to myself. I was currently behind on a self-imposed deadline for two papers I'd hoped to publish early next year, and I had new data from toxicology to input into last month's reports so I could, hopefully, make a final ruling on several cases. Death certainly did not stop for me.

I looked down at the open page of a chunky paperback someone—Waylon—placed on my laptop. The chapter was entitled "The Second Month." I sighed, remembering the midwifery appointment coming up. All of a sudden, I had people pushing me to deal with birth plans and breastfeeding. Decca of all people—being my friend and having heard the endlessly grim realities of fetal and infant mortality rates—should recognize my need for diversion tactics. *If* I even made it out of my first trimester—and that would be an accomplishment itself—I would have another twenty-eight weeks to keep my fingers crossed.

Then there was the birth.

Then there was the newborn period. What if I got postpartum depression? Or postpartum psychosis? What if the daycare worker shook the baby? Or I woke up and the baby didn't. What if I got into an accident?

Oh, God. Car seats.

I slammed the book closed and typed *check Consumer Reports car seat ratings* into the pregnancy to-do list on my phone. So far it was the first item on the list, since my ongoing mental to do list was basically versions of *deny pregnancy to self for as long as possible.*

I sighed. The denial phase was over.

I heard a knock from down the hall and raced to door, forgetting my gentle movements. Luckily, the crackers still held up their end of the bargain.

"Mom. What are y—" She hadn't been to my apartment in months.

"You need to move Waylon's car. George has a pickup."

"I don't think he..." I looked around the kitchen for his keys. Sure enough, he'd left them out on the counter. "His keys," I said nodding, stalling for time. Every solitary moment shared between my mother and I was tense. "I'll just..." I turned around to grab them and she was right behind me.

"Are you bringing Yia-Yiá to church tomorrow? Or don't you have time for your real family anymore?"

"I don't know. I'll ask Waylon if he wants to go."

Her nostrils flared. She barely let me get my words out. "It's all going to be about him now, huh? First, you abandon your family business. And now you have to get permission to attend church? What kind of man have you let into our lives, Athanasía?"

"He's not in your life. He's in mine and I don't even know to what extent. That's why I'll ask him politely if he'd like to go to church with us tomorrow. Because I promised him we'd spend the weekend together to get to know each other better."

"And where is he now, then?"

"Working, which is why I have to move his car."

"He shouldn't have left it there in the first place." She turned around and stomped back into the house. I was glad Decca hadn't invited her to the midwife's appointment. I didn't need her stress competing with my own. Some Yia-Yiá she was turning out to be.

I stepped up into Waylon's truck and started the motor. The engine was loud, and I liked it. It was exactly the opposite of my Tesla, just like Waylon was the opposite of me. The white to my black. The veins to my arteries. I moved the truck in front of the bay door that housed no funerary vehicles and turned it off.

I noticed the bags behind the driver's side door when I hopped back down. There were several of the same, thick white plastic. Waylon had gone shopping. I peeked inside. Books. Well, if the point of this early period was getting to know him, then his choice of reading material was prime criteria.

I pulled out the first book, Ina May Gaskin's *Guide to Childbirth*. The second book, Ina May Gaskin's *Guide to Breastfeeding*. *Spiritual Midwifery*, also by this apparently prolific and very hippy-looking Ina May Gaskin. No wonder Decca liked her. *Childbirth without Fear*—is there an accompanying Pregnancy without Fear? Oh, right here, *Expecting Better*.

I looked in the second bag. How many books did Waylon buy? The titles just kept coming. *Give Birth Like a Feminist*, *The First Time Dad's Pregnancy Book*. (Why fathers needed their own pregnancy book was beyond me. Could they not glean the same information from Ina May Gaskin that a woman could? Or was it bro-advice for *how to deal with a pregnant partner*?) If it was the latter, I had a feeling that feminist birth book might come in handy. In another bag, there was *Lactivate!*, *Hypnobirthing*, *The Feel-Good Pregnancy Cookbook*, *The Birth Partner*, *The Baby Book*, *Diaper Free: The Gentle Wisdom of Natural Infant Hygiene*. It was a good thing one of us was still concerned about the very concerning concerns of this situation.

I started reading the back of *Spiritual Midwifery*. It must be good if this was the fourth edition. But my eyes glazed over after the first few sentences thinking about Waylon in a bookstore, carting *all* of the baby books up to the checkout.

Then it occurred to me: He was really excited about this. I thought he was just being a trooper, making the best out of a bad situation. But seeing all these books, plus the one he had already started to read upstairs in my office... No.

He couldn't wait to be a father.

I threw the books back in the truck and slammed his door. My stomach felt jittery but not because of the morning sickness. I couldn't focus on work so after pacing across the apartment and giving the plants an extra drink and feeding, I took the dog for a run. What I needed was the cerebral focus of fencing class, but that wasn't until tomorrow. It wasn't until after suffering through Decca and the midwife offering their congratulations and well-intentioned instructions and not until after seeing Waylon's eager, *all-too-willing-to-do-whatever-it-takes* face.

Decca showed up first. Bearing gifts of homemade calendula belly balm and herbs for a yoni steam. I pulled her into the apartment as soon as I heard the knock.

"Do you have those cards with you? The ones that gave me that ridiculously happy reading?"

She slapped her forehead. "I didn't even think about a reading. They're in the car." She turned and grabbed her keys, then stopped. "Wait a minute, you don't believe in tarot. You always roll your eyes and tell me the cards are so open ended, I can make them say whatever I want to." I was so agitated I almost missed her concerned look.

"I think I'm freaking out." My voice croaked.

"Soula," she sighed. "Are you just now realizing you're pregnant?" She put a hand on her hip. Her mouth spread into one of her infuriating *knowing* smiles.

"Yes!" This time, she really did know. "I don't even want kids. I didn't even think about it. I just got mad at my mom, who said I didn't have enough love to give to a baby and I decided to keep this baby out of spite. Oh, God. She's right! That's the worst reason to bring a child into this world. That's not even a reason. It's... awful." I was pacing again, more and more frantically. I shouldn't have been left alone in the apartment today. "I'm an awful person. I'm weird and awkward and I don't tell people how much I appreciate them."

"I know you appreciate me. So does Bethany. The way you drop everything to look after Sofia and help her do awesome science labs."

"Waylon doesn't know." I crossed my arms over my chest, then dropped them back down to my sides. I didn't know what to do with my body. I needed to move. But I couldn't concentrate when I moved so I went still again. "He does these little things. All the time. It's like me and the baby... we're always on his mind. And not in an annoying way, either. Like, an unobtrusively helpful way." I shook my head, suddenly very much in awe of him. "And he's so good. Seriously, Decca. He's perfect."

"No, he's not." A sound came from the back of her throat. "You just think that because he's perfect for *you*. He carries a gun for a living.

He's definitely not perfect for me." She shrugged and put the kettle on to boil. "You're soulmates."

"There is no such thing as mates. I don't believe in that."

"I didn't either, but trust me, I've spent enough hours sitting beside deathbeds and hearing the final thoughts of people who knew, without a doubt, that their partner was their destiny from the very first moment they met. In my experience, last words frequently confirm the existence of soulmates." She fished around in the cabinet of teas I kept for her. "Ooh, ginger!" She turned back to me. "You didn't have a moment like that when you first saw Waylon?"

I placed my hands on the end of the island and lowered my head between them, deciding how much truth to admit. "Sort of," I said, reluctantly. "I saw him smiling at me and...." My words trailed off as I thought about the first time I saw him across that bar. He was looking at me. Deeply. Like he already knew me, with an almost puzzled expression. Then he smiled. Smiled sincerely, not like a come-on.

"You went home with him right away. And a condom couldn't keep you two from conceiving your first time. Coincidence aside, that's pretty powerful."

I dropped my hands and started pacing the hallway again. "I still don't know what he's doing with me. I have all the ugly qualities and he's this angel man. He's going to figure out that I suck. And probably not until *after* he's made me fall completely in love with him and then he'll leave. He'll leave me and take the baby because he's going to be a great father and I'm going to be a shit mother because I don't know how to have a baby."

I was so busy spewing out my anxiety I didn't hear the front door close. Usually, the far-left window rattled in its casing. When I stopped walking and turned back to Decca, Waylon stood next to her with lunch and the bags of books from his truck. He must have been standing there for a while because Decca's knowing smile was even bigger than before.

"Caught you." He wasn't smiling. He dropped the books and put the food on the counter before beckoning me to him with one crooked, scolding finger.

It had been so long since I'd seen him, I couldn't help but slink directly over to him. "I didn't say I loved you yet," I said, backing the statement I thought he was responding to.

He smiled and shook his head. His expression was too much like Decca's for my liking. I glanced over as she sashayed into my bedroom and started tidying up. I was right under him, looking up in contrition. His eyes were glossy and they looked like the Earth with their blues and browns. And he smelled good. Like fried chicken. But it also nauseated me.

"You said 'baby.'"

"What?" I asked breathlessly. The sight of him immediately calmed me down. I felt like I had just sparred with a skilled opponent and won all fifteen points in the bout.

"Not fetus."

My cheeks felt warm. "Fetus means baby. In Latin. Basically, it's the same thing." I was floundering in my attempt to be right.

"You can't change the goal-posts from a previous conversation."

"I don't know what that means." I was still pouting.

"It means you're thinking about motherhood. The whole gooey mess of it."

I nodded. "It happened after you left. I had to move your car and I saw the books and I didn't handle it well."

"It sounds like you handled it perfectly. Like a mother. Now can you promise me something before I kiss you?"

I nodded again. I really wanted that kiss. I didn't even care what I was about to promise.

"Can we be happy about this, together? Can we share that?"

I exhaled audibly.

"I don't mean all the time. We're not stupid. We know there's risks and we'll still have doubts about a lot of things. But sometimes, we can celebrate this baby and make plans, and start to love him or her, too. I want to do all that together. I don't want to have to hide that from you."

"Yes."

"Really?" He didn't believe me.

"I'm trusting you. I'm not trusting that everything will be okay, because you have no control over life. But I'm trusting you to be there to help bear this burden—"

He looked away with a frown, but I grabbed his chin and guided his eyes back to me.

"*And* the joy," I continued. "Together. All I want is *together*. Whatever that means. God, you've been gone three hours and I couldn't wait for you to be home. I don't know what's wrong with me."

He nodded solemnly and swallowed. Then his lips parted, and he glanced into the bedroom. Decca was out of our sightline, but he pulled me two steps backward into the kitchen before his mouth crashed down on mine.

The kiss was like an explosion—or maybe an implosion. It unfurled inside me while laughter bubbled up to the surface. Sheer joy radiated from me. From *us*. He picked me up to join him at his level and my feet dangled in midair.

"You're going to make me fall in love with you, too." He said before parting my lips with a searing final kiss.

I LEFT THE GLOWING-EYED optimists, Waylon and Decca to discuss holistic childbirth theories and the optimal pregnancy diet while I took a shower. I was determined to remain at least slightly realistic through this pregnancy. One of us needed to be. I could probably wrangle Bethany onto my side as well. She'd been through the experience of becoming a mother and wouldn't romanticize it.

"Do you have a doula?" The midwife, Claire, asked me once she had me lying on my back. I wasn't expecting her to start providing medical care immediately, especially not in my own bed, but I had to admit, this was much more relaxing than a sterile OB's office.

"That's me," offered Decca.

I glared at her. "You're a death doula. I don't think anything except the title 'doula' carries over."

"Death is just my job. Birth is my hobby. Besides, if I can usher souls out of this world, I am perfectly capable of ushering tiny little baby souls into it." Waylon raised one eyebrow and caught my eye. Even the midwife looked skeptical, which earned her a little more of my trust. I smiled and rolled my eyes at Decca's insistence.

"We'll think about it." I didn't offer more than that, didn't let myself think about more than that.

"If that's what Soula wants, when do we need to hire one?" Waylon asked.

Claire smiled. She looked tired but like someone inherently capable, both of delivering this child and dealing with Decca's exuberant bullshit.

"Athanasía," Decca scolded me. "I am the High Priestess to your Two of Swords. I will not abandon you in your time of need."

That was what I was worried about.

"What is she talking about?" Waylon asked. Decca exhaled audibly and threw her arms down at her sides. She side-eyed Waylon for his remark but I caught a smirk on her face. She left the room to take a call. When she came back in, she was shuffling a tarot deck and paying more attention to Waylon than usual. I knew enough about Decca and her relationship to tarot to know she was doing some kind of reading for him.

Unlike Decca, with her frenetic, over-insistence on... everything, when Claire had walked in about an hour ago, it was like the room was awash in an opium fog. Her presence was calm and reassuring. It was exactly what I needed to counter my... what? Fears? No, that wasn't the right word for it. *Likely outcomes*, more like. Still, I could relax in Claire's capable hands and I wanted to adopt her into our weird little family. Plus, she was serious about only retaining me as a client as long as my pregnancy was considered medically normal—which I was relieved to note she did test with bloodwork, urinalysis, vitals, and everything else they'd do at a doctor's office.

When the fetal heartbeat suddenly swished over the doppler's speaker, as Claire held the lubricated wand over my belly, Waylon's teary eyes met mine and for a moment, probably due to the pure relief of hearing that robotic rhythm, I was almost lost in the hopes and joys I had agreed we'd share.

Decca was called out to another county to look *in situ* at some bones found in a construction site and Waylon escorted the midwife—our midwife, since I had hired her—out. I fell asleep from the exhaustion of pregnancy and the emotional rollercoaster of the day. When I woke, Waylon was leaning back against the pillows, reading one of the Ina May Gaskin books.

I was in heaven.

chapter twenty-seven

Soula—Then

THE DEAD DON'T SIT up.

They don't wave their arms about like a frog attached to a middle-school science student's electrode. They don't groan or speak.

They just kind of lie there and... play dead.

Sometimes you could hear a wheezy, hissing noise if you moved a body. It might even have a slight tonal quality to it. But it was merely the result of gas passing over the larynx. The same mechanisms and tubes that allowed the living to inhale oxygen and vibrate the vocal cords also allowed escape via the same route inside the dead.

It might be fun to speculate over the mysteries of the corpse, especially at Halloween or while debating zombie science, but the biggest buzzkill about the dead (and their bacteria) is that they're lazy.

When a person dies, it's a death of every cell in their body. And while Mr. Jones' family goes into mourning, the bacteria inside Mr. Jones goes into overdrive inside each and every one of those dead cells. Death gives those bacteria your ribosomes, your mitochondria, your cell membranes yearning to break free. And break free they do. Because when bacteria feed on these beautiful, elegant cellular structures, they produce gas. Lots and lots of gas. And that gas needs an escape route. A lazy escape route, at first. Quite often, that route runs right out through the mouth.

So, the next time you hear a dead man sigh, you know it's not great-grandpa coming to. It's just his dead body expressing bacterial farts. And yes, it can definitely startle the living. Even the living-among-the-dead.

When I was in high school, I occasionally did pick-ups when my dad was too busy. Such was life in a funeral home. One time, I had to drive the hearse all the way into Nashville. The decedent had been on his way out for a while and his family had pre-arranged for all the pomp and circumstance you could get. So, I took the "fancy" car.

When I pulled into the cracked concrete driveway the width of a single car, the family was already outside, greeting me with church songs and a certain reverence unbefitting my youth. The family parted like the Red Sea when I asked for the next-of-kin, a man named, Paul. Paul led me inside a sweltering little ranch with teal shag carpeting and matching floral wallpaper. There was a hospital bed in the living room and more family members on each side.

Dear Lord, I hated those living room beds. It meant either an audience or an uncomfortable conversation that amounted to, "Excuse me, but could you leave me alone with the dead body so I can contort it into the positions necessary for a one-hundred-pound girl to get it into this body bag and onto the stretcher?"

A middle-aged woman in scrubs raised her eyebrows when she saw me. She was the hospice nurse, who confirmed time of death. After signing the death certificate, she offered to help me and when I came back inside with the stretcher, I took her up on the offer.

The feet slid into the bag just fine. With the nurse's help, I managed that much with dignity—for both me and the corpse. Then she lifted the trunk to slide the guy over and that's when we heard it. A long, slow, groaning hiss. The nurse and I looked at each other, then down at the little old lady who'd been holding Dead Guy Walter's softly cold hand when I arrived. She was up like a shot, out of her folding chair. "Barbara, for heaven's sake. Get him back in bed. Get my Walter back here. He ain't dead. Oh, Walter, you ain't dead at all."

The old woman was bent over the gurney, kissing and rubbing his hand, trying to warm him up. "Ms. Mae. I'm sorry. He's gone," The hospice nurse said sweetly. "That's just something that happens sometimes. They make that sound, well... it's just the last little bit of air escaping the lungs."

Another woman's voice cut in. "I saw you." She leveled her finger in the nurse's face. "You didn't even try to do CPR. You should've tried to save him."

"Mr. Walter had a DNR. He was in hospice care. He didn't want me to provide CPR." The nurse said it so patiently, as if it wasn't the first time she'd had this happen. Meanwhile, Ms. Mae was pulling Walter's face closer to her, desperate for signs of life when it was obvious there were none.

"You put him back in his bed, girl," the angry woman said to me. I didn't know the protocol for this situation, but not having the inclination to steal a body on this particular evening, I did as I was told. His legs flopped back out onto his hospital bed, and I arranged them closer together.

The nurse took a deep breath before reaching for her stethoscope and listening for a heartbeat.

None.

She opened his eyes and checked his pupils with her penlight.

No reaction. No brain activity.

She even held a mirror under his nose to show the family it wasn't fogging because Walter wasn't breathing because he hadn't been breathing for three hours now. The ridiculous woman thought the nurse had brought a trick mirror until she tested it and her own breath fogged it up. Nevertheless, she told me to "go on back home," insisting their dad was still alive and he wouldn't be left to wake up tonight in some freezer in a morgue somewhere.

I did what any high schooler would do. I hightailed it out of that house, bottomed out the hearse on the edge of the crevasse dividing their driveway from the road, and prayed they wouldn't call us again.

They did call us again. They needed us to transfer their pre-arrangements with us to another Franklin mortuary, costing us even more time just to save themselves from embarrassment when the paramedics showed up and confirmed that based on his internal body temp of 85 degrees, he'd probably been dead for several hours.

Ma blamed me, of course.

Soula—Now

"Am I supposed to be doing that too?" Waylon asked as I did my cross for about the fortieth time in the past hour.

"No. It's just a Greek thing," I whispered, as the psálti chanted lugubriously from the side of the altar—as psáltis famously do. I locked eyes with my mother when Stavros was really laying hard and long on a single syllable, trilling up and down, hitting the full chromatic scale. She rolled her eyes.

Men, she communicated with that gesture. It was the one thing we agreed on. The Chanters of the Greek Orthodox Church thought entirely too highly of their abilities. Well, that and that the delicious, wheat berry-based kóliva should be served for every occasion, not just to memorialize the dead. That sweet dish was so delicious my eyes grew wide with indecent, sugary greed whenever I walked into church and saw the memorial dish lovingly placed to the right of the altar by a grieving family.

There was a memorial today, which meant I would indeed be staying after the liturgy for coffee and the tiny cup of kóliva. It meant Waylon would be introduced to another aspect of Greek Orthodoxy—the decades of mourning after the death of each loved one.

I checked my phone. Eleven o'clock. Father Vasili just finished the Great Entrance so it would be at least an hour until kóliva.

Waylon tried to stifle a yawn. We were up late last night talking about baby names. Or Waylon was. I basically agreed to anything he suggested, not yet willing to bet on that horse just quite yet, but I did like Peter for a boy. In Greek, it meant rock.

Waylon even taught me a few chords on his guitar and when Kudzu jumped into bed early this morning, I was surprised to find myself snuggled up under Waylon's chin, holding onto him for dear life.

I was not a snuggler. Ever. I found it hot and uncomfortable. I liked my skin to breathe at night and previously, I would have assumed any sane person would agree that airflow and physical space provides the most restorative sleep. But shockingly, Waylon seemed as content as I when we were awakened, so I let myself succumb to feeling good. Little by little, I was making choices to let down my guard, regardless of the havoc it was wrecking on my peace of mind.

I did my cross again when the rest of the congregation did theirs and repeated the action several more times. I sat. I stood. I participated in the rituals of my childhood, wondering what Waylon thought about them. Would he want to marry here, in this church where I was baptized? Would he one day learn some Greek words to exchange with the old men who sat in the hall, drinking coffee throughout the service while their wives attended? Maybe my brother would perform the baptism once he graduated, submerging our baby in the same font as all us Smythe babies. All of a sudden, the cyclicality of life was bearing down on me.

Waylon caught my eye and checked his watch, smiling.

"It's almost over," I whispered, trying to maintain as stoic an expression as possible after slipping into an alternate universe where Waylon and I were... a family.

Could he see whatever was going on inside my head? What was my tell? There had to be one. My whole life, people told me they could read whatever was going on inside my mind. I imagined seeing a face like mine during these unguarded moments. Translucent, almost skinless musculature and fearful, lidless eyes, grasping to rest on anything neutral, anything that didn't immediately recall images that conjoined me with another living, breathing thing—philodendrons being the only exception.

His fingers slipped through my own, but Waylon didn't look my way. He squeezed my hand, reassuring me of whatever shadow had passed over my annoyingly readable face. I tried to pull away, but he readjusted his grip, squeezing harder. A tiny smirk played on his lips.

That was what did it. The smirk that told me, *I'm not going to let you go easily*, released something inside me. I didn't know what it was, but my peritoneal cavity grew warm, like I was being blasted with the fifteen-hundred-degree flame of the retort inside our crematorium.

There was a chance that Waylon was so involved so fast because this was all fun for him. Even still, I couldn't help but consider what his turnaround would look like once the fun died off, leaving behind a carcass of my own weirdness and his parental responsibility.

Our relationship hadn't had that swirling, cinematic ease of a couple falling in love slowly and organically. Our times together had been forced and awkward, but not because of Waylon.

I was a forced and awkward person. Either overly proper or overly clinical. Or I was going out of my way not to appear overly *anything* and... it was a bad look. I doubted everyone's every intention and their every word.

I cloistered myself in the morgue because I could trust the dead. I could read their bodies and the stories they told. I could exclude myself from their conversations. I was comfortable among my misfit friends who were in equally misunderstood professions. We didn't have to understand each other. We understood our jobs. And that made us understand each other.

As service lingered, I studied the icons painted on the church walls. I knew them well enough that if I closed my eyes, I could recall every detail from memory. I could mentally trace every curvilinear flourish in the stained glass. It was what I did when my mind wandered. I liked the women of the church the best. The Virgin Mary's outstretched arms covered the half dome behind the altar, the beautiful St. Barbara, and St. Helen, the mother (and boss) of the Byzantine emperor Constantine. My favorite though, was Mary of Egypt, the old woman hermit who lived in the desert and ate locusts and just wanted to step away from life. It must have seemed reckless to those who knew her, but I always thought she was decisive, like me. She had made a decision and that was it. How much flack did she catch from society back then? I wasn't sure when she lived, but did it matter? To this day, if a woman moved to the Egyptian desert to live the fuck alone, society would find a way to punish her.

Waylon was looking too. At the walls, at the Jesus on the dome above our heads, at the mysterious glimpses of the priest and acolytes behind the altar. There was a lot to look at here. It was one of the reasons I didn't mind attending church with Yia-Yiá. I'd brought visitors here and I knew what to expect. But with Waylon, I never saw that common desperate, It's-all-Greek-to-me look on his face when he turned his attention back to me. He didn't even look fazed. Maybe it was that he was a homicide detective and former prosecutor and nothing fazed him.

Or... maybe he liked it.

I factored in the chance that this whole pregnancy predicament was fun for Waylon because he legitimately cared. He didn't have the hang-ups about the living that I did, so why would he lead me along otherwise? He had no reason to play me, which meant I had no reason *not* to trust him.

So I did. I trusted him. Fully. I let my decisive, Mary of Egypt personality play out this time, right this minute, and I took the leap to trust that Waylon was the real deal. That he meant the things he said and he wasn't putting on a show, dangling a carrot in front of my face and waiting for me to finally stretch out my arm so he could laugh when he inevitably pulled it even farther out of reach.

Waylon brushed the back of my hand with his thumb, and I smiled. He couldn't possibly know how much that small squeeze of my hand filled me with such a sense of normalcy. He couldn't possibly know far south of normal I'd felt my whole life. *So, this is how it feels to do what people do. Normal people hold hands. They share family life and responsibilities. They meet and like each other and talk and develop feelings and plan their weddings far too soon.* Normal felt freeing. It felt amazing. *Please, God, don't let me feel less than normal again!*

MY MOTHER WAS THE first to harass Father Vasili when he stepped into the line for a tiny Styrofoam cup of the cheapest brand of commercial coffee on the planet. I saw the light leave his eyes when he heard my mother's shrill Greek, and I didn't blame him one bit. His eyes darted to me as he listened politely, then up at Waylon, then back to my mother when his cheeks took on a rosy glow. In a few steps, he was reaching out his hand for me to shake, congratulating us with "Xrónia

Pollá!" and asking us when we'd need his services for the wedding. Fortunately, for Waylon's sake, he asked in Greek.

I might now trust that it was possible for Waylon to *like* me after the brief period of time he'd known me, but no trust exercise included enthusiastically marrying a person you've known for such a short time.

"Ma, we're going to take Yia-Yiá home, okay? I'll make her coffee at your house. I just... we have plans."

"Plans? What plans? They haven't even served the kóliva."

"Fencing club," Waylon chimed in, easily picking up where I left off. Except he promised actual plans that allowed us our escape. I was only faking.

"You do that on Sundays, right?" He whispered in my ear. I nodded.

"It's okay," Mama said. "I'll bring her home. You two go on."

"Really? You're... okay." I tugged Waylon's sleeve and took off. Then I remembered I hadn't kissed my grandmother goodbye and turned around. It was weird for my mother to give in so quickly, and without a martyred expression, but I wasn't in the mood to question it.

When we finally got out of there, I felt like I could fly. That was probably my favorite thing about church, leaving it. Especially leaving it to play with swords.

"I'm sorry. That was really long."

"Is it usually shorter?" Waylon opened the passenger side door of his truck for me and helped me climb in. My pencil skirt and I were grateful.

"No. It's always that long. But I'm still sorry you had to sit through it."

He was standing with one hand on my knee and the other on the door. "Soula, you can stop trying to make everything sound like it's too big for me to deal with. I had the pew book and followed along when I could. It was interesting."

I made a face despite my trust pact with myself. He stepped closer and moved his hand up to the nape of my neck, sliding me forward. As he nuzzled my ear, his breath gave me chills, even in the early afternoon heat. "I know what you're doing and you're not going to scare me off," he whispered. My eyelids fluttered closed as I waited for his kiss, but it didn't come. He'd slipped away before I could grab him and hold him tight to me.

"We have a day date," he said, climbing into the driver's seat. "And if I can't keep my hands off you in the parking lot of a church, we'll never make it anywhere but your apartment."

chapter twenty-eight

Waylon—Now

"HOW BADLY ARE YOU going to kick my ass at this?" I asked as Soula fitted me with a fencing mask, the kind with the window screening over the face.

I hadn't realized I'd be fully costumed right out of the gate, and I started to change my mind after donning all the protective gear. Surely, she wouldn't try to stab me on my first lesson?

"Depends on how quickly you pick it up. I'm not that good."

"How not good are you?"

"I haven't competed since college." She leveled a sword up to her eyes, peering down the blade before flicking it down. It must have passed her inspection.

"Okay, so you're not Olympics good, you're just collegiate good?"

"I guess," she shrugged, like it was nothing to be an NCAA athlete. "We're going to fence sabre today. I fence foil normally, so it evens the playing field." She thrust a sword at me. It wasn't one of her dainty little Three Musketeers swords, this was a full-on swashbuckling pirate sword.

"Oh, yeah." I whipped it around and swashed at the air. "All I need now is a whore and barrel of rum."

"Well, your whore's not going to be very happy if you don't learn to use your sword right, so let's go."

We left the equipment room for the gym. Only a few other fencers were sparring so it didn't look like I'd make too big a fool of myself today. I was generally athletic and picked up sports quickly, but I didn't often compete with college champions on my first time out of the locker room, either.

Soula stepped onto a rumbling metal strip of flooring, lowering her mask. "Mask on. The head is a target. Fencing is a gentlemanly sport, so we start with a salute and a handshake. I might just kill you, but that doesn't diminish the upper-crustiness of it all." She saluted me with her sword, holding the hilt in front of her nose, then whipping it down and out.

"I will say, you look very regal. And I'll assume you're joking about the killing part."

"This is en garde," Soula ignored me, moving her feet a bit wider, squatting into a prototypical Hollywood sword fighting stance.

"This is surreal. I feel like Inigo Montoya already."

"You won't for very long." She burst my bubble.

After further instruction on basics like footwork, parries and ripostes, what parts of the body counted as a touch, a bunch of French words I'd never remember, and how none of that mattered if I didn't have right-of-way, I was so thoroughly confused, I was about to turn and run like the Six-Fingered Man.

"Hey, Jeff." Soula called out. An older man watching the duels meandered over. "Can you ref for us and give him some pointers?"

"First time?" Jeff clapped a paw on my shoulder. I responded with a sort of snort-laugh and an eyeroll. Anyone could see that I had no idea what was happening.

"I'm Jeff, one of the refs for open fencing."

"Waylon Wells." We shook hands.

"First to fifteen touches wins. Remember, priority wins the point," Soula said as she grabbed her helmet and held it under her arm.

"Oh, we're actually going to do this? We're gonna... duel?"

"Bout. And yes. You'll get a better sense of what it's all about when you see it put together," she smiled. "Isn't this the part you've been waiting for?"

"En garde!" Jeff said, quietly. Even the refereeing in this sport was gentlemanly.

"You really say that?" I asked.

"It means get into en garde. Literally, *be on your guard*," Soula said.

"I'm on guard." I hastened down my helmet and got en garde.

"Prets?"Jeff asked. It sounded more like an announcement.

"Whatever that means."

"Ready?" Soula translated.

"Come at me," I said. I was as ready as I'd ever be.

"Allez!" Jeff called for the bout to begin. Soula advanced toward me and out of nowhere I felt a stab somewhere along my left ribs. I didn't even see her lunge until she was underneath me. And it felt surprisingly... stabby.

"Ow, take it easy."

"Waylon. We're *fencing*." I couldn't see her face, but I knew there was a *what'd-you-expect?* look somewhere under that mask.

Jeff gave me some tips. "For that attack, you can parry Quarte and then riposte to her arm. That's one to Soula."

"Now we go back to our starting points." Soula whispered.

I lifted my mask. "What did you even do?"

"I'll go slower next time," she whispered back.

I lowered my mask. Slower. Somehow, I didn't think that would help.

"I'll let you attack first. Remember your three basic attacks and your parries. Oh, and your footwork. That's the basis of everything else."

I stepped forward, leading with my right foot, toe-heel, toe-heel, and felt like an idiot. The guys over there looked really cool, though. Maybe after more training, this would become fluid, and I could really duel with Soula. We could get the baby a tiny little, all-white straight-jacket like the one I wore, and—

Soula's attack popped me on the top of the head.

"I thought I had right-of-way," I complained.

"Right-of-way doesn't last for eternity. You stopped advancing. While you were busy thinking about making an attack, I attacked you first." She shrugged and lowered her weapon. "Starting places." I turned around and sulked back two steps. This was utterly ridiculous for a blood sport. If a dude pulls a gun on me, I'd never stand and wait until it was my turn to draw. "Hits shouldn't have who-got-there-first rules. A hit is a hit."

"You'd like épée, then." Jeff looked amused. This was starting to piss me off. I hated sucking at something.

"What's that?" I crouched down and lifted my mask off, gasping for air. The mesh didn't inhibit my breathing, but I was suffocating anyway.

"It's a lot like foil, but without any rules." She lifted her mask. She wasn't breathing hard at all. "Actually, there are rules, but it doesn't seem like it when you compare it to the precision and speed of foil. Any part of the body is a fair hit with épée. And you can fight in virtually any position with no right-of-way."

"That sounds more like it."

"It's really hard. I like rules."

"As long as you're the one making them."

"What's that supposed to mean?"

"Nothing." *Shit. That came out really, really wrong.* "Nobody likes rules. That's why I have job security."

"I do. Without rules, you don't know where you stand with anyone. In fencing, I know my own chances for scoring based on your footing on the piste. When is that ever the case in real life?"

"Is that like cold feet?"

Her eyebrows rose. "I suppose so," she muttered quietly. I counted that as my one riposte for the day. Or whatever the right French word was.

"So, Soula uses the rules of fencing to navigate society, huh?" I asked rhetorically. Jeff chuckled but politely refrained from comment. "So that means, if I learn the rules of fencing, I can learn you?"

"I...." She froze. I could see her considering this metaphor for her own life. One that she had created, however unintentionally.

"Think about it and get back to me later. Let's duel."

"This is why I'm better with corpses. The dead don't try to psychoanalyze me through my choice of exercise."

We did thirteen more rounds. Soula won every point, and I didn't mind at all. It was fascinating watching her do this thing she excelled at and loved. And I could see why she loved it. Apart from the highly precise nature of the sport, I suspected she also liked it for the anonymity. Everyone wore the same white jackets and pants. Men could barely be told apart from the women except for the height differential. Here, she could be the nameless, faceless, person she couldn't be elsewhere. Death didn't follow her onto the gym floor. Her family didn't hound her here with their legacy that left her lonely and sad elsewhere. And she could work out her aggressions physically, which I was quickly learning was her favorite way to emote. She drew strength from physicality.

It didn't matter if it was fucking or fencing, a sword was a powerful thing in Soula's hand.

chapter twenty-nine

Soula—Now

WAYLON'S JAW DROPPED WHEN I stepped out of my fencing knickers. "*That's* what you've been wearing under those pants? I didn't even know they made thigh-high tube socks. How is it that fencing never became widely known as the sexiest sport?"

"Well..." I thought for a moment, placing my foot on the bed to roll down my socks. "Because there's swimming, track, gymnastics, beach volleyball. And those are just the overtly female-sexy ones. Thank you for the compliment, though. I don't normally wear these. They're very old school."

Waylon moved my hand off my sock. "Beach volleyball," he said in a low voice. "Bikinis have nothing on these socks. And that white onesie that covers both your entire neck and your butt crack. So sexy."

I couldn't tell if he was teasing or turned-on. Both, maybe. I laughed and climbed up on the bed, straddling him, then wrapping my sock encased thighs around his body. He groaned and his head slumped forward, resting on my brow. "I thought fencing was a safe way to pass the time. I didn't know it was going to dress you up as my teenage wet dream." He took a deep breath. "Soula, wait. I didn't mean to sound like a jerk, earlier. I really don't want you to think I was playing mind games or shaming you for what works in your life."

"Okay." I was confused. He really needed to talk about this?

"Okay, but... really? Because I feel like I made things awkward back at the club."

"You think *you* were awkward? That's a first. Making people uncomfortable has been my M.O. since childhood. I didn't know it was possible for suave, handsome devils like you." I leaned forward and bit his lower lip, ever so gently tugging at it.

He groaned. "Soula," he countered.

"Do we really need to talk about this? Because I'm okay. Really and truly okay. You told me you're sorry if you made things weird. I appreciate your apology, but you didn't. Can you just trust me that I'm not upset?"

I leaned down again, and he leaned away, frowning. "Well, there is *one* thing upsetting me." I teased. Or so I thought.

Waylon lifted me off him and pinned me down to the bed in a frustratingly un-sexy way.

"Really? You know what this pregnancy is doing to me," I whined unapologetically.

"Making you horny?" He got off the bed and started taking off his own pants, knowing full well the effect his body had on me. That long, rather unremarkable form that I had begun to crave. It was his body that was upsetting me. Specifically, that his body wasn't already performing amazing acts on mine. It wasn't even just sexual, this ravenousness. I loved the very insistence of his thighs under mine. When he shuffled me off him, my body immediately missed his. When I straddled him, my legs had to spread wide to accommodate his, but the stretch felt exactly right. Just like his penis when it initially slid inside me.

Ugh! These pregnancy hormones were agony. I was a sex-crazed maniac. *How was I even going to get through the workday like this? Maybe he could stop in on his lunch breaks. I could get a slipcover for that scratchy couch and—*

"Soula. Did you hear me?"

Yes, unfortunately. I was jolted out of my reverie about sex with *conversation* about sex.

"I don't like that word." I cleared my throat, and with it, my dirty mind—hopefully.

"Something's telling me it's not the pregnancy that's making you... *thirsty*. Have you considered that it might be the fact that this is your first relationship in... how long?"

"Ever."

"It's been a while for me too." He leaned back over the bed to kiss me quickly. "I have very high standards."

"Is that what we are? In a relationship? You're my boyfriend?" I curled up and leaned back against the pillows, repeating the immature phrase, *I have a boyfriend*, to myself. The words were so foreign. But not out of place.

Realistically, it was accurate. I was in a relationship with a good person, a handsome man whose every move released my *thirst*. He wasn't scared away by me or my family. He was everything I thought would never ever happen to me, a life I'd already disallowed myself. I should feel giddy. And I did. But also, at my age, it was embarrassing that I'd never experienced this before.

"Of course we're in a relationship. It might be a *little* soon-ish, but not really. It's a little soon to be starting a family, too, by conventional standards." He grinned so big. "But I love that we're unconventional. What else could we be? A squeamish detective and a swordfighting medical examiner?"

"I've never been in a relationship." I said quietly, still stunned at the use of that label that now seemed so obvious. *At some point, that label gets slapped on every relationship, right?* It's probably a bit exhilarating for everyone. Maybe not accompanied by tears, though.

Waylon stopped undressing. "How is that possible? You're gorgeous and smart and funny. I'd think any man would beg on his knees for a date with you. And anything else it took to keep you around."

"I've never had the opportunity. Please don't act like you don't know why."

"I'll drop it then," he said. "We have other things to talk about today and I'm taking a shower. Now, I know you can't resist my amazingly average body, but *please*, do not follow me. We need to actually talk. About us. About how the zero-VOC painting's just about done at my place and when you want to move in." He said that last part from the bathroom as he started the shower. Maybe I hadn't heard him right. We'd never talked about moving in together. "I'd like to hash out some logistics before this weekend's up," he said from the bathroom. "And if we're going to get any of that done, we need to do it where we can't be tempted by a bed."

I wasn't hearing him anymore, not that I could hear him very well from inside the shower.

Moving in with him, though. Neither of us had breathed a word about it before. I didn't know he'd been having his house painted. I didn't know he'd gotten his floors installed.

I stood up and finished changing out of my fencing gear, throwing on a pair of loose jeans that were getting less loose and a plain black t-shirt. I wasn't thinking. I wasn't feeling. I was just an automaton. Out in the living room, I watered my plants again. My Monstera was now edged with brown and the fiddle leaf fig was dropping leaves. Even my Pothos had some crispiness creeping in. My plants were dying. What did that say about my ability to nurture a relationship? A *child*?

Maybe the plants could do with a change of scenery. They might be happier at Waylon's place. The baby would be better off there, too. *Me*, though?

We strategized through dinner and our walk back home from downtown. We were doing this. Living together. Pretending to be a family. We had plenty of time for me to settle in and "nest" before the baby arrived. (His word. I doubted I had any kind of nesting instinct.) He'd leave all the design choices of the renovation up to me, he said, sipping on the beer I practically forced him to order. He didn't think it was fair since I couldn't drink.

Since he watched the house shows, I tossed that decision-making hot potato right back into his lap. He could do whatever he wanted with the interior on the grounds that he let me fiddle with the landscaping.

"Maybe next time you can teach me hockey," I said later that night when we were lying in bed with our limbs mixed up together. I thought the suggestion was both generous and considerate of the idea that he'd want to show off his own physical prowess.

"Or next time, I'll sign up for a fencing class, so you don't have to teach me all my moves." He rubbed my arm absentmindedly.

"You'd go back to the fencing club?" I twisted my head back to look at his face. "I thought it was a novelty for you. Seriously though, I'm pretty coordinated. And I can skate. I'm willing to try your things too."

Waylon stroked my hair. No one had ever stroked my hair. It seemed like something I'd hate, those whispery fingers raking across my scalp, trailing long strands up and away from my face. But I loved every way Waylon touched me. He intuitively knew how. I shivered and reached down to rub the goosebumps off my legs. He pulled the comforter up around my bare shoulders and tucked it around us.

"I might be shit at fencing, but it's something you like and it's a way—maybe the only way—I can prove to you that I'm in this with you. For you. Not for—" He stopped moving his hand and I felt something heavy on my head. His chin. "Not for any other reason. Soula, I know it's going to take a lifetime of convincing you, but there was something..."

He didn't finish.

"What?"

"Listen, there's no rush to move in. There's no rush to get everything in." He gestured to the both of us. "The baby doesn't put us on a deadline. There's no expiration date arbitrarily stamped on our relationship. I keep getting the feeling you see us as a quart of milk—something that's destined for the garbage disposal once that date passes." He lifted my chin with a finger, forcing my gaze up. "You don't realize it yet, and that's okay—healthy even—but we're not milk, we're Twinkies. It's going to take an apocalypse for us not to work."

I didn't say anything for a long time. His chin started to get heavier and his hand slipped off my shoulder.

I couldn't sleep. At dinner, I thought it would be okay, this pretense. A happy little family. It seemed to make him happy just a few hours ago. But now he wanted to wait. Was he was having doubts now, after I thought I'd finally released my own? If both of us were reluctant now, I didn't see our happy little family lasting long—not apocalypse long.

This afternoon, for the first time in my life, I felt the overwhelming rightness of being with Waylon. We were developing a companionship I never hoped to have. I didn't want it all to slip away just as suddenly. When I finally fell asleep, it was on a wish for something to suture us together.

chapter thirty

Soula—Now

"HAVE YOU MET THEM yet?" Tiff asked, raising her camera to her eye as I removed the chest plate.

Under the ribs, the pericardium had bulged out into a bluish, blood-filled balloon. Tiff looked over at me with her eyebrows raised.

"Cardiac tamponade?" She asked.

I nodded. It was near certain. It was just a matter of determining what had caused the rupture in the heart and precisely where it was located. I ladled the excess blood into a container to be measured before carefully incising the tissue.

Still, some of the congealed blood oozed out of the pneumothorax, causing my stomach to heave. This wasn't a decomp case, but the scent of that much iron attacking my hyper-sensitized olfactory sense wasn't much more pleasant.

Tiff snapped a few more photos as I worked. "Have I met whom?" I snipped. I had a headache from the decrease in my caffeine consumption and besides that, I didn't like to bring personal conversation in the autopsy room. Tiffany knew that, but she also wasn't the type to care.

"Wells's family," she said.

I dropped my arms. "No."

"Isn't that a little odd, Doc? I mean, you hate your family, but you guys are around them all the time. I would've thought he'd introduce you, like, weeks ago."

"I don't *hate* hate my family."

"You just cringe when any of them walk in here."

"Just George."

"And your mom."

I thought about it for a minute. It was so difficult to describe our relationship. We lacked all pretense of boundaries. We weren't very nice to each other. But it also didn't seem to bother either of us much. I shrugged. "Mom's never forgiven me for leaving George alone to run the business. Coming here reminds her that she's mad at me, which reminds me that I'm mad at her. We don't hate each other. We have a lifelong truce. Bethany helps."

"What do I help?" Bethany grunted as she pushed a gurney through the double doors.

"Speak of the devil... I forgot you were coming today."

"Bethany's a saint," Tiff said, nodding a greeting to our visitor. "She works closer with George than anyone and I've never met a bigger prick. And I know a lot of attorneys."

"Ooh, Tiff." Bethany shimmied as she said it. "I don't think anyone's ever used the word "saint" in the same sentence as my name, but I'll definitely accept *that* compliment. You have no idea how much I put up with."

I severed the blood vessels that would allow me to remove the lungs and heart in one block. "I'm starting to feel uncomfortable around Wells. Or maybe I just feel like I *should* feel uncomfortable. Do you think I should push the issue? Or drop it?" If I dropped it, it would probably be the final straw in our short-lived romance, which had a note of inevitability but at the same time, already made me feel lost.

"Wait. Waylon? What could he have possibly done?" Bethany huffed out a breath as she parked the gurney in front of the dairy section. Her hair was falling out of her bun and into her face and she was wearing scrubs. I'd never seen her looking more harried and I was certain that was George working her to death.

"Wells is making you uncomfortable? *Detective Wells?* Isn't he your baby daddy?" said a deep voice behind me.

"What was I saying about attorneys?" Tiff asked.

"Speak of the devil," I repeated.

" ... And he shall appear," Ewen finished the statement. Of course, he relished being compared to a devil.

"How did you know about Wells and me?"

"Tiff told me," he said, biting into a green delicious apple. I glared at Tiff.

"What?" She shrugged and looked away. Guilty. "You know you can't eat in here, Ewen." Tiff said.

"Just an apple." He held out his hands. "Wells told me, too, by the way. But I think it was a territorial thing." He winked at me.

"Ewen, do you really have to be told you can't bring food into the autopsy room?" I asked.

"No kidding, dude. Isn't that common sense? You're revolting." Bethany hopped onto the empty gurney. I didn't know if she was disgusted by the idea of eating while this gory scene was taking place, or at Ewen Cameron and his overpoweringly boyish charm. Or what he thought was charm.

"*He* doesn't make me uncomfortable," I said. "The thought of moving in with him makes me... nervous." I lifted out the block of heart and lungs and maneuvered them onto the sideboard.

"*That* might be the most disgusting thing I've ever seen," Ewen said, taking another bite of his apple.

"And yet, you're eating," Bethany said.

"Nicely done." Tiff praised me and glared at him. He ignored the look.

Ewen took another bite of his apple. "If you're going to end up with anyone other than me, I approve of Wells. He seems like a good guy. Smart, too." *Crunch.* "He remembered something from Benton County that I might be able to show Judge Taylor." *Crunch.* "He actually seemed pretty excited to become a dad, too. More so than I would be." He threw the apple core into the biohazard bin.

"Big surprise." Bethany said it, but we were all thinking it.

Tiff jumped on Ewen's back before I could. "Hey! We pay an outrageous biohazard disposal fee—"

Ewen picked up on Bethany's comment. "Unless she's already got kids. Bethany, doll, you just name the date and I'll let you take me out." She smacked his shoulder.

"Seriously, though." Bethany turned her attention back to me as she hopped down from the gurney and her feet hit the floor. "If you're not sure about Waylon, don't move out of your apartment. I can tough it out under the same roof as George for another few months."

"Who's George and what does he have that I don't got?"

"Ewen," Bethany linked her arm in his. "You're a man-slut but I'd take you any day over the sadistic asshole who thinks he's my boss. I just don't know what I ever did to him."

"You didn't do it. Eleni did," I said, placing the heart on my cutting board. "After she had sex with Gus. Not only did he swear off women after she left, for the last four of those ten years he swore off vacations, sex, weekends, and anything that might be construed as fun. And he holds us all to that same standard." I sighed. "Maybe I am glad to be leaving."

"Wait," Tiff chimed in. "Gus? The Gus that's in seminary to become a Greek Orthodox priest? Slept with his brother's wife?"

"Is there a better reason to go to seminary? I'd want to hide out too, if I crossed that line," Ewen said.

"Really, Ewen?" Tiff's fingers hovered over the keyboard as she narrowed her eyes at him. "I honestly didn't think you had limits."

"I don't have many." He shrugged.

"Oh, Lord." Bethany crumpled. "I knew she cheated, but I didn't know it was with his brother. That's... shit."

"Yeah, she was. Pure shit. The whole thing. It was... not good." I wasn't very eloquent, but it was the best I could do to describe the situation.

"But Gus... George and him are tight." Bethany knew how it was in our house. She lived with it. "How'd he handle it? How is Gus still alive?"

"It was bad for a long time. Then, Dad hired you and all George's leftover anger pivoted in your direction," I said, jokingly, before I realized the unfunny truth of my own statement. I resumed my task and sliced the heart in half inch, sagittal sections that I could examine in greater detail. It was a normal part of every post-mortem exam, but vital to a heart that caused a bleed of this scale.

I tried not to think back on the post-Eleni period of Smythe family history. The whole household walked on eggshells for years afterward, whenever Gus was on break from his seminary in Massachusetts. A few months ago, Bethany arrived and George started being a dick almost exclusively to her. I hadn't put that puzzle together before now. I'd been overly self-involved lately. I'd have to talk to my stupid brother. It was something I generally avoided, but Bethany was worth the price of ten uncomfortable minutes with George so I could figure out what was going on with him.

I thought about my brothers' unlikely path toward reconciliation. It wasn't complete, and I didn't know that it ever would be, but they were at the point they could have normal conversations again, laugh about Dad's seeming unwillingness to eat a full family dinner, pretend to banter about sports.

"I think it helped that Mom couldn't bear it otherwise. Greek moms and their sons have a bond I can't fathom."

Bethany nodded. She was still pondering silently.

"That, and George drove Gus to daily AA meetings for an entire year afterward, insisting he did what he did because was an alcoholic. You also know how much he likes to be the father figure to us all."

"Welp, sounds like you've got yourself an interesting dynamic there, Beth." Ewen said. "Let me know how it goes, or if you want to throw it in this guy's face that you still know how to have a good time. Bye, ladies."

"I'll keep you in mind, Ewen." She didn't bother looking over at him as he left. She was still leaning against the gurney with her arms crossed, deep in thought.

I stepped around the table to weigh the left lung before sectioning.

"690 grams." I reported to Tiff. "I do want to move in with him. I just want to make sure *he* wants me to move in with him." I knew it was immature as soon as I said it. I was a grown woman. I could put myself out there first. Wasn't that the fertilizer that lovvv . . . ing-type relationships grew on? Risk and assertion?

"Why don't you just demand to meet them? Rip off that band-aid." Tiff said, awaiting my next notation.

"Who?" I sliced into the lung with my bread knife. "Evidence of intra alveolar hemorrhage present in left lung."

"His family."

"Oh. Let's just drop it." I sighed. "My problem seems trivial in comparison to Bethany's. I've never seen her look so glum."

"I should be nicer to him," Bethany decided.

"Right lung, 708 grams."

"Who?" Tiff asked, her horrified face fearing the reply.

"George. I didn't know all that. That he experienced that kind of trauma. I thought it was some kind of game and we were both playing it. I've been a jerk right back to him from the start."

Tiff looked at me like Bethany was nuts. George had a reputation everywhere he went for telling people how to do their jobs while insisting they get out of his way so he could jump in and do his first. Whatever the opposite of a team player was; that was George. He needed a wide berth, not lenience.

"You need a break from living with him. No one should have to share a bathroom with a man they hate. I'm being too precious about Waylon. So what if he doesn't want to show me off to his precious family? *He and I* might be excited about this pregnancy, but I can't expect other people to be on the same page of our fairy tale. Besides, now that I think about it, I don't know if I'm ready to add another family dynamic yet."

"I'm sure Wells has his reasons, Doc." Tiff said. "There's no way he's embarrassed of you. It's probably them he's ashamed of them. Javi told me he already threatened Waylon twice that if he doesn't stop talking about you constantly, he will be writing every report until the baby comes.

Secretly, I was thrilled. I took a deep breath and looked down.

"Oh, here we go." I said, returning once again to the bleeding organ on my cutting board. "Evidence of ruptured myocardial infarction of the left ventricular lobe." I palpated the slice of the decedent's heart, examining the section for further signs of disease.

Bethany sighed quietly, but I caught it during the lull. "There's a hole in his heart." She said, sadly.

chapter thirty-one

Soula—Then

THE BLACK OUTSIDE THE basement windows was broken only by flashes of lightning, highlighting the rain drops melting into streaks and pools on the surface of the panes. A veritable panorama in strobing blacks and whites.

That should have been enough to make me think twice about working in the embalming room. Or at least enough to forewarn me it was destined to be the night that changed everything. But George promised he'd be down there with me the whole time.

Not that I was scared of a thunderstorm. Especially not in such a clinical environment as the preparation room, with its stainless steel tables and the soothing clickity-clicks of the embalming machine. And we had two backup generators. Even if the lights went out, as they often did upstairs, it would only be five seconds before they'd kick on again down here.

Dad had just made George a full partner after coming back to us from his apprenticeship in Murfreesboro, and I was between undergrad and a faulty year of grad school in Knoxville, both of us recently returned after flying the coop.

But, while my career trajectory hadn't even taken off yet—I had years more education to complete before I could start seeing regular paychecks—George's was already on the downswing, having reached his goals as a funeral director.

He owned a lucrative, recession-proof business and he was fully engaged in the career he was born to do. He even managed to marry that stuck-up girl, Eleni Kiklis, from my Sunday school class. Five years older than me and his life was the same as it was ever going to be for the next fifty years, unless he died prematurely.

Thinking about that made the night even gloomier, but I kept it to myself.

"Drying gel or powder, do you think?" I asked.

George stepped over and let the tissue slide between his fingers. "Powder first. Then suture as tightly as possible. Even then, maybe glue over it. These long bone donations can weep. We still might use a unionall. I'll go grab one from the supply closet."

He hit the button to start the embalming machine on the decedent he was preparing across the room and left, the door shutting with a snick. I continued the process of replacing my corpse's donated left femur with PVC pipe, sprinkling drying powder on the cut edges of the tissues and suturing the skin closed as tightly as I could.

The local AM radio station was on, but WAKM was cutting out on George Jones as the storm moved closer.

After my fifth suture, the radio went silent. My eyes flicked up to the radio sitting in its usual spot on the ledge of the ground level window. There was just enough time for my eyes to light on the silver speakers before a curtain of darkness fell around everything.

I waited, counting out the seconds in the eerie silence until the generator kicked on.

I had been standing, bent over the corpse, holding the needle driver and forceps to pull the black cord taught, drawing together the severed edges of skin made by a hospital pathologist. But I couldn't do anything in the pitch black. I lowered my tools momentarily to stretch my arms above my head, relieving some of the pressure on my back. George would check the generator any minute and we could resume operations. Until then, I might as well get comfy with the scent of the cocktail of embalming fluids lingering in the room and the carwash noises of the rain smattering the window.

"George?" I called out. A flash of lightning was my only reply. It illuminated the stainless-steel cabinetry around the room, a flash of silver from the tools on my tray, and the two corpses who were now my only company in the blackness.

The thunder answered after two *mississippis. When would the generator turn on?*

"Soula?"

Fear shot all the way down my body and straight out my toes as my hip hit the table and sent it flying. My forceps pinged against the linoleum and my needle driver jabbed the curved needle right into my fingertip. "Shit."

"What happened? Are you okay?" George asked, coming quickly to my side.

"I'm fine. I'll just need antiseptic when we get upstairs. Why aren't the generators working?"

He sighed. "I shouldn't have had you here so late. We've just been so busy, I thought I could get some work done tonight. The generators are hooked up to the coolers. We're going to have to stop where we are. Get these guys back into the coolers. Help me real quick?" George's hand clapped firmly on my back. Together we worked by flashlight, zipping both decedents back into their thick plastic bags. I flipped the lock on the wheels and moved to the head to push the gurney out the door and that's when I heard it.

The moan.

It was low and guttural. Hauntingly supernatural considering our surroundings. I froze, my hands tightening on the cold chrome handles of the gurney. I willed myself to look down at the body I was wheeling.

No. I shook it off. Now was not the time to start believing in ghost stories. I knew these corpses hadn't made that sound. Not even escaping gases from the dude inside this body bag could have accounted for it. I didn't even get most of his body cavity stitched up. The groan must have been my imagination. But damn, that's exactly what it was. A groan.

I cleared my throat and stepped forward, my chucks squeaking on the tiles.

There it was again.

My eyes shot to George. Maybe my ears were playing tricks on me. It had been a long day with two funerals. That was the reason I was still down here lending a hand at ten o'clock.

In the flashlight, his eyes caught mine and he smiled a little. "It's nothing. Just the wind. Come on, I'll get the door." But he opened the heavy, wide door just an inch before we heard something else, *a sigh.* We both knew that door only hissed on closing, operated by well-functioning hydraulics, so it couldn't have been that. It had to be something else. Some*one* else. George held the door steady, open those same few inches.

The lightning flickered over his face long enough for me to see him staring down at the floor, listening. He swallowed. He didn't make a move for another two mississippis until the thunder boomed, rolling through the corridors and the prep room, rattling the tools we hadn't put away yet. But that low roll carried another sound, a stifled cry.

George jerked his head to me. His jaw tightening and twitching as he clenched his teeth, a silent cough shuddering deep in his chest. In the span of a moment, he desperately sought my understanding or my compassion or my *God-only-knew-what.*

Our eyes were locked together. I watched him disappear into himself, his expression morphing from surprise to anguish to disgust. Finally, the lines softened as his face took on a truly horrific quality. Apathy.

Since that night, I've never once seen him release that death mask.

I didn't know it then. I didn't understand anything that was happening. How could I have? In five minutes, we went from embalming together and making fun of old country songs, to... whatever was happening now, that George confirmed by his reaction. He was turning to stone right before my eyes.

Quietly, he put his hands on my gurney, not wheeling it out the door, but firmly pushing me back, pinning me against the cabinets. He ran his hand through his hair, raking his nails across his scalp before finger combing his hair back into place. He always had great hair, even in the creepy, greenish light from the flashlight lantern. Pure black, thick but soft, and kept just long enough to be precisely and respectfully molded. Those were the kinds of specific details I always remembered with ridiculous clarity.

He opened the door and left me in the preparation room, his steady footsteps receding down the corridor. I wiggled out from behind the gurney and followed him. He didn't stop me. He probably didn't realize I was there.

He was already there in the old prep room. The one no one used anymore. The door to the old room had no hydraulics. It just opened. And stayed open. I flew around the corner and my chucks squeaked against those tiles at the same time I heard another moan. I stood behind George, looking at movement writhing in the blackness.

The lightning flashed again and instead of live motion, I saw a montage of still shots. Perfect, half-grapefruit breasts plastered onto a woman's chest; long, smooth legs wrapped around longer, hairy legs. My brother's gross balls. Her gaping mouth.

"You motherfucker."

The statement was so quiet, so... resigned, I wasn't sure who said it. Nor to whom it was said. Probably George. It had to be him that said it. He was the one whose heart was being ripped out and stomped on in front of our very eyes. The room was black again as the thunder rolled. I debated going back for the flashlight when George said, "Soula, get out of here. Please." His voice broke on the *please.*

But I physically couldn't leave. I was paralyzed. I recognized enough of the horror to realize that stupid, self-serving bitch, Eleni was getting fucked on the embalming table by the wrong brother, but while it should have been a *turn and run* situation, it was a *holy shit, my body will not move* situation.

That's when the power came back on. The overhead fluorescents flickered, shrouding my brother and my *other* brother's wife's nakedness in a sickly green cast. She pulled the cups of her bra back over her new implants and Gus tucked himself away in his jeans. After that, no one moved. Eleni sat there, her legs still parted wide, staring George down with a sick expression on her face, daring him. To do what, I didn't know. To come close her legs? Cover her up? Find any shame in her performance?

Gus looked contrite enough. But it was almost like he didn't even matter at that point. George didn't spare him a glance. It was a situation we'd all been dreading. The whole family had seen the flirtations; Gus's flirtations with anything female and Eleni's flirtations with anything that could hurt George. The inevitability of this moment was starting to sink in.

But somehow, George was blindsided. His eyes remained in a deadlock with Eleni's, but she just kept smiling lazily, snaking her long, heavily highlighted waves across her shoulder.

"You wanna come finish me, baby?" She widened her legs even further. George's heart that had turned to stone in the next room protected *him* from further pain, but she didn't just ruin her husband that night, she ruined all the Smythe siblings.

Soula—Now

Packing my apartment to move in with the man I was almost sure I loved should have been a joyous lovefest.

There should have been music and dancing barefoot around the cardboard boxes. There should have been kisses and pausing for quickies because we couldn't keep our hands off each other. There should have been Chinese food on fancy china—or was that unpacking? Because damn it, that was the bliss I was promised by the media.

Well, I didn't get my bliss, but it was almost as good. Decca's high spirits and impromptu three-card tarot spreads provided the entertainment, and Sofia was now an enthusiastic convert to Decca's ecclectic brand of spirituality.

Waylon wasn't here. He was called to a scene. But even before that, he hadn't been coming around much. For the past few weeks. Actually, I knew, because time now revolved around my pregnancy rather than an actual calendar, it was exactly two weeks and four days that he hadn't been as present as usual. We still went out. He took me on a string of dates, brunches at the Bluebird café in Nashville, bluegrass concerts along the Harpeth. We even took Sofia to watch classic movies in Pinkerton Park when Waylon wasn't on call.

Our moments together were always easy. I'd never spent so much time away from my home or office. But Tiff had me suspicious about what he might be hiding.

"The Four of Wands, Soula. Do you know what this means? With the Page of Cups?" Decca was covering her mouth.

"No, Decca, I have no idea what it means. Bethany, you're keeping these bookends and all the tchotchkes, right?"

"I'm keeping everything that's not in your office. I want Sofia to have a blank canvas before we decorate her room and I know you don't feel like packing up anything besides your books and clothes."

"I'm going to paint it green," Sofia said.

"That's cool, but before we paint, all those books need to get packed up, so get started." Bethany handed her daughter a jumble of empty boxes.

Decca continued with her reading, "First of all, this is the marriage card, so it's pretty obvious you made the right choice moving in with Waylon. The cards are honoring that and want you to celebrate this season of hope and promise in your lives."

Bethany and I exchanged a look when Decca uttered the word marriage. After the infamous Celtic Cross spread Decca had done before I realized I was pregnant, Bethany and I were both starting to give an inch on Decca's tarot skills.

But marriage? Moving into his house, as a concept, still seemed like it could just as easily be a step closer to co-parenting instead of a sign of deepening romantic commitment. I was embarrassed to admit it, but I had been trying to avoid asking him what it meant. Until I worked up the courage to have that potentially horrible conversation, I was withholding final judgement on the tarot thing. And I was a pro-level avoider.

"The Page of Cups, though... I don't think that's about you," Decca brought out her guidebook and perused the glossary.

"Yeah, I think it's about Decca trying to avoid lifting heavy book boxes," Bethany said. Decca didn't hear her. She was in a groove.

"I think it's about Waylon. We know he's a wonderful human. We love the way he treats you, Sou. He even gets along with George." Her eyes turned to the steps as George's head appeared, then his arms, loaded with flat-packed cardboard he found in the garage below. He gave Decca the side eye, practically growling at what he heard as he dropped the boxes on the floor.

"Okay, maybe that's a stretch. No one gets along with George," Decca continued, "but Bethany's right, we all want someone like Waylon."

George grimaced at that, too. I tracked his eyes over to where Bethany was dumping paperbacks into a box, trying to read her expression. I was doing that a lot lately, trying to read the two of them. I wasn't naturally gifted at reading people, but I was trying to get better. The energy surrounding them had been different since I told Bethany about Eleni and she started to accommodate his anal retentiveness a bit more. George picked up a tape gun and started to tape up the boxes. *He was actually being helpful?* And he hadn't given a single directive in the minute since he stepped foot in my (now Bethany's) apartment. That must have been a record.

"Still, the reverse of the Page of Cups makes me think he feels unaccepted." Decca sighed, still considering Waylon's card. "I mean, his card isn't reversed, but there's always an element of that. The thing with his family is still an issue, right? Or are we the ones who made him feel unaccepted?"

"I don't know if it's an issue—" I started.

"Wells, feel unaccepted? I think Soula's taken care of that," George said.

"You are aware that people can still harbor feelings from their past, right? We can't all shove it down and flip the switch like you," I reminded him.

"You're one to talk," he shot back. His retort didn't have the same edge it usually did. Maybe something was wrong with him. Maybe he was diagnosed with an illness. That was the only reason I could see for this... softening. Bethany shrugged. She'd noticed it, too.

"You think you can read my fortune next?" George asked.

"I don't read fortunes, I practice a little cartomancy, but mostly I just use the cards to intuit events in your life you already know about," Decca's eyes flickered over to Bethany, "but maybe you aren't ready to explore yet."

"This should be illuminating," Bethany said over the ripping of the tape gun.

Decca looked at George for a long while as she shuffled the cards.

"Cut the deck into thirds, please."

George did as he was told. He didn't love this. I could tell by the tightening of his jaw, but the fact that he was participating—that he had *initiated*—this reading, was a big leaf he was turning over. Decca continued shuffling.

"Anything you want to ask?" George shook his head slowly. Bethany and I had stopped packing and gathered closer to the kitchen island to peer over Decca's shoulder.

"I bet he gets The Devil," Bethany whispered to me. I laughed. Suddenly, there seemed to be a lot invested in this reading. Decca shuffled a few more times before fanning out the cards in an arc.

"Pick three," she said. George complied. She pointed to where he was to place them, then she stacked the cards again and began.

"So, I did a basic past, present, and future spread. The Four of Swords—your past—indicates to me that you let yourself get run down by work. You needed to take a break but didn't let yourself and now you're exhausted." His jaw flexed but he cocked his head to the side, perhaps conceding Decca was right.

"Next," he said.

"Um...the Six of Pentacles tells me you still need to find that balance." Her eyes were hesitant to meet his. I got it. George was intimidating when he wasn't getting his way.

He opened the fridge, bending down to peer inside. "You don't have beer?" he accused me.

"She's pregnant." Bethany rushed to my defense.

"Um, the Six of Pentacles also makes me feel that you want to enact positive changes, but maybe you aren't sure how to proceed, so..." Decca trailed off as George hovered above her.

"Yes," he prodded.

"So stepping aside and letting others help, delegating responsibility and showing compassion will be life changing for you."

"Ha! I told you that. And that's why *I'm* here, Ladies and Gentlemen," Bethany waved her invisible hat in the air. George glowered at her and rubbed the back of his neck.

"Next," he said.

"Okay, the Two of Cups. Your new partnership shows promise." Bethany gloated at the news. Decca looked closer at the cards. "But I'm getting the strong sense that your alliance might be more than just business. I feel like this is a partnership of your whole selves joining, and both of you will thrive and grow from this relationship." Everyone was quiet for a while, until Sofia came out of my office asking if she could go home to play video games with Gus.

"Sure, baby," Bethany kissed the top of Sofia's head, and her daughter took off.

"Thanks for your help," I shouted after her.

"Well... that was fascinating," George said, straightening from leaning on his elbows. "I guess I don't believe in fortune telling after all." He raised an eyebrow and sauntered down the stairs, careful, this time, to avoid Bethany's eyes.

"I think I've become a firm tarot believer," I said, watching Bethany's shocked expression as George left.

chapter thirty-two

Waylon—Then

THE FIRST DEATH I watched was my grandad's.

I was nine and already wise to the way my family dynamic played out. Mom would occasionally take me and my sisters to visit him in the nursing home.

I hated that place. I hated the way it smelled of food and ammonia, I hated the hallways that twisted on and on in an endless labyrinth like a Hitchcock movie, and I hated the way Grandad always looked so sad. I hated that place so much that I dreaded seeing the man, which made me feel guilty, which made me dread the whole ordeal even more.

We didn't visit often enough. I know that now, but as a kid, it seemed like we were always there. It couldn't be the easiest thing to cart three kids around a nursing home, but Mom barely tried. Only when she needed money. The last time I saw him was one of those times. Mom got our rent money from him as usual. Bringing us along usually won her a little extra for groceries and this time was no exception. Hint: she never bought groceries with his little extra.

She couldn't even be bothered to stay in the room long enough to ask him herself. That responsibility fell to me while she stepped outside to smoke a cigarette.

I asked. He handed me the check. Then his body stopped working.

There was a call button somewhere. I stood paralyzed for a few long seconds, then my brain finally kicked in. After a frantic search, I found where it had slipped under the hospital bed, and pressed it. I kept pressing until a nurse came.

She silenced the alarm and called his name a few times, leaning over to grasp his shoulders and gently shake him. No response. She straightened her back and checked his pulse before her concerned eyes darted to me, then my little sisters', then back to my grandfather as she bit her lip.

The nurse wasn't even trying to revive him and all I could do was stare in disbelief. I couldn't remember the words to yell at her, make her lift her arms, do mouth-to-mouth, whatever it was I saw on ER. The lunch cart rolled down the hallway and the scent of institutional chicken wafted into Grandad's room. No one was helping him.

"He has a DNR," Mom said, from the doorway. I didn't know what that meant. "You get the check?" she asked me.

I nodded. Good timing for her, then.

My sister, Loretta cried as we left. Patsy didn't. She wasn't old enough to know any better. I didn't cry either. I was too old and knew enough to know I had to be the one to help them through this—whatever this next phase was going to be, where we didn't have Grandad as a backup for when Mom couldn't pay for us to live.

The second death was my baby sister's. A standard overdose. A cliché, really, when you came from our background.

When a young person from a rich white neighborhood died, people said it was a shame. They blamed big pharma and the Opioid Epidemic. When a young person from a trailer park in rural Tennessee died, people didn't say anything. They shrugged.

"*Well, what did you expect?*" everyone thought.

It wasn't that they said it outright, they just didn't offer much sympathy that wasn't tempered with some not-so-subtle victim shaming.

The third death was my mother's. And I was the one shrugging when she died. Hers should have been the first. I'd still have my sisters. They were only family that mattered to me. But Mom lived through the same epidemic that took my sister, only to die a relatively peaceful death of fatty liver disease. We hadn't spoken to each other in over a decade by then. I had started building up my boundaries at Grandad's deathbed and I didn't stop putting up walls until she was finally gone.

It was funny, really, that Reyes told me I needed to build up my walls. *What did he call me? A sweet angel baby?* It was an act. Being raised by a drug-addicted single parent had taught me walls, alright. Growing up with constant anger, fear, and the powerlessness of youth had taught me to erect whatever walls I could, wherever I could.

But I had done the work to overcome those tendencies. I had gotten help. I was lucky. Or blessed, maybe. I operated in a state of hyper-consciousness, making good, wise-mind choices instead of falling back on what my childhood trauma had taught me. My sisters hadn't—Patsy was dead, and Loretta had never lost her co-dependent tendencies, vilifying me for setting boundaries with Mom before she died—namely, for not giving her most of my paycheck. Part of me would always take responsibility and mourn that my choices had ultimately failed them, but another part was finally recognizing that I was coming out of the tunnel after all those years of choosing loneliness over bad relationships, kindness over knee-jerk reactions, and lots of cognitive behavioral therapy.

I'd punished myself for a lot of years and I wasn't going to do it anymore. And I couldn't punish Soula either. It was time, not only to step outside the wall, but to tear it down completely for her.

Waylon—Now

There was something missing between us.

Or maybe instead, there was *a thing* between us, since the tension it created felt more like a physical block, preventing us from closing that last gap toward the full actualization of our relationship. If I could hazard a guess, it was my family.

No, I *knew* it was my family. She thought I was avoiding introducing her to them. That I was embarrassed to bring her to some delightfully cheery home with roosters printed on the kitchen wallpaper, me holding her hand and, through joyful tears, telling them they were going to be grandparents. The idea made me laugh. They would never have been grandparents. I never knew my Dad, and I would have never allowed Mom near my child if she were alive.

The thing holding me back from even talking about my family wasn't some dark, nefarious secret. It was simple. It was too hard to emotionally unpack something that was so far behind you it really and truly didn't matter anymore.

How was I supposed to convince her that everything was fine with me, despite my past, and it would be fine during our future together? How was I supposed to show her that I didn't need to revisit my childhood history of abuse and neglect and those subsequent years of therapy with her in piteous detail, just to get her believe that it wasn't and wouldn't be an issue for me?

I knew what the expectation would be once I brought up my family history; she'd need to ensure that I was okay. *But how do you even do that?* What could I possibly tell her to drive home the point that this shit didn't bother me anymore? With my background, how could she trust that I wouldn't, at best, emotionally check out on her and the baby, and at worst... I wouldn't think about the worst.

I kept likening my situation—my cowardice about not having *brought up the situation*—to fencing. You could parry all day, deflecting from the coming onslaught, but if you dropped your guard right after that, you'd miss their riposte, and they'd slowly beat you. I'd been parrying, which was keeping Soula and me in a holding pattern, with me scared to take that final step closer, with her not knowing what that step was.

It was act now or slowly ruin the best thing that had ever happened to me.

Soula had dropped in my lap, a perfect specimen of the woman I didn't know I needed or wanted. The baby solidified my luck, forcing her to accept me when she would have otherwise let us lapse into a story of *what-might-have-been*. She came through on her end. She had been brave. I was still trying to deflect.

All I had to do was take her there and let her see. The graves would speak for themselves. I'd fill in the gaps, of course, as would her inevitable questions, but the more I put it off, the bigger it seemed. I needed to lay all of my history on the table so she could examine me under the cold lights of the autopsy room. And I would... someday.

chapter thirty-three

Waylon—Now

"YOU PAINTED THE BABY'S room black?" Soula asked when she arrived with the moving truck.

It seemed like a good idea to match the walls of the nursery to her womblike office in her apartment, but now, as she stood in the room for the first time, it was stupid that I hadn't consulted her before choosing Campfire Soot as the wall color.

"It's supposed to be dark grey. But it's just paint, Soula. We can fix it."

"I would have picked yellow, because that's what you're supposed to do when you don't know the baby's sex."

"Yellow will be good, too." I nodded. "I just had to give the painters the colors and—"

"No. I hate yellow," she said, turning to me. She didn't shy away from eye contact as much with me anymore, but the unanticipated reaction was that I now remained constantly under the spell of her huge, brown cow eyes. "I love this. It's so cozy. I want to live here."

"Your office," I said as a way of explaining. "I figured it was your favorite room in your apartment. I wanted to make this one of your favorite spaces as well."

"It already is. But, um... this seems dumb to ask at this point, but do I have a room of my own, or...?"

"Well," I took my time, trying—and failing—to read which way she wanted this to go. "I figured we'd share a room, like most couples. But if you want your own, there's the upstairs, it's just not—"

"No. I want that. I want to share a room with you. God, I sound like a toddler, I know, it's just, when we talked about moving in together, I thought maybe I got us all wrong. I still doubt myself and anything that's not explicitly communicated. I thought maybe you wanted to share a dwelling just for the baby, but I guess that's not what either of us wanted."

I'd listened to her ramble enough. I walked closer to her, shaking my head. But I couldn't help smiling. I loved that she was so unassuming. That her first reaction was to jump ahead, then doubt it later. She never had to doubt with me. She didn't know it yet, and that was my fault because I still hadn't shared much of my past and I knew that's what she craved, but deep down, I was tied to her. I was fully aware that she was my future. And the selfish part of me just wanted to savor every moment of our brief courtship, including this one, where I could still seduce her with paint colors.

Days later, the baby's room was a failure in seduction. Soula was growing increasingly tentative around me, and I knew it wasn't the pregnancy hormones. She kept hinting about my family. I kept putting her off even though it made me feel like shit. Here I was, trying to present the idea that I was this great and honorable man, ready and willing to do the right thing and stand by her and our child—and that much was true—but what I really was, was a coward.

I couldn't chalk our distance up to our jobs anymore. We hadn't talked, hadn't shared a meal together, even during our days off, in a week. And last night, she slept on the couch after working late. That cold, empty bed had been the clincher. I didn't want the mother of my child living in another room. I was honest about us being together. I'd want her to spend the rest of our lives in our bed even if she wasn't having my baby. It was time to bite the bullet.

"Are you busy?" My voice creaked from non-use over the weekend.

She looked up from her laptop. She'd just come from fencing—I didn't go—and some of the hair that had escaped her ponytail was floating loose around face. Her chest was still red from the exertion and her belly was showing, ever-so-slightly under her tight t-shirt. She looked back down. "I guess not." She said it like she couldn't come up with an excuse fast enough.

"I'd like to take you to meet my parents." I threw it out there fast, so I couldn't reel it back in before I'd finished.

"Oh." She looked up. Really looked up this time. "I thought you didn't want—"

"What you thought..." I paused, then started over. "What I led you to believe was wrong. I'd like to show you. Are you up for a drive?"

"I just need a shower."

"No, you don't."

"Um, I'll just change, then." She was wearing a pair of my sweat-pants and a V-neck tee.

"Seriously, Soula. You don't."

"But—"

"Do you trust me?"

She nodded. God love her, she trusted me. I couldn't help but smile. "Then get in the truck."

AFTER A STOP AT Biscuit Love—because Soula and food—and thirty or so miles East on 96, we ended up at Puckett Cemetery. Soula looked at me but didn't say anything as we bounded along the bumpy dirt road leading into the new section near the back, toward my people. She didn't even speak when I turned off the engine, nothing in sight but a handful of shiny granite markers. I slumped over, barely noticing when my forehead bumped the steering wheel. I hated coming here. Hated to bring Soula here. But she had to know. And maybe I could let a piece of that hatred finally die.

I felt her small hand on my back. She reached out to me in a way that didn't come naturally for her. Rubbing back and forth, the firm pressure of her hand washed away my reticence. Without picking my head up, I looked over at her. She was perfect. Strong, sympathetic, without pity. She smiled. This was why I wanted her, that night at the bar. They didn't make many of her kind, at least not that I saw. The kind that suffered her world, making it better as much as she could without losing herself in the process. There was no one like Soula and if I was going to be her partner, I needed to show her all of me.

"Are you ready?" she asked.

I nodded. I hopped out of the truck and jogged around to her side to help her down. She didn't need the help yet, but she reached out for my hand as we walked through the graves.

"No." I stepped away from her. "Not yet. Not until you hear what I have to say." If she was surprised, she didn't show it.

We got there. Mother's grave. I stared at the words etched on the face of the marker until the wind stung my eyes. I wasn't really seeing though. I was remembering.

Raelynn Wells
1967-2020
Beloved mother and grandmother
And I will dwell in the house of the Lord forever.
-Psalm 23.6

"I'm sorry—" Soula started to say as I interrupted her.

"It's bullshit, that last part." *Great job, Waylon. Start out with the harsh.*

I shook my head. "It's just something Loretta thought sounded fancy. If there's anyone who won't be dwelling in the house of the Lord, it's Raelynn." My country accent was coming out just being back on the outskirts of this town.

"Loretta?"

"My sister. One of them. She lives in Murfreesboro with her husband and kids. I think she's okay. Married a cop and I don't think he's one of the good ones. She won't talk to me anymore, since Mom died, so I don't really know. It's hard when you go through too much, too young, the way we were brought up. And then you get out and... don't come back for them. She hasn't forgiven me for giving up on Mom. Patsy's over here."

I walked a few steps to the left, to my sister's grave. Just the name, Patsy Wells, and the dates were engraved on hers. No ludicrous Bible quote junking up the granite. *I* ordered this stone. It was clean and simple. In memory of a life cut short because I wasn't there... I didn't come back for her.

"You've never spoken of her." Soula was right next to me, but she didn't touch me like she did in the truck. She could probably sense the shame wafting off me. I didn't blame her.

"It was my fault. Not at first. Not when we were kids. But I got out of that house. Got a baseball scholarship and that was it. I cut ties. Never looked back, even when I should've. *Especially when I should've.* I should have been fighting for custody of them as soon as I left for North Carolina. I should have applied somewhere closer. Then afterward..." I let my words die. It wasn't healthy to think this way, but I couldn't help it whenever I saw her name on a grave.

"I image you were thinking about what you had to do to make a better life, which is more than what most seventeen-year-old boys have to think about." Soula moved in even closer. "I don't know what your mom did, and you don't have to tell me if you don't want to. I've seen the effects of abuse often enough throughout my career to imagine your young life quite well based off the hatred that's directed at that tombstone right now."

"You don't understand." I sat down in the dry grass and plucked a few blades, spinning them between my fingers. It hadn't rained in a few weeks and the humidity wasn't enough to keep it from browning. "During college, even after, I just... wiped it away. While my sisters were still in the thick of it. They're younger than me."

"What kind of home could you give them in college?"

"A home where Patsy could've stayed clean. Maybe. I don't know. We would have been poor, but that was nothing to us. We were always poor. Working two minimum wage jobs to keep afloat would have been better than the despair she faced with our mother. I'd rather her and I both come home smelling like burger grease than her not come home at all."

She sighed. It was a smart move. There was nothing she could say that I hadn't already argued my way out of, then argued right back into.

"I didn't come back for them after college either." I took a deep breath, but it didn't do anything to ease the lump in my throat. This was the shitty part, admitting that my pride was what killed my sister. "All my life, my teachers told me I was smart. Or I would be smart if I could learn to apply myself. Once I figured out how to apply myself, I let it go to my head."

"How exactly did she die?"

"OD." I shrugged. It wasn't the most original of deaths. But the fucking normality of her death made it a tragedy of greater proportions. "Fentanyl. Heroine. Crack. Whatever else she could find. It was three years ago."

"When you stopped being a lawyer?"

I nodded. Or tried to nod. It was too much. I shouldn't have brought Soula here. This was a childish idea. I thought I owed it to her to give up every last barrier, and this was my big one, but I was wrong to think it wouldn't place a burden on her. "Too many fucking drug arrests with too few convictions. It was driving me insane. I couldn't do it anymore," I said. "The worst part is that now I'm doing a career that I started right after college. I worked my way through law school being a cop. I know now that this is a better fit but if I hadn't let my pride get in the way, if I wasn't so hardheaded, I could have discovered that a lot of years earlier and saved myself a lot of misery, maybe even my sister's life."

"Surely you recognize that you're not to blame for your sister's death. Even with our flawed system, it's so hard to outrun childhood trauma. And she made choices—"

"Yes. I know. She was always a risk-taker. No matter how much I'm blathering on, I promise I don't accept *all* the blame. I don't even blame it all on my mom. The years have taught me that. I'm not a martyr. But haven't you ever looked back on a moment of your life and thought, '*If only I could go back and make a different choice...*'"

I couldn't help it but my eyes flicked down to Soula's belly. She placed her hand there. It was a gesture I hadn't seen her make yet in her pregnancy. Maybe she'd done it out of protection. Maybe tenderness.

"No," she said quietly.

"No? You'd make every choice the same? No re-dos? Even your career? Even the baby? Even... me?" I could barely get the words out. I wasn't sure if they were audible.

"Yes." She dropped her hand and stood a little taller. "So far, every choice I made, conscious or unconscious led me to standing in this cemetery with you. And somewhere in your blathering, I realized that this is what I've been dreaming of my whole life."

"Standing in an ugly cemetery in the heat of summer?"

"Finding love with a man like you."

"You can't be serious."

"I'm always serious." She looked so adorably confused.

"You're telling me you love me? In a cemetery?"

"You have to admit, it fits us." She smiled and stepped toward me.

"No, it's just..." I blew out an exasperated breath and closed the distance between us, taking her head in my hands. "I came here to fight for us. You're making it too easy."

She looked confused. It was little wonder since I wasn't making sense. I tried to clarify, "I thought you still weren't getting it. I thought this might be the last thing I could drop at your feet to make you believe in me. Believe in us." I shook my head, angry that the words weren't coming out right. "This was the last thing I could strip off, to lay myself bare in the hopes you'd see me and want to build a life with me as much as I want a life with you."

"Are you saying I beat you to the punch?" She asked innocently.

"Essentially."

"You thought you had to reveal your every insecurity and moment of shame. That I had to get you emotionally naked before I loved you?"

"Did it work?"

"No," she said.

I dropped my hands and turned around. "Then what more can I do? There's no more of my soul that I can bare to you. After this," I gestured to the cemetery "it's all pizza toppings and childhood stories. All that's left to really know about each other are inconsequential details that take a couple years to discover."

"Oh, I see." She smiled and looked down, quiet for a minute. "Waylon, I love that you told me about your background, but you didn't need to do any of this. You just needed to ask."

"Ask what?" Oh God. I had the worst feeling all this shit I'd been feeling could have been cleared up with a conversation months ago. That lump reformed in my throat.

"You never asked me to be with you," she said. "I would have said yes."

"The first night—"

"You said, 'You can stay if you want.' That's not asking. That's like when my mom told me I could go to medical school but to this day, she holds it against me. If you asked me to stay... I would have stayed."

"Soula?" I didn't know if I was mad or ecstatic. Shit. I needed a drink. "You realize I have been asking, right? This whole time?"

Now it was her turn to get mad. Or something else. "You know I'm not good at communicating. I need things spelled out for me."

"So does everyone else when it comes to relationships, sweetheart. You don't need it spelled out. You want it spelled out because it gives you the power. It's no longer nuanced. It's just one simple decision. Yes or no. Yours."

Her breathing deepened and she swallowed. Maybe she had a lump, too. "Is it too late to say yes? Oh, God, what am I even saying yes to?"

"You're saying yes to me." I grabbed her arms. "To being all in with me. To the messy, complicated non-verbal cues and the slightly unclear verbal communication. If you need clarifying, tell me. Because I want my life totally, messily, complicatedly intertwined with yours."

"I want that, too. All of that. I'm placing my order. Waylon, I love you."

I couldn't say it back. Not right away. I took a deep breath and held her out so I could examine every last detail of her frightened, open, sincere, beautiful face. But her eyes became too insecure, her lips too needy, and I had to pull her closer. I couldn't breathe unless I was breathing in her scent. I couldn't see anything but her eyes, so dark even under the bright sun there was barely any delineation between the pupil and the colored part (she'd know the right term for it).

I slid my hand up the back of her neck, pressing her forehead to my lips. Her skin was hot and damp. My breath hitched as I kissed my way down her temple, across her cheekbone. By the time I reached her mouth, we were both in a frenzy to take in as much of each other as we could. She stepped closer, pressing her body against mine. We no longer fit together the same way. We weren't the same puzzle pieces. Now there was another form between us, a tiny convex presence. I smiled against her mouth, thinking about that beautiful little belly and the life we created together. "God, Soula, I love you," I said, breaking the kiss. "I didn't think it was possible to feel so much."

"Does it feel more than the guilt?" She asked, wiping her mouth and breathing like she'd just fenced a bout with a much better fencer than I.

"So much more."

"And more than anything else this cemetery represents to you?"

I nodded. "You mean more than all of it."

"Then, can we go home so I can better communicate how much you mean to me?" She asked.

"Fuck, yes."

"Because you know I express myself better through sex than with words." She said, quite clearly.

"Yes, I know." I nodded and we were once more entwined in each other's arms.

"And I really, really want to show you how much you make me *feel.*"

"Soula! If you don't start walking toward the truck, I'm fucking you right in this cemetery."

She recoiled. "Ew, no. It's two o'clock in the afternoon and the sun is way too bright for that."

epilogue

Soula—Then

I DIDN'T KNOW WHERE I was when I came into consciousness. My neck ached and the lights were too bright. My room was never this bright first thing in the morning. Opening my eyes, still groggy with sleep, I looked down at my physics textbook, lying open across my lap. Jeez, I had really slept here the whole night? Seriously? No one in my family thought to wake me so I could go to my room?

There was a gasp from the doorway and my head swiveled to my right, searching for the sound. A cluster of middle-aged people wearing their funeral blacks were filtering into the room. A family.

I groaned and wiped a stray hair from my forehead.

"It's moving," said a boy's voice.

I closed the book, knowing any minute my mother or father would chastise me for being in this part of the house, let alone the casket room, while a family was planning the funeral of their loved one. I didn't blame them. A teenaged Dracula wearing jeans and a sweatshirt and lugging a physics book wasn't the most respectful sight for a family making burial preparations.

"Uh, I'm so sorry. Just give me one...." I stepped out of the casket—our cushiest one with the full mattress, satin lining, and memory foam pillow—and my sneakers caught the edge of the carpet. My right ankle rolled, my left foot hooking the casket lining, pulling the whole thing onto its side. The open head panel hit the bar of the half-casket above it, the one that was formerly attached to the wall, displaying the various metal and wood finishes we could order. My feet couldn't stop. They propelled my body forward. My arms stretched out in search of something, *anything*, to grasp onto to stop the forward momentum of my windmilling legs and give me balance.

The epic crash of those heavy wooden coffins tumbling onto the showroom floor sent my brothers flying onto the room through the door opposite the decedent's family. That was the exact moment my hands found purchase on the first thing I could use to right myself; the large, protuberant breasts of an elderly woman, presumably the decedent's wife. My brothers were followed closely by my mother, still holding the boiling honey and clove syrup for the baklava she was making. Gus snickered. Even George hid a smile behind his hand. He couldn't help himself. Mama was mad enough when she saw that the expensive caskets had been ripped off the wall and were now lying in a heap of splintered wood. When her eyes caught the stunned expressions of the mourning family, their bodies paralyzed with horror at the scene unfolding in front of them while my groping hands froze to the old woman's breasts, the pan slipped, and molten honey syrup poured down Gus's left arm.

He wasn't badly burned. After a visit to the emergency department and a prescription for burn cream, he was still laughing at me. The decedent's family laughed, too, once they realized I was not a vampire or a corpse, but merely a high schooler who fell asleep in a top-of-the-line casket after seeking refuge in the quietest room of the house. They even bought the $18,000 casket when they realized that if it was comfortable enough for living person to accidentally drift off (and sleep through the night), it would more than suit Grandpa's eternal repose. Only my mother never forgave me for that. But she never forgave me for anything.

Soula—Now

We'd made it out of the cemetery, but only as far as the truck. It was awkward with my changing body proportions and the cramped quarters. I couldn't express the full extent of my feelings for Waylon, but it relieved some of the pressure for both of us. By the time we got home, after stopping for the barbeque we ordered from Puckett's Grocery, our friends and my family was already starting to arrive for a surprise housewarming—no thanks to Waylon who hadn't let me shower or change out of gym clothes before the cemetery.

Decca brought out her witchy kit that made my mother cross herself, but by the time the smudging ritual began, Yia-Yiá was asking her all sorts of questions and it turned out that she performed her own, similar ritual with a candle that she brought home from church every Greek Easter. Since Decca geeked out over anything spiritual, she became enamored with my Yia-Yiá and in turn, Yia-Yiá insisted she be adopted into the family alongside Bethany and Sofia. Decca even gave Gus a run for his money when it came to theological discourse and the two shared thoughts and beers on the back porch most of the evening.

Even George was in high spirits (for him) considering Bethany was the one who prompted this little get-together. He spent most of the time out back with Sofia and Waylon, throwing horseshoes at a length of rebar he drove into the ground—something that would be removed immediately after this get-together, my morgue experience telling me this was an impalement waiting to happen. Still, when George was forced to be in the same room as Bethany, even I could tell the situation was coming to a head. I feared for everyone within blast radius when those two finally blew up.

Mom brought baklava. It was my favorite Greek dessert, and she hadn't made it since the time she burned Gus's arm. Waylon barely left my side from the time he saw her car pull into the driveway and it felt good to have an ally, but I knew the baklava was a peace offering, her way of trying. We had a long way to go, but I counted myself lucky I hadn't had a childhood like Waylon's, where I felt the need to distance myself from my family. They were annoying, but apart from personality clashes, diagnosis denials, and career disappointments, it wasn't anything I couldn't shrug off.

THAT NIGHT, WAYLON AND I lay in bed. Not entangled. We'd already done the tangling. I was on my half and he on his, lying on our sides facing each other, feeling the mental togetherness of us. I never thought I'd experience anything more than physical release with another person and yet, Waylon was here. He had found me. He kept finding me, never stopping until he dug deep under my concrete and mildew and rot and grime until he made me his. He made *us* his. Me and the baby.

I turned on my back, wondering about the baby inside me. Waylon must have been thinking along the same lines, because his hand settled over my belly, and he inched closer. I knew how genetics worked. Punnett squares were middle school biology, for God's sake, but I allowed myself to think, for just a second that there might be something happening in my uterus right now to form the same mesmeric eyes as Waylon's. What if my eye color wasn't dominant? What if, when we looked in our baby's eyes, we saw the whole blue and brown world swirling in his irises? What if—

"Did you feel that?" Waylon's own blue and brown worlds collided with mine and somehow, we connected even more completely than we had the minute, the *second* before.

"Yeah," I said dreamily. "I've been feeling it for a few days, I've just been telling myself I haven't. But you...?"

His hand slid up from my belly, fingers tracing over my t-shirt and neck before weaving into my hair and pulling me into a deep and frantic kiss. His face was wet. He was laughing. And crying. And it was making me love him even more.

The house wasn't anywhere near ready for a baby. We had furniture to purchase, a kitchen and two bathrooms to renovate, not to mention landscaping the apocalyptic wasteland that was our yard. Finishing the house would be an exercise in trusting the living. That was what you bargained for when you purchased a murder house.

Being with Waylon would mean forever trusting a skill set I didn't have. People. Honesty. Openness. I never bargained for any of that. I parried and counter-attacked that trust, but it beat me anyway. If I learned anything in the past few months, it was the deeper understanding of the word *touché*; a word I thought I had long been familiar with.

In fencing, it was simply an acknowledgment of a touch. Translated to my own life, it was to acknowledge *his* touch. My opponent had come out of nowhere and touched me at what turned out to be my most vulnerable point; my heart.

I couldn't think of a better way to lose.

The Smythe family saga continues with George and Bethany's sultry, spicy, enemies-to-lovers story, Undertaking Love.

author's note
& acknowledgements

I'VE HAD A LIFELONG love of death that spans all disciplines, from the technical/medical to the cultural and historical practices of body preparation, grieving, and mourning, to the art of the gravestones. My first tattoo was a 17th century New England gravestone rubbing.

I love the creepy/spooky/gothic/ stories, horror novels, all things witchy or skeletal, Elvira, Tim Burton, Victorian hairwork jewelry, Mozart's Requiem, and all the vibey aesthetic trappings of death.

It goes without saying that I'm a Halloween Queen.

But I hoped to achieve something more with this book besides providing kitchy, attention-grabbing fodder; I wanted to shed light on the inner lives of those who work with the dead. Soula, Bethany, and Decca represent just a fraction of the spectrum of careers in deathcare and in this book (and their sequels), I tried to present those careers as accurately as possible—from the mundane to the fact-is-stranger-than-fiction details—while giving them great character-driven love stories in the process.

I came into this project assuming I was well versed enough to write off the cuff about a forensic pathologist with only minimal research. I was not. There is no greater turn-on than competency, and for me, that extends to fictional careers and hobbies. So, it wasn't enough for me to write a cardiac tamponade into my story, I had to portray it in a way that wouldn't make a real-life forensic pathologist roll their eyes.

I thank Darin Wolfe, MD for being my guide in the morgue, and for answering my highly specific questions. I would have had blood gushing out of a peritoneal cavity and onto the floor had he not told me that the blood in my story was already congealed by the time of autopsy. (That would have been embarrassing).

In the name of fiction, I changed Tennessee from a coroner state to a medical examiner state. I based this decision on Dr. Judy Melinek's memoir, *Working Stiff* and therefore I apply her interpretation of the different systems here. A coroner is an elected official who does not perform autopsies (unless they happen to be elected officials who are also board-certified forensic pathologists). Typically, a coroner heads a team of medicolegal death investigators and issues death certificates once an independent forensic pathologist performs the post-mortem exam. A medical examiner has all the duties of a coroner *and* a forensic pathologist, and also has a medicolegal team (whose members are sometimes also referred to, confusingly, as medical examiners). MEs can do it all. The terms can vary slightly from state to state. I wanted Soula to have complete control over the system in Tennessee, so I changed the system for her.

This is an #ownvoices Autism book, but it's not intended to be a book about Autism.

I'm grateful to Michael Vitoux from The Pointe fencing club in Urbana, Illinois for graciously answering my questions and providing me with a tour of the facilities and an impromptu sabre lesson.

Thank you, Holly and Esther from Wildly Tarot Podcast for teaching me about how fun and interesting tarot can be. (Decca's readings in *Morgue* were actual spreads that I drew for my characters, but I tried to interpret their meanings through Decca's eyes. "Soula's deck" is the Antique Anatomy Tarot by Claire Goodchild from *Black and the Moon*. No cards were changed in the process.)

Thanks to my family for supporting my vampiric work schedule, and to all the Last Responders who never get enough credit for the work they do in deathcare to support the living.

Thanks to my readers, who stuck with me through this weird journey.

(an update to the pulp edition: Thank you to Kris Madden, for painting and designing the book of my dreams! I've always wanted my books to look like the old pulp crime novels of the 1960s and now they're PERFECT! Thanks isn't enough for what you've done.)

about the author

Megan Montgomery is a multi-award winning author of steamy, smart, character-driven romance.

Her debut novel, WELL...THAT WAS AWKWARD, described as "a big, juicy bite of Chesapeake Bay culture," was inspired by her homesickness for southern Maryland. She now lives among the cornfields of Illinois with her family--but don't ever mistake her for a Midwesterner. A goth at heart since age 12 (if not younger), she loves the color black, Mozart's Requiem, and the history of death and burial rites.

When she's not writing, reading, or cooking dinners her son won't eat, you'll find her volunteering at the library or the medicinal herb garden, or cackling over a cauldron during a full moon.

Her books have received the B.R.A.G. Medallion, Best Indie Book Award for romance, the Indie Reader Discovery Award for chick lit, the Rudy Award for contemporary romance, and were finalists in the Page Turner Book and Screenplay Awards, but she's most thrilled when she makes personal connections with readers.

Scan here to join the morgue & subscribe to Megan's newsletters!

further reading & listening

Books

- *Confessions of a Funeral Director,* Caleb Wilde
- *All the Ways the Dead Still Speak,* Caleb Wilde
- *Smoke Gets in Your Eyes: And Other Lessons from the Crematory*, Caitlin Doughty
- *Will My Cat Eat My Eyeballs*, Caitlin Doughty
- *Death's Acre: Inside the Legendary Forensic Lab the Body Farm Where the Dead Do Tell Tales*, William M. Bass
- *The Handbook of Zombie Forensics and Medicine: A New Theory of Zombiology and Why Humans Will (Probably) Survive the Apocalypse*, Darin L. Wolfe, MD
- *Stiff: the Curious Lives of Human Cadavers*, Mary Roach
- *Working Stiff: Two Years, 262 Bodies, and the Making of a Medical Examiner*, Judy Melinek, MD & T.J. Mitchell

- *Past Mortems: Life & Death Behind Mortuary Doors*, Carla Valentine
- *The American Way of Death Revisited*, Jessica Mitford
- *Mortuary Confidential: Undertakers Spill the Dirt*, Todd Harra and Kenneth MacKenzie
- *The History of Death: Burial Customs and Funeral Rites, From the Ancient World to Modern Times*, Michael Kerrigan
- *How Not to Die: Surprising Lessons from America's Favorite Medical Examiner*, Jan Garavaglia, M.D.
- *Corpses, Coffins, and Crypts: A History of Burial*, Penny Colman
- *Written in Bones: How Human Remains Unlock the Secrets of the Dead*, ed. Paul Bahn
- *Exploring Tarot Using Radiant Rider-Waite*, Avia Venefica
- *The History of Tarot Art: Demystifying the Art and Arcana, Deck by Deck*, Holly Adams Easley and Esther Joy Archer

Podcasts

- *Wildly Tarot Podcast*
- *The Momento Mori Oracle Podcast*
- *Knife after Death: The Official, Unadulterated Podcast of*

Autopsy, Forensics, and the Freshly Dead

- *The Mortuary Show*
- *Dead Men's Donuts*
- *Death in the Afternoon*
- *Forced Proximity Podcast*

books by
megan montgomery

A Small Town Chesapeake Romance:

Well . . . That Was Awkward
(winner: Best Indie Book Award & IndieReader Discovery Award; B.R.A.G. Medallion honoree; Page Turner Book Award & Screenplay Award finalist)

A Last Responders Romance:

Morgue to Love (B.R.A.G. Medallion honoree)
Undertaking Love (Rudy Awards 1st place finalist)
The Bones of Love (coming soon)

Scan the QR code for book links

undertaking love
chapter one

Bethany

My body was broken.

I blinked hard to lubricate my eyes, struggling to stay awake behind the wheel. The vent blasted tepid air into my face, trying its damnedest to desiccate my skin and sabotage the efforts of my latest hyaluronic acid injections.

My stomach churned from too much coffee and too little sleep.

A sweat broke out under my arms and boobs.

Great. Now I could smell all that coffee excreting from my pores and ruining my favorite silk blouse.

I glanced at the man in the passenger seat.

George's pores were looking perfectly dry, as usual. He wouldn't think of sweating, even from the most strenuous effort.

I'd seen him pull a rotund, decomposing man out of that impossible space between the toilet and the bathtub and plop him on a mortuary cot in an un-air-conditioned, third-floor apartment in the middle of August without breaking a sweat.

The man never had a hair out of place, was never not freshly shaven, and he never forgot to button his suit jacket when he stood, or unbutton it when he sat.

And he was a consummate professional—as long as you didn't work with him.

And as long as your name wasn't *Bethany West.*

I breathed in a lungful of stale air. Even now, in the mortuary van, George managed to smell fresh, yet intensely masculine. The faintest notes of sandalwood and citrus wafted toward me as he fiddled with his ear, pushing his earbud deeper in.

I suspected he wasn't listening to anything producing actual sound; the earbuds were just a tactic to try to keep me from making "unnecessary" conversation.

I was almost too tired to care.

I stifled a yawn, hoping he wouldn't catch it.

He did, of course.

I saw the tick of his jaw from the corner of my eye. Glaring at the screen of the laptop balanced on his crossed legs, his flexed fingers hovering over the keyboard, a ballpoint pen clutched in his teeth.

I'd never seen the man smile except for a wince-like approximation of the real thing, and he saved that stingy expression for our clients.

After an entire life spent in the trenches of the funeral business, his handsome face was permanently etched into a show of bland sympathy—except when he scowled in contempt.

That expression was reserved exclusively for me.

I shifted in my seat. This road was designed to induce drowsiness. It snaked around low hills as the primordial forest crept closer. Tree limbs reached over the roof of the van like a giant's greedy arms snatching up a matchbox car.

Scrub brush and broken-down barbed wire fencing lined short stretches of road, while ancient pavement crumbled away at its edges—chunks of gray rock giving way to tall grasses disguising deep gutters, the kind that would break an axle if I accidentally swerved to the right.

The last of the afternoon sun broke free, painting the scattered cornfields behind the tree line with a golden, Maxfield Parish light. Then, just as suddenly, the oaks, hickories, and honey locusts, with their inch-long thorns, encroached again, cloaking the van in shadows.

Those colors might have been something to look at if my eyelids hadn't been fluttering shut every few minutes on this endless drive.

My ass hit the seat with a thud I felt clear up in my chest.

I must have nodded off and hit a pothole.

George's scowl deepened as he glanced halfway in my direction.

He couldn't be bothered to turn his head completely.

I wasn't worth the effort.

But falling asleep while driving was a new low—even for me—in terms of work/life imbalance.

I exhaled slowly, visualizing the stress of my thirty-six-hour *shift from hell* leaving with my breath. So far, I'd already done one (literally) shitty body pickup. I'd also embalmed, prepared, and casketed two people for tomorrow's services.

I just had to get through this one last pickup, then my daughter and I would spend a dead-people-free weekend eating Chinese food, watching screwball comedies with Cary Grant and Clark Gable, and taking turns beating each other at Monopoly.

I reached for the radio, turning down the local country station in a desperate attempt to stay alert. Not that it would help. I took a deep, yoga gulp of oxygen, holding it at the top.

Turning again to my business partner, I tested my earbud theory.

"What are you listening to?" I asked so quietly George would never be able to hear me if they were producing sound.

Was I picking a fight to stay awake? Absolutely.

"Podcast." He didn't bother with articles of speech, or even eye contact. I bit my lip to hide the smile of my secret knowledge.

The man may have *thought* he hated me, but he was so highly attuned to my presence, he couldn't bear to leave my question unanswered.

That definitely wasn't hatred.

He typed a line. Paused. Referred to his paper notes.

"Did you remember to book that follow-up with your dentist?" I asked.

No response.

Hmm . . . Just when I thought I might have to reevaluate the stunt AirPods, he flicked his eyes over to me, nodding once.

Theory confirmed.

But still no argument. That had to be a record for him. Usually he detonated at the first sound of my voice.

"What did Soula say about the Fair Street shooting? Is she releasing the body?"

"The family wants us to do the services," he said to his screen. "Dad'll pick him up on Tuesday. You'll do the prep."

"You're better with gunshot wounds," I flattered, counting on him to take the bait this time.

He looked up from his notes, one thick black eyebrow raised. The fish was hooked.

"Doesn't matter. It's not a facial reconstruction. I think he was shot in the chest, so his clothing will cover any restorative work. As long as you seal the wound properly."

I was expecting that, goaded it on even, but his dig still stung. I'd never not sealed a wound properly. There were basic mortuary techniques for that.

I kept pestering though, relishing how it felt to push his buttons. "Or, you could prepare him and I could take the Jones viewing that evening."

"Bethany." He finally gave me his full attention. "It's Tuesday. Guitar lessons. I scheduled you for the prep so you'll be finished in time to pick up Sofia from school. Did you forget your own schedule?"

"I didn't forget. I'm just surprised you memorized it."

"I'm your boss. Of course I memorized your availability."

"You're not my boss. But . . . you can always buy out my half if you hate working with me so much."

"How much?" His nostrils flared. He knew better than to ask.

"Five million."

He snorted. "The entire business isn't valued at five million."

"It priced you out, didn't it," I taunted. Really, I didn't care how much my half of the funeral home was worth. I'd never sell.

"My own father priced me out. That's why he sold to you."

"Jim sold to me because I knew what was best for the company, in spite of you."

He looked over in the general vicinity of my knees. As if it pained him to move his eyes any farther up. He gripped the pen so tightly in his fist I expected to hear the crack of the cheap plastic.

"*I* know what's best for my company," he said.

"You *think* you do."

The argument followed the same format as usual. He'd offer *(threaten)* to buy out my 51 percent share. I'd throw out some ludicrous number, far beyond what I knew was in his bank account.

Earlier this year, I'd paid slightly more than what my half was worth, but Smythe Mortuary was my dream job. The sentimental value far exceeded the market.

His jaw tightened as his eyes lingered too long on my bare thigh peeking out from the slit in my suit skirt. I bit my lip to hide a smirk. I liked his eyes on me a little too much.

A lot too much.

I knew I shouldn't, but I just wanted to break him. Even if it was just for a minute. *A second.* For once, I wanted his face to read something other than platitudes and business duties.

George had a heart once, or so I was told. It was broken in the cruelest of ways and if it healed at all, it healed with a hell of a lot of scar tissue. God help me, but for some reason, I wanted to be the one to rip open those old wounds, clean out the festering scabs, and let that tissue heal smoothly again.

Despite our bickering, despite his feigned hatred for me, despite all his emotionally damaged, anxiety-riddled, trauma-surviving flaws, *I wanted him.*

I wanted his impeccably coiffed hair and the five identical gray suits he wore on repeat. I wanted that perfectionism and anal retentiveness that was manifesting in his cracked molars and TMJ.

And somewhere deep down—in that small part of him that was still testosterone and bone and blood rather than output code of 1s and 0s—I knew he wanted me too.

Made in the USA
Monee, IL
26 November 2024

71084231R00184